The Alehouse Murders

A Templar Knight Mystery

Maureen Ash

BERKLEY PRIME CRIME, NEW YORK

THE BERKLEY PUBLISHING GROUP
Published by the Penguin Group
Penguin Group (USA) Inc.
375 Hudson Street, New York, New York 10014, USA
Penguin Group (Canada), 90 Eglinton Avenue East, Suite 700, Toronto, Ontario M4P 2Y3, Canada
(a division of Pearson Penguin Canada Inc.)
Penguin Books Ltd., 80 Strand, London WC2R 0RL, England
Penguin Group Ireland, 25 St. Stephen's Green, Dublin 2, Ireland (a division of Penguin Books Ltd.)
Penguin Group (Australia), 250 Camberwell Road, Camberwell, Victoria 3124, Australia
(a division of Pearson Australia Group Pty. Ltd.)
Penguin Books India Pvt. Ltd., 11 Community Centre, Panchsheel Park, New Delhi—110 017, India
Penguin Group (NZ), 67 Apollo Drive, Rosedale, North Shore 0632, New Zealand
(a division of Pearson New Zealand Ltd.)
Penguin Books (South Africa) (Pty.) Ltd., 24 Sturdee Avenue, Rosebank, Johannesburg 2196,
South Africa

Penguin Books Ltd., Registered Offices: 80 Strand, London WC2R 0RL, England

PRINTING HISTORY
Berkley Prime Crime mass-market edition / September 2007
Berkley Prime Crime trade paperback edition / September 2010

ISBN: 978-0-425-23831-8

PRINTED IN THE UNITED STATES OF AMERICA

10 9 8 7 6 5 4 3 2 1

Berkley Prime Crime titles by Maureen Ash

THE ALEHOUSE MURDERS
DEATH OF A SQUIRE
A PLAGUE OF POISON
MURDER FOR CHRIST'S MASS

For my daughter, Tammy;
husband, Robert;
and good friend Rick
with gratitude for your constant support
and encouragement

One

⁜

Lincoln
Summer 1200 A.D.

Ⱨᴇᴀᴛ ʜᴜɴɢ ʟɪᴋᴇ ᴀ ꜱᴏᴅᴅᴇɴ ʙʟᴀɴᴋᴇᴛ ᴏᴠᴇʀ Lɪɴᴄᴏʟɴ town and the surrounding countryside. The air was heavy, almost too thick to breathe, wrapping itself around mouth and nostrils like a linen shroud. It made the atmosphere seem ominous; a feeling enhanced by the distant sound of thunder as it rolled and crackled, but did not give the gift of rain.

On the banks of a stream about two miles from the walls of Lincoln, a hawking party was engaged in the hunt. From behind the shelter of a stand of trees the sheriff of Lincoln, Gerard Camville, and his wife, along with their companions, watched as a falcon circled like a small speck high in the ceiling of the sky. Directly below the bird, hidden in the reeds of the river bank, lay the sheriff's falconer, directing her movements. At his signal the kennel master released his hounds and they surged forward, barking and yapping at the ducks bobbing unsuspectingly on the gently rippling surface of the stream. In alarm, the waterfowl took to the air and, as they rose up like a whirring cloud, the peregrine stooped, plummeting like a ragged stone to strike on a fat mallard that had been a little slower than the rest. The talons and notched beak of the falcon quickly extinguished the life from its prey.

The falconer swung his lure in a wide circle above his head, attracting the young peregrin and tempting her from her kill. Soon she was hooded and resting securely on her trainer's wrist, the tidbit he fed her disappearing quickly down her sharp curved beak, while servants ran to secure the mallard in a rough cloth sack. The bird skittered and bobbed on the falconer's wrist, pulling against the thongs that bound her. He calmed her by dribbling water from his mouth over the feathers on her back.

"Good man. Well done." The thickly muscled figure of the sheriff, Gerard Camville, left the cover of the trees. He walked lightly for so large a man, but there was no doubting the aggressiveness of his personality. It was there in the forward thrust of his jaw and in the restless darting eyes. "You have trained her well, Eubold," he said to the falconer. "I was right to buy her. These birds from the cliffs of Wales are far superior to those of Norway. I remember King Henry losing a fine gyrfalcon in combat to one of this strain some fifteen years ago. We will get some good sport from her."

"And some tender morsels for the table as well, I trust." Nicolaa de la Haye came to stand beside the sheriff. They were an oddly assorted pair, the sheriff's powerful figure seeming to diminish that of the small plump woman who was his wife. But only the most unobservant would not have noticed that they were more than equally matched in temperament. Camville's fractiousness washed over the calmness of his wife's demeanour with the futility of a winter storm beating upon a rock. Both in their midforties, they had been married for more than twenty years, and although time had not softened the contrast in their personalities, it had taught them both to tolerate the differences.

The rest of the hawking party came to where they stood.

It was a small group, with only a handful of the castle's household knights and a few servants to carry the food and wine for their midmorning meal.

"We will go downstream," Camville announced, "towards the marsh. Perhaps we will find some heron on which to test this beauty." He reached over and took the bird from the falconer, securing her to his own gauntleted wrist and setting the bells on her jesses tinkling.

"Do you not think, Gerard, that it would be best to keep her to smaller prey at first?" Nicolaa asked her husband. On her own gloved wrist perched a merlin, the small falcon deemed suitable for a woman's use. It was one of her favourites, and sat quietly, the rough spotted feathers on its breast ruffling lightly in the breeze. "Your bird is young yet; she will lose heart if you set her too hard a task before she is ready."

Gerard turned to debate the point when he noticed a thin trail of dust rising above the trees that lay between the stream where they stood and the stone walls of Lincoln. Soon the muffled sound of hoof beats, moving at speed on the hard-packed dirt of the forest track, reached them and, moments later, a horse and rider broke through the cover of the trees into the clearing at the side of the stream. It was a man-at-arms from the castle garrison; the twelve pointed red star of the Haye family showing brightly on the breast of his tunic. Sliding to a stop in front of Gerard and Nicolaa he dismounted, leaving his horse standing foam-flecked and with heaving sides as he went down on one knee before the sheriff and his wife.

"Christ's Blood," Camville swore, "what is it now? Can we not have a morning's sport without interruption?"

"My lord, my lady," the soldier panted, "Ernulf has sent me." The man-at-arms was young, with a pasty face liberally scarred with boils. Sweat ran in rivulets from the lank brown hair that stuck out from beneath his leather cap, caused not only by the heat and the exertions of his ride, but also nervousness at being the center of his master and mistress' attention. He hoped to draw the sheriff's well known irascibility away from himself by making it clear that it was the captain of the castle guard, not he, that was the cause of the intrusion.

Camville swore again, but Nicolaa laid her hand on her husband's arm. "Ernulf would not spoil your pleasure on a whim, Gerard. It must be important."

Although Gerard was sheriff it was Nicolaa, through the inheritance of her father, who was castellan of the castle and responsible to the king for its security. Ernulf had been in her father's service since she had been a child. His loyalty to her was unquestionable, as was his devotion to her well-being. If he had thought there was reason to disturb her, it would not be for naught. "What is the message from Ernulf?" she asked of the young soldier.

The lad took a great gulp of air, thankful for Lady Nicolaa's calm authority, and now with relish he repeated the words he had been told to say. "There has been murder done in Lincoln town, my lady. Four people dead in an alehouse off Danesgate. All stabbed to death. Sir Bascot and Ernulf have gone to the place and to see the priest of St. Andrew's. It was the priest who reported the crime." The young man-at-arm's face grew even redder with the excitement of his tale. The boils looked ready to burst.

"May God's angels weep," Camville exploded. "As if this hell-sent weather wasn't enough, we now have a murderer loose in Lincoln. And the fair about to begin. Someone's guts shall spill for this."

Although the news had shaken Nicolaa as well, she reacted with more restraint than her husband. "If these unfortunates were found in an alehouse, Gerard, they may only be drunken sots who have killed each other over a game of dice, or a woman. It is most likely something of nothing."

Camville was not much mollified, but he did grunt in assent to her reasoning, and he gave her no argument when she suggested that she return to the castle immediately to find out what was the truth of the matter. "It may be some hours before all the details are known, Gerard. I will go now and you can return at your leisure. There is no need for both of us to lose the morning's sport."

At the sheriff's nod of agreement Nicolaa spoke to the messenger. "Return to Lincoln. Find Ernulf and tell him I am returning directly. Tell him also to be discreet and that he and Sir Bascot are to report to me with all haste, before this news is bruited abroad and alarms the townspeople and the visitors who have come for the fair. I shall await them in my private chamber."

As the man-at-arms put his heels to his flagging mount and sped away, Nicolaa herself moved to depart, motioning for one of the servants to accompany her. "God grant these deaths were caused by nothing more than an alehouse brawl, Gerard. But if they were not, we shall need some good meat for the table to fortify ourselves for any trouble that may come. Perhaps I was wrong about your new falcon. It may be time to try her on a larger quarry."

With a smile she disappeared down the track, the servant following behind. It was an old game between her and her husband. She bought his complaisance by pandering to his taste for the hunt and his disinclination to attend to the details of running the shrievalty and castle. In return she retained the power in her own hands, managing the garrison and Haye lands as her father had done before her. It suited them both.

Two

✠

LINCOLN CASTLE STANDS HIGH ON THE SUMMIT OF A hill, sharing the height with the Minster and cathedral. Bisecting the area between the castle on the western side and the Minster on the east runs the old Roman road of Ermine Street, which continues down the precipitous southern slope of the hill and converges at its base with the River Witham. On either side of this main street and below the confines of the castle and Minster lies the town, stretching out on either side like the outer edges of a leaf from the main stem. All of this area—castle, Minster and town—are encircled by a stout stone wall with an additional parapet encasing the top of the hill, which can be sealed off from the lower reaches in case of attack. Within the large bailey of the castle, beside barracks, stable, chapel, smith and storehouses, are two keeps, one newly built and an older one which, although showing signs of disrepair, is still sound enough to house the armoury and a few sleeping chambers.

When one of the town watchmen brought Ernulf the urgent message from Anselm, the priest of St. Andrew's,

Bascot de Marins was breaking his fast in the hall of the new keep. De Marins was a Templar, a member of the religious military order of the Poor Fellow-Soldiers of Christ and Temple of Solomon. He had arrived in Lincoln a few months before, in the dead of winter, clad in the white surcoat of a Templar, with the blood red cross of Christ emblazoned on its breast. He had been emaciated and weary, his only companion a young Italian boy, Gianni, riding pillion behind him. The boy, who was a mute, had looked in no better state than his master, for he was thin and shivering in the cold of a climate with which he was unfamiliar.

After a brief conference with Nicolaa de la Haye, the Templar had been given a room to himself in the old keep, and had not been seen for many days; only the boy appeared to take him his meals and bring back the empty vessels on which the food had been served. The boy, too, had otherwise kept to the chamber, seeming fearful of any who approached, and attempted communication only with the cook. To him, through a series of hand gestures, the boy conveyed the needs of himself and his master and gave his thanks by means of a shy smile and a grateful glance from beneath his mop of brown curls.

No one had been told why the Templar was in Lincoln. Gerard Camville had said in passing that de Marins had been on crusade in the Holy Land with the now-dead King Richard back in '91, and had been captured by the Saracens during a skirmish near Acre at the end of that year. After eight long years of captivity he had recently escaped. It was obvious that he had been tortured during his incarceration, for he wore a leather patch over the eye socket of his missing right eye and walked with a pronounced limp. When, early one morning, he came into the hall to break his fast after attending Mass in the castle chapel, all eyes had turned his way but, although polite, he had said nothing of his past and seemed disinclined to talk about it. Any question put to him that referred to his ordeal was met with a disarming silence and then a deliberate change of conversation that left no doubt that while he did not wish to give offence, neither did he want to confide.

He was a man of medium height, with skin burned by the sun to the colour of old copper, and hair and beard of dark brown that was prematurely threaded with grey. His one remaining eye was blue, so pale in colour that it was startling in the burnished darkness of his skin, seeming like a piece of ice that the sun had failed to melt. As he began to recover his health, he had taken to practicing his combative skills in the yard, first with a blunted sword against the wooden stake erected for the purpose, and finally with Ernulf in mock battle using both sword and shield. While he seemed to have regained his former weight, his prowess with a sword was hampered by the lameness of his leg and the blindness of one eye. For all that, he still made a formidable opponent for Ernulf, who needed all the tricks he had learned in his many years as a soldier to keep pace with the Templar.

When Ernulf went into the hall that morning seeking someone in authority to accompany him in answering Anselm's summons, there was little of the castle retinue stirring. A few servants had set out trestle tables and laid them with platters of cold meats and early summer fruits. The night shift of the castle guard were seated at the rear of the hall downing mugs of ale and some cheese before returning to the barracks for a few hours sleep. A couple of clerics and a smattering of Haye personal servants were drinking watered wine and munching on day-old bread while, in a corner, some of the pages were playing a game with a set of polished rabbit bones. Beneath the covered walkway from the kitchen to the hall a pair of serving maids giggled behind their hands. The heat of the last few days had permeated even the thick wall of stones with which the keep was built and the air was stuffy, redolent with the smell of smoke from the torches that lit the inner confines of the room mixed with the scent of the pungent herbs that had been scattered amongst the rushes on the floor. Of the household knights there was little evidence. Those that were not out on the hawking party with the sheriff and Nicolaa de la Haye were still in their beds sleeping off the effects of last night's wine. Only Bascot sat at the table below the dais that was usually used by those of knight's rank, with the boy Gianni standing behind him in attendance.

When Ernulf approached and told him what had happened, the Templar readily agreed to accompany him to St. Andrew's, asking only if the church was a far distance.

"Too far for you to walk," Ernulf had said baldly, making a pointed reference to Bascot's crippled leg. "I will order mounts saddled."

The Templar gave the serjeant a small smile and rose from the table. He had a liking for the grizzled old campaigner and had learned that while he was phlegmatic and brusque, he was not surly. He also treated the men-at-arms under his command with a rough fairness that had won de Marin's respect.

Gianni was hovering at Bascot's elbow with an anxious face and didn't seem at ease until his master spoke to him quietly and told him to wait in the hall for his return. Nodding, the youngster turned and slipped away to a corner of the large chamber, curling up between two of the castle hounds that lay there gnawing on the discarded bones of last night's meal. His eyes followed the Templar as he and Ernulf left the hall.

Outside the pair made their way to the stables, pausing only for Ernulf to call to two men-at-arms lounging in the doorway of the barracks to accompany them. Once mounted, the small party headed out of the castle ward and, passing under Bailgate, the main gate into the town, they turned down onto Steep Hill. It was an apt name, for the drop it made from the higher ground on which the castle and Minster were situated down into the town itself was deep. The group rode their horses carefully on the cobbled pavement before turning off onto Danesgate, a side street which led off in an arc towards the east before swooping still farther down the hill to Claxledgate. They passed a few early risers amongst the townspeople, but otherwise the streets were empty and it was not too many minutes until they were in front of the church of St. Andrew. At the mouth of a small side street was an alehouse, the sign of an ale-stake hanging over the doorway. Beside the sign was bunched a sheaf of greenery, the usual signal to let customers know a new brew was ready for consumption.

"The watchman told me that the alewife discovered the bodies earlier this morning," Ernulf said to Bascot as they dismounted. "Luckily she went running straight to the priest at St. Andrew's instead of screaming her head off in the street. The priest had the presence of mind to calm her, then went to the alehouse and barred the door before he sent to inform Lady Nicolaa. Probably be best if we went to see the alewife and the priest first."

Bascot nodded and followed the serjeant's squat figure as he led the way into the church, a small one in comparison with many others in Lincoln, and down into the shadows of a short nave that was lit at one end by a torch flaring in a wall sconce. By its flickering light brightly painted scenes depicting stories from the Bible could be seen on every wall. Across the empty space, below the altar, Bascot could see the priest standing over a woman seated on a low stool. The woman was crouched over her knees, her broad shoulders shaking beneath the plain gown that she wore. Her sobbing was loud and grating. Upon her head was a piece of crumpled linen, looking as though it had been hastily donned for a makeshift covering. As Bascot and Ernulf approached she looked up and, at the sight of them, began to moan and cry in heartrending gulps. She was about fifty years of age with a florid face and pale eyes.

Wisps of fine grey hair escaped from the confines of her slightly askew coif. Despite the ravages of time and her present distress, there could be seen the shadow of a once fresh-faced comeliness. Her hands, wringing themselves together in her ample lap, looked strong and capable.

The priest, Anselm, a handsome full-faced man of about forty years of age, looked relieved to see Bascot. He had met the Templar once before, soon after Bascot had arrived in Lincoln, and he murmured a greeting before patting the distraught woman's shoulder and saying, "Now, Agnes, you must compose yourself. Sir Bascot has come from the castle. You must tell him what you found this morning, just as you told me."

The alewife gulped and, with an effort, managed to stem her tears. "I came down this morning, from my bed in our chamber above the taproom. I thought it strange that Wat— Walter—that's my husband—wasn't in bed beside me, but I thought as maybe he'd got up early like. He does—did— sometimes, if he'd taken too much ale the night before and it made his stomach bad."

She stopped for a moment and wiped her running nose on the sleeve of her gown. "I went down to the taproom and opened the door, thinking I'd pull him a draft, just to set him right, you know. When I went inside, it was still dark from the shutters being closed and I went . . . I went. . . ."

Here she broke down and began to sob again. Father Anselm took up her tale. "Apparently she went to open the shutters and stumbled over something. As she fell she re- alised it was a person lying on the floor. She was not alarmed at first. It seems"—and here he looked down with a stern but understanding expression at the woman, who was again hiding her head in her hands—"that there are of- ten patrons who spend the night on the floor after they have had more ale than is good for them. However, when she managed to get the shutters open she found that there were not one but four prone figures on the floor, and that they were not insensible from drink, but dead. One of them was her husband."

Bascot regarded the nearly incoherent woman and spoke to the priest. "The serjeant and I will go and see for ourselves what is at the alehouse. Please keep Mistress Agnes here until we return."

Father Anselm, with a resigned sigh, agreed to do as he had been asked. The corners of his mouth turned down in an exasperated grimace as they left him to the difficult duty of trying to console the unfortunate alewife.

Coming outside from the dark interior of the church the light of the sun, which even this early had more heat than was usual, dazzled their eyes. They went across the cobbles to the door of the alehouse, ignoring the stares of a small crowd that had now begun to gather about the horses and men-at-arms, and removed the bar which the priest had placed across it. From the outside it had the appearance of a moderately well-run establishment. The walls had been freshly limed and the shutters were clean and in good repair. The sign above the lintel had been recently repainted. But as Bascot pushed the door open the smell of heat and death, wrenchingly familiar from the time of his captivity, rushed out to meet him. No amount of cleanliness or industry could defeat that stench.

Ernulf told the two men-at-arms to remain where they were, then he and Bascot went in, finding themselves standing on a small threshold just inside the door. To the right was the entrance to the taproom, in front of them a passage with what appeared to be an open door leading outside at its end, and to their left a flight of narrow stairs presumably giving access to the floor above. Both men drew their swords and, moving swiftly, made a thorough search of the premises. They found no sign of any intruder.

Returning to the taproom they stepped inside, the death smell more pungent here. The interior was dim, lit only by the glare of the sun glancing off the wall of the building opposite through the one open casement which the alewife had unshuttered. The bodies lay like piles of unwashed linen on the floor and Ernulf stepped around them to throw open the other casement. The scuttling of rats could be heard, and the insistent drone of flies.

The task was unpleasant, but necessary, and one by one Ernulf and Bascot went to each body and examined it. There were three men and a woman. One of the men was elderly, and wore the long beard of a Jew. Nearest to the door, he was half-propped against a three-legged stool. At the front of his gown was a long rent through which the marks of a dagger thrust could be seen just below his heart; a thin trickle of blood mixed with the grey hairs on his chest. The exposed tissue had a drained look and was tinged a bluish white. His face was the colour of clay, the mouth hanging slackly and the lids of his eyes not quite closed. His hands lay one on each side of his body, loosely, palms up. The left one bore evidence that the rats had begun to feed.

The body in the far corner was that of a young man, plainly dressed in sturdy clothes. He was fair of hair and face with a broad sprinkle of freckles across his nose. A crease of skin at the side of his neck showed the scar of an old injury, possibly a burn. This victim had been stabbed from behind and he was slumped forward, as though he had obligingly offered his back to his attacker. Again, there was only a small stream of dried blood from the wound on the back of his jerkin.

Bascot and Ernulf moved to where the woman lay, halfway between the Jew and the young man, in front of one of the casements. It must have been her body that the alewife had tripped over. She was slightly turned onto her side, and one arm was flung out in front of her as though in useless supplication. She was wearing a gown of cheap but bright material with sleeves of green. There was no covering on her head and her hair, the shade of pale honey, tumbled down her back in riotous disarray. Nearby lay a wig such as those worn by prostitutes, made of hair taken from the mane and tail of a horse and dyed. The colour of this one was a deep dark red. Ernulf turned her over. Even though dead, she had a fair prettiness that was marred by the vermillion face paint daubed on her cheeks. Like the Jew, her breast bore the marks of a dagger thrust above the low neck of her gown, with a small stain of blood smearing the lace just below it.

The last victim was a man of late middle age, with thick shoulders and a large stomach barely contained by the black leather belt that encircled it. He was sprawled on the floor beside a cask of ale, face down in the rushes, his limbs stiff. The back of his skull had been smashed in. Beside him lay two empty ale cups.

None of the victims had purses at their belts or were wearing jewellery of any kind. If any of the men had been equipped with dagger or sword, these too had vanished and there was no trace of any blade that might have been used in the stabbings.

Bascot looked at Ernulf. "Except for the alekeeper, these bodies have been dead longer than since curfew last night."

Ernulf agreed. Both were too familiar with the state of bodies during the aftermath of battle to mistake the length of time it took for the telltale signs of deterioration to show.

"The death rigor has come and gone except for Wat. And there's precious little blood for three people stabbed. The walls would be spattered with it if the deed was done in here. And there's no sign of a struggle, either."

Bascot knelt down beside the Jew, the nearest corpse to him. He lifted the hand that had not been molested by the rats. The nails were free of any skin or material that might have been torn from an attacker and, apart from the rent made by the dagger, his clothes seemed untouched. The young man and woman's bodies and clothing were in a like condition. "I would think that all three were dead before they were stabbed," he said. "The blood had already settled and the hearts ceased to pump when these wounds were made. There are no bruises. Whatever the means of their deaths, it has not left a mark." He looked up at the serjeant. "Do you recognise any of them?"

"Two," Ernulf replied succinctly. "The Jew—his name is Samuel. Cousin of Isaac that lives in the big house in Mikelgate. And the one over there"—he nodded in the direction of the body lying beside the ale cask—"that's Walter, the alewife's husband. The other two I've never seen before. The girl looks, by her dress and wig and face paint, to be a harlot, but she's not a regular from the stewes down in Butwerk. I'd recognise her if she was." He rubbed his stubble-encrusted jaw. "'Course, with all the strangers that we've got in Lincoln right now she could be some newly arrived country girl who decided to turn bawd in the hope of earning a few pennies. If she is she might have strayed out of the whores' patch."

The serjeant waved his hand towards the young man. "Don't know about the lad. Could be a visitor come for the fair, or perhaps an apprentice new to Lincoln."

If Ernulf did not know the two young people then it was most probable that they were strangers. In his short time at the castle, Bascot had come to realise that Ernulf seemed to know every person that dwelt within the precinct of the town walls as well as having an almost intimate knowledge of most of the buildings. Since Ernulf had spent all his life in the town, except for occasional sojourns abroad in the service of the Hayes, this was not surprising.

As fresh air came into the room from the opened shutters, it became a little easier to breathe in the fetid atmosphere. Bascot and Ernulf moved back towards the door. Near the entrance was a table, on its surface a candleholder with a burnt down stub and a pair of dice. Apart from that, and the two empty tumblers on the floor, the place was tidy and seemed to have been scrubbed within the last few days;

even though the reek of ale was exceptionally strong, there were no obvious spills and the rushes on the floor looked fresh.

"Why bring three dead bodies in here and stab them?" Bascot mused. "Why not leave them wherever the deed was done? It is most strange."

The serjeant shrugged. He had seen death too often to be much affected by it, and the bodies in the chamber were not, as far as he knew, anyone of importance—two strangers, a Jew and an alekeeper. "I'll send for the infirmarian at the Priory of All Saints. The monks'll take the bodies and see them ready for burial—the Christian ones, that is. The Jews'll want to take care of their own, I reckon. Good fortune that one of the dead was a Jew. Otherwise the whole lot of 'em would be blamed for the murders. That's usually the way it is. And that's the last thing Lady Nicolaa needs, right in the middle of the biggest fair of the year, a hue and cry after any member of the Jewish community. Not good for trade, is that."

Bascot flinched inwardly. His enmity towards the Jews had been the same as that of every other good Christian until he had been captured by the Saracens. It had seemed logical and just that they were to be hated as the race who had crucified Christ. But during his years of captivity there had, at times, been Jews imprisoned with him, especially after the great infidel leader, Saladin, died and his unruly family fought for control of the Muslim world. Bascot had come to know one of them well, a young Jewish lad named Benjamin. He and the Jew had never become friends, but with the enemy a common one, they had helped each other and it had been Benjamin who had been instrumental in Bascot's escape from his Muslim captors. That Benjamin had lost his life in aiding the Templar was a fact that Bascot found hard to forget, just as it also made it difficult for him to blindly accept the premise that all Jews were unworthy of any emotion but contempt from a Christian.

Uncomfortable, he made no reply to the serjeant's comment and Ernulf continued, "Will you want to talk to the alewife again? Seems strange she slept upstairs all night and didn't hear her husband havin' his head bashed in."

Bascot, remembering the near hysteria of the alewife, reluctantly agreed that it seemed necessary to question her again and instructed Ernulf, while he was seeing her, to send news to the Jewish community of Samuel's death.

Ernulf nodded in a brisk fashion at the instructions. "I'll send one of my lads to do that after he's been to the Priory. In the meantime, I'd best stay here. That crowd outside is not going to be satisfied until they find out what's happened and it might need a firm hand to curb their questions. When you're ready, we'll go back and report to Lady Nicolaa."

Bascot nodded, taking a last look at the bodies, particularly those of the woman and the young man, before he left. Death was fast removing the bloom of youth from the faces of these two, but there still remained vestiges of their vitality: the smoothness of the unlined cheeks, the bright hue of their hair, so similar in colour. It had been too soon for them to die, these two youngsters, especially from a cause as foul as murder. To die on a battlefield was one's own choice; for a life to be taken in stealth and for the purposes of another was a grievous offence, not only to man but to God Himself.

Outside, as Ernulf had predicted, the number of curious people had grown and they were pestering the two men-at-arms, who stood firmly silent, about what had happened. When Bascot appeared, they drew back a pace, respectful of his knight's rank and not a little intimidated by the small replica of the Templar badge he wore high on the shoulder of his tunic. He walked, unaccosted, across the street and into the church. The coolness of the interior and the smell of incense were welcome after the stifling aroma of death.

Three

✦—✛—✦

SEVERAL HOURS LATER, IN A SMALL CARPENTRY SHOP hard by the church of St. Mary Crackpole near Mikelgate, the alewife, Agnes, sat with her sister, Jennet. She had ceased to cry but an occasional sob would still shake her ample frame and she was having difficulty sipping the posset made of herbs and honey that Jennet had prepared for her.

The two sisters were very different in appearance, for Jennet was tall and slim and the carrot-coloured hair that framed her thin sharp face still bore no traces of grey even though she was only three years younger than Agnes. In one respect, however, they had a similarity, and that was in strength. Agnes possessed it in her thick bones and sturdy flesh; in Jennet it evidenced itself in her mind, which was aggressive and quick.

The younger sister regarded the older. Jennet bore no grief that her brother-by-marriage was dead. She had thought Agnes a fool for marrying him and was not sorry to see him gone except, perhaps, for the manner of it and how it would affect her sister.

"You must try to calm yourself, Agnes," she said sternly. "The monks have taken Wat. They will see that he is prepared right and laid out for his burial. Which won't be delayed too long," she added thoughtfully, "because of this hot weather."

This unfortunate but true observation set Agnes off into a fresh paroxysm of tears and Jennet lost her patience. "Why do you carry on so? Wat were not a good husband to you, as I've told you many a time. How many beatings have you had off him since you married him two years ago? More times than you can count, I'll warrant. I thought you would have learned your lesson with that other wastrel our da wed you to when you was young. Even though he didn't raise his hand to you, he was the laziest swine I've ever met in my life. And when he died, not beforetimes I might add, from drinking too much ale, you went and married another useless oaf, twice as worse. And he was your own free choice, too. God forgive me for saying so, but it's maybe not a sad matter that none of your babbies survived to grow. They'd never have thrived, not with the husbands you've had."

"Oh, Jennet, don't scold me," Agnes sobbed. "It's bad enough Wat was killed the way he was, and those others— stabbed right in my own taproom. But I could have been murdered, too. Haven't you thought of that? It's making my flesh creep, knowing I was there while . . . while. . . ." She started to cry afresh.

"Well, you weren't murdered, were you? Whoever did it wasn't after you, was he? If he had been, you wouldn't be here in my house now."

Jennet looked at her sister, purposely stifling the pity she felt. She had learned through their years of growing up that if you once gave Agnes any compassion she would

give herself over completely to self-pity. The only way to get
her through any difficulty was to bully her out of it. Their
father had been the same, and Jennet had learned how to
deal with Agnes by watching their mother. As Agnes began
to recover somewhat and took a sip of her posset, Jennet
looked at her consideringly. There was something more to
Agnes' tears than grief. She was frightened alright, but Jennet was sure there was something else, something she was
not telling. Agnes could be sly at times and secretive, just
like their old dad, but Jennet could usually worm any secrets out of her sister, most of them anyway.

"When Father Anselm sent for me and I came to the
church this morning, that Templar knight was asking you
some strange questions. What did he mean about anything
hidden in the ale house?" Jennet had arrived at St. Andrew's
just as Bascot was about to leave and had only caught the
last part of the conversation between him and Agnes.

"I don't know, Jennet, truly I don't." Fear now completely took over Agnes. It was plain in the way her hands
and voice shook. "He said that them bodies—the others,
not Wat—might have been in my house or yard the day before. But I never saw anything. We had our custom as usual
and I served up the ale. The taster even came and said I'd
made a good brew. I don't know anything about any bodies,
or anything else. . . ."

Jennet took a seat beside her sister. The table at which
they were sitting was good and solid, as were the four chairs
arranged around it. She was proud of the few bits of furniture she had, for her husband, Tom, who was a carpenter,
had made them. He wasn't a master craftsman, but he belonged to the town guild and earned a reasonable living
making simple items and doing repairs in the yard out behind their little house. He was a good man, worked hard
and never took too much ale or hit her even though, by law,
he was allowed to strike her if she gave him just cause. And
they had raised three children; the two girls married well,

one to a freeman with a small holding outside Lincoln and the other to a tanner, while the boy, her youngest, helped his father. She felt pity again for Agnes in her plight and unhappy life, but quashed it down. She didn't want her to start crying again.

"Did Wat come to bed with you last night? Or did he stay up?" Jennet asked.

Agnes looked at her sister, then her eyes slid away. Jennet knew there was something she was not telling. "He always stayed up after curfew, just for a little while usually. To have a last glass of ale, or . . ."

"Play at dice?" her sister finished knowingly. "But last night? What did he do last night?"

"The same," Agnes mumbled.

"If there was something different, you had better tell me," Jennet said firmly. "If that murderer missed you by mistake and you know something—well, he might just come back to finish you off. If there's anything you haven't told, the more that know it the better. You'll be safer that way."

Agnes' eyes rolled in her head and she began to shake again. Jennet gripped her by the arms with surprising strength in her bony fingers. "What happened, Agnes? Tell me."

"Wat said . . . Wat . . ." Agnes began to stutter and Jennet shook her so hard that her sister's large bosom wobbled beneath her gown.

"Tell me," she demanded.

Agnes gulped. "Last night Wat told me to go up to bed and not to come down, not for anything. He said if I did, I'd be sorry. When I asked him why, he said someone was coming to see him and whoever it was wouldn't take kindly to me being about. I thought it was just another of his dice games and said so, but he gave me a slap and said I'd better keep my mouth shut and put myself out of sight." Agnes stopped for a moment and wiped the wetness of her tears from her face with the hem of her gown.

"And . . ." Jennet prompted. "Did you not hear anything,

screams or summat? With four people being murdered, I'd have thought there would have been some sort of ruckus."

"I heard nary a sound. I did just as Wat had said. I didn't want a beating. Wat had a heavy hand, as well you know." Here she hastily crossed herself, for forgiveness in speaking ill of the dead. "But, Jennet, that morning Wat had told me not to touch anything in the yard. I was just to pour the ale, not draw it. And he wouldn't let me even go out to the latrine, at the back. I had to use our old pot in the house. But, Jennet, if Wat had known there was to be murder done, why was he murdered himself? It doesn't make any sense."

"Did you tell the Templar about this when he asked you?"

"No, he scared me. He looks so . . . like a heathen, with his dark skin, and there's that eye patch. It's like he could be a murderer himself."

"That's silly," Jennet exclaimed. "He's a Templar, swore his life to God's service, he did, and spent years in a cell at the mercy of them same bloody infidels you say he looks like. If you could trust anyone, it's him. Even more than the priests, because most of them are more interested in the pennies we give than in saving our souls. You don't see them giving up everything they possess for the love of God, like he did."

"Father Anselm isn't like that," Agnes protested. "He was kind to me this morning and helped me when I was all alone." There was an accusatory tone in Agnes' voice, as though her sister should have known of her distress and been there when it happened.

"Well, some of them are alright," Jennet conceded. "There are a few good ones, I suppose, even if Father Anselm is a bit too well favoured for a priest, and knows he is, and all. But the Templar is from Lady Nicolaa, not from her husband, the sheriff. Gerard Camville is none too gentle a creature, as you well know. If he sends one of his men-at-arms to question you, you'll be made to tell what you know, right enough. And they won't be asking you quiet like the Templar did. They'll take you up to the castle and beat the truth out of you."

Jennet wasn't too sure if this was true or not, about the Templar being sent by Nicolaa de la Haye, but she had heard a man-at-arms from the castle telling the Haye serjeant that Lady Nicolaa would be waiting for their report in her own chambers so there was a good chance that the castellan had sent them. Whether it was so or not, Jennet wanted to scare her sister into doing as she was told, and Sheriff Camville was enough of a devil to scare anyone.

"Oh, Jennet," Agnes wailed, "what am I going to do?"

"Tomorrow we'll ask Father Anselm to tell the Templar you want to see him, and then you're going to repeat what you told me. I'll go with you," she added, seeing the distraught look on her sister's face. "The sooner the task is done, the sooner you'll be easy." She looked down sternly at her sister. "There isn't anything else you're not telling me, is there?"

Agnes shook her head and swore that there wasn't. Jennet was not confident that her sister was telling the truth, but she decided not to press the matter because Agnes truly did look as though she might swoon from the torment of emotions that her ordeal had caused. Later, when Agnes had rested, Jennet would question her again. She was sure there was something her sister was hiding.

Finally allowing the compassion she felt to come to the surface, Jennet took her sister by the arm and led her up a flight of narrow stairs to a bedchamber above. "You lie down on our pallet and sleep now, Agnes. I'll come up later and fetch you a bit of food for your dinner."

Willingly letting her sister take charge, Agnes crawled under the thin cover and closed her eyes. She didn't know what she would have done if she hadn't been able to come to Jennet.

Once Jennet heard her sister's breathing begin to grow slow and regular, she left her. There was more to this coil than could be seen, she was sure of that. Just as she was also sure that Agnes could be blamed in some way, if not for the actual killing, then for having a helping hand in it. She hadn't suggested that to her sister, for it would scare her even more than she already was and, besides, Jennet was sure that Agnes was innocent. She was a trial sometimes, and could be unexpectedly stubborn, but she would never hurt anyone. Why, if she had been that kind she would have fought back at Wat when he hit her. She had enough strength to lift a cask of ale, she could have defended herself. But even when she was being beaten she had never tried to hurt the one who was doing it to her.

Of one thing Jennet was sure, and that was that she didn't really want her sister to be taken in for questioning by the sheriff's men. Gerard Camville was a brutal man, and crimes committed by anyone other than himself were harshly punished. And he would be looking for a solution to this murder. It would be bad for custom in the town to have an unknown murderer on the loose and he was fond of his silver, was the sheriff. Just let him see a drop in the tolls and taxes the fair would bring and he would be angry, angry with that cold fury he was capable of—and would look for someone to blame it on. No, she had to get Agnes to tell what she knew and preferably to someone not directly connected to Camville. If she had put the right interpretation on what she had overheard, then the Templar was Lady Nicolaa's knight, not Camville's, and it would be much better for Agnes to be under the jurisdiction of the castellan rather than the sheriff. Lady Nicolaa was stern, but she was fair, unlike her husband. Yes, Jennet decided, she would take Agnes to the Templar. Besides, he was a monk, God's own man, and despite her remarks to Agnes about clerics, she did believe that some of them were good, especially one who had risked his life in the service of Christ amongst

the heathens. Muttering a prayer beneath her breath she
asked for God's help and that her instinct about the Templar prove true. She had always tried to protect her sister
and often failed; she implored God for assistance in safe-
guarding Agnes now.

Four

⊹

AFTER HE AND ERNULF HAD MADE THEIR REPORT TO Nicolaa de la Haye, Bascot left the keep, motioning for Gianni to follow him. Outside, the bailey of the castle was a mass of moving men and animals as visitors arrived for the fair and castle servants rushed about unloading baggage and arranging for it to be stored. Along the perimeter of the castle walls outbuildings were packed close together—smithy, granary, the garrison sleeping quarters and stables, and space allotted for use to the carpenters, fletchers and coopers. There were also pens for sheep and swine, an area for poultry and, at the far north side, walled in for protection against a stray four-footed intruder, Lady Nicolaa's herb garden. Adjacent to the garden were the mews where the castle hawks were kept.

Bascot and Gianni threaded their way through the crowd, making for the tall tower of the old keep, and Bascot's room at the top. The Templar knew it was a rare privilege, and in deference to his standing as a member of the Order, that he had been given a private chamber, for the

majority of Haye retainers made up their pallets on the
floor of the great hall. Although he was grateful for the privacy, the room was almost at the top of the narrow tower,
and he cursed his aching ankle as he climbed the circular
stairway to the third storey. Once inside, he sank down
gratefully onto the shelf that held his pallet and told Gianni
to pour them ale from a leather flagon standing in the corner. Reaching into a bundle by the bed, Bascot brought out
a small leather sack. In it was a supply of the lumps of boiled
sugar that were sent to England from Templar property in
the Holy Land, made from sweet canes that grew in the
fields near Acre. The Arabs called them *al-Kandiq*, but in
England they were known simply as *candi*, and were one of
the items the Templars used in trade to raise funds for the
upkeep of their Order. Bascot was very fond of them, even
though they made his teeth ache if he ate too many. He
tossed one to Gianni and watched the boy's delighted expression as he popped it into his mouth and let it roll on his
tongue.

Bascot sipped his ale and sucked the *candi* thoughtfully,
his mind on the meeting from which he had just come.
Lady Nicolaa's husband, Gerard Camville, had been present,
just returned from a morning's hunt. Bascot was reserved
in his opinion of the sheriff. Ostensibly the Templar was a
guest in the retinue of his wife, for it had been to her that
his introductions had been directed when he had arrived
last year, but Camville was her husband and, as such, was
lord over both her and her offices and possessions. The
sheriff was an impressive man, massive with thick black
hair cut high on the nape of his neck in the old Norman
fashion and a heavy jaw that he kept clean shaven. He
seemed as broad as he was tall, with thick shoulders and
thighs that swelled beneath the rust-coloured jerkin and
hose that he wore. But his unpredictability disturbed Bascot, for his moods were as restless as his body seemed to
be. All the time Bascot and Ernulf had been giving a report

of their findings at the alehouse, the sheriff had prowled back and forth in front of them and behind. It was as though he found the walls of the private chamber in which they were holding the meeting too small to contain his wide frame.

When the tale had been finished, Gerard had muttered an oath and said, "And tonight we can expect a deputation from the town officials, come to complain about a murderer being loose, spurred on by their wives and daughters. Every female in Lincoln will be seeing a bloody fiend behind her bed curtains, or lingering malevolently near her privy. Damn the deed, and him who did it! My men are stretched as far as they can be at the moment, protecting visiting merchants from outlaws on the road and from thieves in the town. I cannot spare any to go hunting this miscreant."

He banged the wine cup, from which he had been drinking, down on the table in front of his wife. "And, if these two strangers are found to be of more than lowly station their relatives will come dunning me for recompense. It all means more silver to be paid out, silver I will have to make up out of my own coffers, for the king will say it is my responsibility, not the crown's."

Lady Nicolaa had sat silent throughout her husband's tirade. What Camville had said was all too true. As sheriff, he was responsible for the safety of travellers to the fair and if he was found wanting in his duties, he would have to pay the cost for that failing to any family member who had suffered from the loss of the deceased. Even villeins, absconded from a lord, would merit a few pieces of silver as a consideration to their master. Bascot knew that Camville was nervous of the new king, John, who had ascended to the throne the previous year after the death of his brother, Richard. This was so even though, while Richard had been away on Crusade, Camville and Prince John—as he had been then—had conspired to overthrow the chancellor that

Lionheart had left to rule England in his stead. Reprisals had been heavy on Camville when Richard returned to England after being imprisoned in Austria on his way home from the Crusades. The king had taken the shrievalty away from him. Although John had restored it when he had gained the crown, the new king was not as trusting as his brother and watched Camville with a wary eye, for he knew how easily he could be swayed to betrayal. Had it not been that John regarded Nicolaa de la Haye as an old and trusted friend, it was doubtful he would have reappointed Camville to his post, and the sheriff was aware of how tenuous his position was. If the people of Lincoln complained loud enough about their sheriff, the king would have no recourse but to listen and perhaps give the lucrative post to another.

When Nicolaa spoke, it was quietly. "The alehouse is on land held in fee from the Haye demesne, Gerard. Anything that happens on property from which the Haye coffers gain revenue is ultimately my responsibility. It is, therefore, right and proper that I personally oversee the search for the perpetrator of these murders. At least initially, just until the fair is over and our visitors have left, which is only a matter of a week or so. And, I think, the townspeople will accept my guidance. If they do, it will soften any complaint they may make to the king."

Camville relaxed enough under her suggestion to stop his pacing. He nodded. "You will use Haye men?" he asked.

"De Marins and Ernulf have already viewed the bodies. They can make further enquiries into the matter and I will inform the coroner what is being done."

Nicolaa, with a concise movement of her hands, pressed them down on the table top and rose, signifying the end of the discussion. "See if you can find out the identity of the two strangers, de Marins. Also enquire about the Jew—his own people may be able to tell you if he had incurred the enmity of a disgruntled creditor or was, perhaps, at odds with one of his own race." She thought for a moment, then said, "This alewife—were she and her husband complaisant with each other, I wonder? It may be she knows more than she is telling. Could she have been responsible for the deaths, do you think?"

Bascot shook his head. "She has the strength, I think, but not the wits or the boldness. And it took wits and boldness to kill and hide three bodies unseen for at least a day."

Lady Nicolaa gave his words some thought. "Still, it is worth investigating," she said. "See her again. Be discreet, but thorough. You may call on Ernulf whenever you require his assistance."

With that, he and the serjeant had been dismissed and Bascot had left the chamber, feeling a tinge of admiration for the economy of Lady Nicolaa's direction and the ease with which she had quelled the uncertain temper of her husband. Such diplomacy was a rare gift.

Bascot ruminated on the task he had been given as he sipped his ale and enjoyed the delicious sweetness of the brew. How was he to set about finding out the identity of two strangers in a town half-full of people not ordinarily resident here? The smell of the ale in his cup rose strongly to his nostrils and he felt a jog at his memory. The reek of ale in the taproom earlier that day had been just as powerful, the room filled with the odour even though there had been not a drop poured in any cup, and the room clean of spills. It was not unusual for a taproom to smell so, but it had been powerfully strong, almost overwhelming, as though a barrel had been standing open in the middle of the floor. Even the bodies had stunk of it.

He began to ponder on this when Gianni made a movement and attracted his attention. The lad, though mute, had developed a series of gestures that Bascot easily interpreted. Now the boy was rubbing his stomach and pointing to his mouth. Bascot grinned. It was time for the midday meal and Gianni was hungry.

"I cannot face those stairs again in such a short time, Gianni. Go down and see the cook. Get us some food and bring it back here. When we have eaten, there is work to do."

The boy scampered away, and Bascot lay back on his pallet and lifted the patch that covered the place where his eye had once been, rubbing the socket gently. Not vanity but pride accounted for the fact that he did not like anyone, even Gianni, to see the wound uncovered. It was a grisly sight and for a moment the pain that had burned and taken away his senses when a Muslim lord had ordered the hot iron to sear his flesh returned like a flash of lightning, then receded. He would not think on that, he decided, the memory was too painful, not for the loss of his eye but for the helplessness he had felt afterwards, and the deep anger that followed.

He got up and moved to the tiny window slit. Overhead the sky was a clear translucent blue, a heat haze shimmering over the fields and woods beyond the castle walls. Down in the bailey he could see Gianni running back across the ward towards the tower, the dark curls on his head bouncing as he struggled to balance two wooden bowls filled with food, one on top of the other. Bascot was glad to see that the boy was beginning to fill out, to put some flesh on his slight frame. When the Templar had found the lad on a wharf in Palermo the boy had been fighting with some mangy street dogs over the body of a dead pigeon, his bones protruding sticklike under a thin covering of skin. The lad had been starving, covered with the festering sores of malnutrition and eyes no more than black circles of pain. Bascot, his soul stirred by the utter desolation of the boy's expression, had taken pity on him and given him food, then made him his servant, training him and teaching him his letters on the long journey back to England. He had been rewarded by finding that the boy had a quick and intelligent mind hidden beneath his inability to speak. Bascot did not know how old he was—nor did Gianni—but it was a reasonable guess that the young body had been stunted by lack of food and that he was older than his size would suggest, and was probably about eleven or twelve years of age. Not being able to speak his name, if he had ever known it, Bascot had christened him Giovanni, after the saint of the day on which he had found him. This had soon been shortened to the diminutive, Gianni. The boy was devoted to Bascot and, in return, the Templar had come to regard the lad in almost the same light he would have had he been his own son.

Gianni's light footsteps pattered on the stairs outside and, as Bascot slipped his eye patch back into place, the door was pushed open to reveal the boy and his burden. One bowl, on the bottom, was filled with chunks of bread; the other, on top, was brimming with a hearty meat stew thickened with root vegetables. Carefully Gianni set them down on the floor then, removing the bread, he poured a smaller portion of stew for himself into the empty bowl and served Bascot with the remainder, laying chunks of bread beside his master on a clean cloth which he had carried folded in his belt. Two wooden spoons appeared from the folds of his tunic and he carefully polished one of them with the hem of his shirt before laying it beside Bascot. Looking up at his mentor with liquid brown eyes, he waited until Bascot gave a nod of approbation before sitting down cross-legged on the floor and hungrily attacking his own food.

As they ate, Bascot thought again about the events of the morning. In a sense, Lady Nicolaa was not only giving him a duty to perform, but a test of his capabilities. She had taken him into her household on the recommendation of the Templar master in London, who was an acquaintance of hers. When she had learned that Bascot could read and write she had asked him, after he had regained some of his strength, if he would assist her in carrying out some of the tasks of running the demesne. Literacy was uncommon, even amongst the nobility, and she had need of someone trustworthy to aid her and her overworked bailiffs and clerks in preparing the records necessary to overseeing her lands. Nothing too onerous, she had explained, or unfitting to his rank, but she herself had so little time and it would bring her great relief if he would agree. Bascot had smiled at her guile. Since he was eating her food and accepting the shelter of his room he could hardly refuse, but she had given him the courtesy of putting the request in the form of a favour to her, not as payment for her generosity. He had agreed to do as she asked and she had given him her thanks.

So far, since coming to Lincoln, his duties had consisted of visiting some of the lands belonging to Haye and overseeing the tallies of sheep and grain, recording the stores that had been used from the castle stock and helping with the many accounts that had to be kept of wages paid to knights and servants. Now, it seemed, Lady Nicolaa had given him a task that would stretch his capabilities, see if he was able to cope with a situation that gave him more responsibility, albeit on her behalf.

He wondered why. There were other knights in her retinue to whom she could have handed over the responsibility of investigating the murders. He was, after all, not strictly in her service, but only a guest. She knew he could have refused but she had also surmised that he would not. Why had she chosen him? Was it just convenient, or had she done it deliberately? Her calm face, slightly round with a margin of red hair turning grey showing beneath her coif, had regarded him steadily, her pale, slightly protuberant, blue eyes deceptively innocuous. She had held his own gaze as she spoke. She seemed to be defying him to refuse. Why?

At last he shrugged and left his pondering. When the Saracens had first put him into a prison cell after his capture during a skirmish on the road to Ascalon, he had asked himself a similar question. Why had God chosen that he should not die along with his comrades; why had he not fallen with honour and glory, as they had? Why had the Muslims not killed him? No ransom was ever paid for a Templar. It was a rule of the Order to bolster courage and reinforce dedication. But his captors had not killed him. Instead they had kept him as a slave. And he had never understood why. From prison cell to base servant in the household of a Saracen lord to chained oarsman on an infidel pirate ship, through all these happenings he had asked himself the purpose of such a fate. Shipwrecked and washed ashore on the coast of Cyprus, as he had lain recovering from his injuries in a Templar hostel on the friendly island, still he had questioned what the good Lord above had chosen for his destiny. Then, during the long journey home, by boat to Sicily where he had found Gianni, and then on horseback through lands both hostile and friendly to an English knight, he had wondered until finally he had arrived in London and found that the family he had left behind—brother, father and mother—had all, in various ways, perished while he had been in captivity. Then he had ceased to ask or to care. God had forsaken him, forgotten his existence. No longer could he find consolation in the vows he had taken on that far gone day when he had joined the Templar Order. The faith that had burst forth so joyously when he had pledged himself to Christ had dwindled, becoming no more than the flicker of a feeble rush light.

It had been because of this lapse of faith that the Templar master in London had suggested he leave the Order for a space and recover his health within the shelter of the royal castle of Lincoln. Usually, any Templar knight leaving the Order had to enter a regime that was stricter in its rules than their own, but in his case Bascot knew that the Templars hoped he might return to their fold. Sending him to Nicolaa de la Haye had been a way of releasing him, but not quite letting him go.

Bascot knew this and accepted it. When he had first ar-

rived at Lincoln he had just wanted a quiet place to recover
from the rigours of his captivity and the shock of learning
about the deaths in his family. So far, he found himself content. He was well fed and had slowly, by dint of steady
bouts of exercise on the practice field with Ernulf, found
his body responding so that he had recovered much of his
former strength. Lady Nicolaa, he suspected, had purposely
allowed him this space of healing. Now he thought that she
gauged him ready for something more and was challenging
him. Was he being manipulated and, if so, to what purpose?
Once again, he put the question aside.

Gianni had finished his stew, the bowl wiped clean with
a chunk of bread, and that chunk devoured. Bascot gave
him his own utensils to carry and they made their way out
of the chamber into the passage where, set into the wall of
the tower, was a latrine. Nearby a cistern had been fashioned with a tap that sluiced rain water from a tank on the
roof and flushed the waste into a midden on the lower floor.
After using the facilities, Gianni carefully rinsed the tumblers from which they had drunk their ale and put them
back in their chamber. Then they descended the stairs, Gianni
running ahead to return their eating bowls to the kitchens
while Bascot headed for the stables. If he was to discover
the identity of the two dead strangers he would need to
have a more careful look at their faces, and their clothes.
Mounted once more on the grey gelding he had used that
morning, and with Gianni riding pillion behind, he headed
for the Priory of All Saints, set in the ward of the cathedral.

The priory was an ancient institution, inhabited by Bene-
dictine monks in one part and, behind a high wall that sepa-
rated its buildings from the rest, a nunnery of the same order.
Bascot dismounted at the gate and, after informing the
porter of his errand, was ushered into the presence of the infirmarian, leaving his mount with Gianni in the priory yard.

Brother Jehan, the infirmarian, was tending a few sick

and aging monks in the long low room that served as a hospital. He listened attentively while Bascot explained his errand. The monk was an elderly man, with white hair ringing his tonsure and a face creased with lines of care. He seemed to Bascot almost as frail as his charges until he bent to administer a draught of some herbal mixture to a young novice raging with a fever. The patient, in his delirium, fought against the cup held to his mouth and Brother Jehan, revealing an unexpected strength in his long bony fingers, gripped the young man by the shoulders and forced him back so that he could tip the contents of the cup into the gaping mouth. Smoothing the brow of his charge with fingers now gentle, he gave instructions to an assistant to watch the patient and motioned for Bascot to follow him.

The infirmarian led the way out of the chamber and down a passage to another room, this one smaller and in semidarkness. The shutters were drawn and only two candles, set in holders below a crucifix hung high on one of the walls, gave any light. In the centre of the room, on trestle tables, lay two linen covered mounds. The odour of sweet-smelling herbs was strong in the air, along with the aroma of incense.

"These are the earthly remains of the alekeeper and the boy whose identity is unknown. The female is with our sisters in the nunnery," Brother Jehan informed Bascot. "The bodies have been cleansed and wrapped in their shrouds, and Masses will be said for the repose of their souls in chapel tonight, where they will lie until they are interred. Ordinarily the alekeeper would have been laid out in his home, but since it was the place of his murder, his wife's family has asked that we keep him here."

"I would like to see the stranger's face again, Brother," Bascot said, "and would also ask if there were any marks, other than the dagger wound, on his body. It appeared, to the castle serjeant who was with me when we examined the bodies, and to myself, that all except the alekeeper had been dead for more than just the previous night, and also that the knife thrusts in both the young man brought here, as well as the woman and the Jew, were not the cause of their demise, but had been inflicted after they were dead."

The monk had been nodding as Bascot had spoken. "Yes, when I was laying out the young man I thought it strange myself that there was so little blood around the wound."

He walked over to one of the trestle tables and drew back the linen cover, revealing the face of the stranger. The skin was now waxy and covered with a slight sheen of putrefaction. Against the pallor of his face the freckles stood out on the bridge of his nose like spatters of blood. The old scar at the crease of his neck could be plainly viewed now that his tunic had been removed and the shroud left open about his face. It would not be sewn closed until the body was ready to be sealed in its coffin. The young man's hair was still crisp and fair, curling in a parody of life over the fast deteriorating flesh.

Brother Jehan sighed. "So young to be taken from life," he murmured, crossing himself. "It would appear that he was dead for some few hours at least before he was stabbed. His life blood had settled in his extremities and so there was little left to spill from the wound.

"There were a few welts on the body," Brother Jehan continued, "on the back and across both knees, but none of any such magnitude that would cause death."

"What, then, do you think killed him? Poison?"

"Possibly. There are many fatal mixtures that can be made from plants and herbs growing in the countryside and few that would leave traces of their ingestion. Or he could have been rendered unconscious by a similar mixture and then suffocated whilst out of his senses."

Bascot agreed that the latter was a possibility, then asked, "The stranger's clothes, Brother—do you have them here?"

"They are in the next room, awaiting cleansing, as are the alekeeper's. The alekeeper's, of course, will be returned to his widow once they are in a state that will not upset her. The stranger's I had thought to give to the poor, or to the leper house outside Pottergate. Do you wish to dispose of them in some other way?"

"No," Bascot assured him. "I would just like to see them. Perhaps they may give me a clue to the identity of their owner."

The monk left the room for a few moments, then re-entered, carrying a bundle of clothing. His expression was one of distaste. "I have no discontent in dealing with stains of the blood with which our good Lord sustains life, but the stink of ale is offensive. The room where they were found must have been awash with it."

He handed the young man's tunic and hose to Bascot who had already, at the approach of the monk, smelled the acrid reek of old ale. There were few stains on the clothing however; rather it seemed that the odour had permeated the cloth without wetting it.

He looked up at the monk. "I think, Brother, that I may have some idea of how this stench adhered itself to the fabric, and also where it was that the young man spent the hours after his death."

He shook out the garments, thinking as he did so, then asked, "When the clothing has been cleansed, may I have it for a time? I will return it for you to give as alms wherever you choose, but this cloth is of a fine weave and, to my eyes, looks distinctive. It may be that its origin will be recognised by one of Lincoln's weavers, either as their own, or as that of a competitor in another town. If it can be determined where the cloth was purchased, we may then discover where its owner came from."

The monk readily gave his acquiescence to the request and then Bascot asked if he might speak with Jehan's counterpart in the nunnery. "I would ask her the same questions about the dead female that I have asked you about the young man, and I would also like to see if the cloth of her garments can be identified as to the maker."

Brother Jehan arranged for Bascot to enter the nunnery through a small door kept for visitors, and the Templar was ushered into a tiny guest room. After a few moments a nun came in, leaving the door open. Outside, within sight and earshot, was another habited figure acting as companion. The nun who had entered was in her middle years, with a broad heavy face that wore a look of inner contentment. She sat herself on a small stool, her hands folded into the sleeves of her gown, then bade Bascot be seated also.

"I am Sister Bridget, the infirmarian. Brother Jehan has told me you have some questions about the unfortunate young woman brought here today?"

Her voice had a singsong quality about it that was calming. Bascot imagined she would be a comforting presence to the sick or dying. He asked her, as he had Brother Jehan, about any wounds or marks on the body of the dead girl and got almost the same reply.

"Yes, some welts on her legs and across her back, but nothing else," the sister said. "Poor pretty young thing— for pretty she was once, Sir Bascot, even though death has taken the bloom from her cheek."

"Her clothes, Sister, do you have them?"

"Yes. Like our brothers in the priory, we were going to give them to the poor once they had been cleansed of blood. It was not so much, just a little on the lace in front. They are not costly garments, but will be welcomed all the same by those that have only rags, even though they are a bit gaudy. But that can be put right by taking off the sleeves and putting in some of a darker and more sober colour. An easy task since the green ones were only loosely sewn. They were already half out of their seams, which was strange . . ." Sister Bridget's eyebrows pulled together in what Bascot was sure was an unaccustomed frown.

"Why strange, Sister?" he asked.

"The gown was large on her, too big for her small frame. There should have been no strain on the stitching," was the reply.

"Perhaps she could not afford her own and was forced to wear another's, like one of your alms-takers," Bascot suggested.

"That could be so," the sister agreed, "or it may be that since she was with child her own would not fit and so she was forced to have some made larger for the time when . . ."

The sister would have continued on, but Bascot stopped her. "You say the young woman was enceinte?"

"Yes," Sister Bridget replied, her expression showing surprise that he had not known. "She was about halfway through her time, and not much more than a child herself." She shuddered. "Such evil in the world outside. Not only was the poor girl murdered but her unborn babe was killed by the same foul act. My sisters and I will pray for both of their souls, and say a special novena for the blameless one of the child."

Bascot recovered his composure while the sister talked on. This piece of knowledge would not please Gerard Camville at all. Nor did it please Bascot. He had no doubt that the townspeople of Lincoln would feel, as he did, an outrage that a defenceless unborn child had been killed along with the mother. It was unlikely that the news could be suppressed for long, and it made it all the more imperative that he discover who the two dead strangers were. He asked the sister if he could see the girl's clothing and she brought it. Like the garments that he had examined in the priory, these also stank of ale.

Sister Bridget promised, after cleansing, to despatch the clothing to the castle, along with that of the young man. Bascot gave her his thanks and half of a silver penny for the poor box, then left the way he had come, going through a door in the wall to find himself back in the yard where Gianni was waiting. When both were once more mounted, Bascot left the priory and turned his horse in the direction of the alehouse. If his suspicions were correct, he now knew where the bodies had been before they had been found on the taproom floor—in empty ale casks, pushed in so that the staves of the barrels had carved welts on the flesh of their backs and knees and their clothing had become contaminated by the ale-soaked wood.

Five

✦✚✦

IN A FINE STONE HOUSE FRONTING THE MAIN THOR-
oughfare of Mikelgate two men sat in a small private room.
One of them was Isaac, dead Samuel's cousin, and the
other, also a cousin, was Isaac's younger brother, Nathan.
The chamber in which the two men were ensconced was
richly furnished with tables and chairs of oak. On the
walls hung brightly coloured tapestries and the gleam of
gold could be seen in the cups from which they were
drinking and in the seven-branched candlestick that stood
on a chest at the far side of the room. Both men were
seated, their faces drawn in concern as they listened to
the voices of women from a nearby chamber raised in
soft tones of lament. Their clothes were of fine wool,
worked at hem and cuff with strands of silk. Isaac was
some years older than his brother, his long dark hair sprinkled with grey amongst the curls that hung down from his
head and beard. He had an astute look, tempered by the
slow easy movements with which he smoothed and
straightened the parchment lying on the table in front of

him. Nathan was fairer and more aggressive in the carriage of his body.

"You will take Samuel's wife into your own household, Isaac?" Nathan questioned.

Isaac nodded. "She cannot be left to fend for herself. Samuel was a poor provider, but he was all she had since her own family was slain at Stamford ten years ago."

Both men sat in silence for a moment, remembering the relatives and friends they had lost when, on the occasion of King Richard's coronation, anti-Jewish riots had broken out all over the kingdom of England and resulted in the loss of many Jewish lives, most notably at York.

"Even though one of our own was killed, I have no doubt that it will be determined that a Jew was responsible for the deaths of the three Christians found with Samuel." Nathan spoke with great heat, his light brown eyes showing in the intensity of their gaze the depth of his anger.

"Be easy, Brother," Isaac soothed him. "The castle is nearby, and Lady Nicolaa is our friend. She will give us shelter should there be an outcry against us."

"That is only because the king values us for our gold, like a herd of cows to be milked. We are only allowed to trade in usury, yet it is because of that very trade that we have silver and gold that can be stolen, and that we are resented for our riches. Nicolaa de la Haye merely protects that which is precious to her king, no more. It is even rumoured that it was her own husband who led the raid on Stamford all those years ago. Camville will do little to protect us."

"There will be no need, if we are circumspect." Isaac leaned forward towards his brother. "Tell me again of the errand that Samuel was on when he was killed."

Nathan shrugged. "As you know, I did not trust Samuel with any matter of importance. He was not of the greatest intelligence. Small tasks he could carry out, and did so for me. But in anything involving greater sums, he became uneasy and invariably offended the client, or miscalculated the figures. Yesterday, I sent him to the manor of Alan de Kyme. . . ."

"Is he the de Kyme that is nephew to Philip?" Isaac interrupted.

"No, this is a cousin of the baron's. They are a large brood, the de Kymes, and this is one from a lesser branch of the family. He and his wife have only a small manor house along with a few acres and a mill."

Isaac thought for a moment, then nodded. "Yes, I know him now. Go on. . . ."

"De Kyme wanted to borrow a few pounds only. His mill is in need of repair, and he was to give Samuel his note of debt in return, promising to repay the debt, with interest, after harvest in the autumn. It was a simple enough task for Samuel to carry out. He left in the morning with the silver and the note for signing. That is the last I heard of him. I did not worry when he did not return last night, thinking that he may have travelled slowly in consideration of the heat of the day and not arrived home until late. It was not until this morning when I called at his house and his wife told me that he had not returned that I began to be concerned. But then, with Samuel, as I said, anything could have delayed him. His mule had thrown a shoe; he had fallen asleep under a tree. You know what he was like."

Isaac nodded, and waited for his brother to continue. "But I was worried. There are many outlaws outside the walls of Lincoln and although Samuel had only a little money on him, those robbers will cut a man's throat for half a penny, and I did not think the sheriff's men would be overconscientious about reporting the death of a Jew. Then, just as I was calling for a groom to saddle a horse so I could go in search of him, one of the men-at-arms from the castle came to tell me that Samuel had been found dead in the alehouse." Nathan shook his head. "What would he have been doing in an alehouse, in the company of Christians?" The thought of such an unlikely happening made him shake his head again in disbelief.

"And you found neither silver nor note of debt on his person?" Isaac asked.

"Apart from the clothes he was wearing, he had nothing on him, not even the purse that would have held the money. I could understand that there might have been an attempt to rob him, either going to de Kyme's or returning, but then he would have been found somewhere on the road, not in a Lincoln taproom."

"It is a mystery," Isaac agreed. "But we must be careful what we tell anyone who comes to enquire into his death. First, a rider must be sent to see if he reached de Kyme's."

"I have already done that," Nathan replied, then gave a wry grimace. "Of course, if de Kyme did receive the silver and now knows that Samuel is dead, and no trace of the debt on him, then he may deny that he ever saw Samuel, and keep the silver for his own, free of repayment and of interest."

Isaac leaned back and smoothed the curls in his beard thoughtfully. "Samuel may have been seen along the road. We must make enquiries, but carefully, Nathan, very carefully. Of the most importance, even more than finding Samuel's murderer, is that no blame be attached to any Jew. For the safety of our people it must be shown, without doubt, that Samuel was as much a victim as were the three Christians murdered along with him."

Six

✦

Bascot and Gianni arrived at the alehouse to find the guard that Ernulf had posted at the door still keeping to his duty. He nodded to Bascot as the Templar lifted the bar and went inside, Gianni close behind. They came first into the taproom which now, in the light and heat of the day streaming through the open shutters, had lost most of its smell of death and ale and stood empty, and somehow forlorn.

Bascot had told Gianni what they had found earlier that day on these premises and what he now hoped to discover. The boy, although mute, had sharp ears and even sharper eyes. It was as though his lack of speech had made his other senses more vibrant, a necessary aid to survival when he had been a wharf-urchin in Palermo. With his own sight diminished by the loss of his eye, Bascot had come to rely on the youngster's quickness in taking in the details of his surroundings.

After first making a cursory search of the taproom, Bascot went into the passage that connected the front of the alehouse to the back. To one side were the stairs leading upward, in front the passage that went out into the brewing yard. First they climbed the steep stairway to the bedchamber above. Aside from one room which appeared to be used for sleeping, there was only a small cubbyhole with an old wooden pail and some sacks of dried herbs.

Bascot went into the bedchamber. First he examined the bed. There was nothing secreted either within the mattress or among the folds of the thin woollen blanket that served as a covering. Beside the bed was a sturdy wooden chest, well made but plain, with a candle and holder sitting atop its lid. Removing the candle Bascot looked inside the chest. He could hear Gianni behind him, searching with small fingers among the rushes in the corners of the room and under the bed. Inside the wooden coffer there were some clothes, obviously belonging to the alekeeper and his wife, but nothing else. Sprigs of dried lavender had been placed among the folds of the clothes and Bascot thought once again that the alewife was a woman who kept her premises remarkably clean. There were no vermin in the mattress on the bed, nor among the clothing in the chest.

Bascot looked at Gianni and the boy shook his head. They descended the staircase and went out into the yard. There was an open-fronted large shed with a quantity of ale kegs stacked within, as well as a number of other vessels of varying sizes, all for the filling and transport of ale. Most of the smaller ones were made of leather and coated with pitch—blackjacks and piggins. There were some wooden communal drinking mugs, fitted with pegs to mark the space where a man could draw his share and remove the peg before passing it on to his neighbour, and a couple of large tankards fitted with a lid and spigot for purchasing ale to take away from the premises.

At the end of the yard, away from the alehouse walls, was a stone hearth on which rested a huge cauldron and nearby were small drying sheds for the grain of the malt.

Behind this, set on a slight slope so that it drained away from the yard itself, was a privy, with loose planking forming a lean-to for privacy, and the midden behind.

On wooden trestles laid across two blocks of wood were the large smooth stones that were used for crushing the grain once it had been soaked and dried. Underneath, pinned by the weight of the stones, was a stack of clean linen cloths necessary for straining the malt after it had been brewed.

On one side, under the shelter of a shake roof, was an open wooden cart and a set of casks containing a little of the old brew for adding to and starting a new batch. Bascot motioned to Gianni and the boy clambered up into the cart. There were some empty barrels sitting on the floor of the cart, the lids removed. Gianni, reminding Bascot of a ferret after a rabbit, dived into each of the barrels, his dark curly-topped head reappearing after a few moments, each time shaking his head.

They next tackled the barrels that were stored in the shed. Few were full, for any good alewife does not keep her brew too long, but makes fresh batches almost continuously so that it would keep its flavour and be passed as drinkable by the official taster of the town. Between them, they inspected every barrel, working smoothly as a team, with Bascot, his weight set firmly on his sound leg, doing the heavy work of lifting the barrels down and removing their lids while Gianni, with his lithe and agile frame, crawled inside and felt around the murky interiors. It wasn't long before the boy's clothing reeked of old ale much as the corpses' had, and there were no barrels left that had not been examined.

Bascot was disappointed. He was sure he was right in his surmise that the two strangers and the Jew had been murdered somewhere else and then secretly brought to the alehouse in empty ale kegs, but they had not found anything to confirm his suspicions. He had been hoping for some sign—a missing purse belonging to the Jew or the young man, perhaps a belt buckle or a thong from a shoe, a few strands of hair—any item that would have given his premise credence. He shook his head. Even if they had found such a thing, it would not have proved who the two strangers were, or where they had been murdered, or by whom. But it would have helped him, in his mind, to know that he was beginning to unravel the slightest part of the mystery that surrounded the deaths.

As he stood musing, Gianni had been clambering around amongst the barrels, looking at the planks and wheels of the ale cart, lifting the smaller vessels for carrying ale. Suddenly he clapped his hands together in triumph and Bascot turned to see him standing by one of the sturdy posts that formed the mainstays of the open-faced shed that held the ale casks. Gianni was pointing upwards, with a grin of triumph on his face. Bascot went to where he stood and saw, just above the height of his shoulder, a splash of bright colour caught on the rough wood of the post.

Reaching up, Bascot unfastened the scrap of red cloth that was caught amongst the splinters. It was only a few threads, no wider than a sparrow's feather and slightly longer, and caught just where, if a man were to take a body from one of the barrels and hoist it onto his shoulder, it would catch and snag as he adjusted the weight. Bascot had no doubt that it had come from the dress of the dead girl. He cast his mind back to try and remember what she had worn. Sleeves of green—such as harlots wore, and cheap stuff—plain lace at the neck of her gown, the bodice and skirt a tawny yellow. But there had been red, too, at the back, a panel of it below the bodice and attached to the lace, as though it were an undergarment and not of the dress itself. He looked closely at the scrap of material in his hand. Lincoln was famous for its red cloth, called Lincoln Greyne or Grain. The colour came from the juice of an insect which was dried and crushed and was in much demand not only from the area around Lincoln, but from the rest of England

and as an export to the continent. Bascot was almost certain that this was a small piece of that very cloth. If it was, it was expensive for a harlot to be wearing and, although it would not prove the girl was from Lincoln, it was probable that the cloth for some part of her gown had been purchased in the town. If she was a bawd, how had she come by it? From a rich patron? Or had she, in fact, been a harlot? Had she been merely dressed and her face painted to make her look like one? Was this scrap of cloth a piece from her own clothing, left underneath and covered with the tawdry gown which Sister Bridget had said was too large for her?

These questions and others flooded Bascot's mind like a gush of ale from a barrel newly drawn. He did not know the answers, but suddenly it became important to him to try and find them. Perhaps the dead girl's unborn child had prompted his determination; maybe his mind was beginning to recover from the trials of his captivity and the deaths in his family. He did not know, but of one thing he was sure: his premise that the bodies had been hidden in ale barrels was the right one. A scrap of cloth too expensive for the alewife to wear, and too high for her to snag it if she had, proved it. Even though he was no closer to discovering the identity of the two strangers, he felt elated.

Taking some *candi* from the leather pouch at his belt, he tossed one to Gianni, then popped one in his own mouth, and they sat upon the hard-packed earth of the yard and slowly sucked them, relishing not only the taste but their accomplishment.

Seven

✦✦✦

Having decided that it was necessary to visit the alewife again, Bascot and Gianni left the alehouse and crossed over to St. Andrew's church and enquired of the priest where she might be found. On learning that she was staying with her sister near Mikelgate, Bascot sent the man-at-arms on guard outside the alehouse to the castle, instructing him to bring back the serjeant, Ernulf.

It was but a short space of time before Ernulf arrived, looking a little disgruntled, for it was now coming up to the hour for the evening meal. Bascot told him what he and Gianni had found and Ernulf quickly forgot his irritability.

"So, the victims were already dead and in the yard before they were placed on the taproom floor," he opined. "Then the alewife . . ."

"Unless she is deaf and blind, and has less wits about her than she appears to have, must have seen something. It is her task to brew the ale, cleanse the empty barrels, tidy the yard. She must have known there were three barrels that were either not empty or held a brew that was most definitely not drinkable."

They set off down to the end of Steep Hill where it turned into Mikelgate. To assuage Ernulf's hunger, Bascot bought a meat pie from a passing vendor whose tray was nearly empty. He also bought one for Gianni, whose capability for devouring anything edible was prodigious. Ernulf pronounced the pie stale, but Gianni seemed not to notice. His pie had disappeared down his gullet before Ernulf had even time to chew his first mouthful.

As they rode slowly through the press of people still busy readying the town for the next morning when the fair would begin, thunder began to rumble in the heavens. At first it was low and far off, but soon it came closer, and was so loud in their ears that the church bells ringing the hour of Vespers could hardly be heard. Just as they passed the large street that intersected with Mikelgate, called Clachislide, a procession pushed past them. It was led by a few of the more prosperous merchants of the town, including Rolf the Draper, Aeltheburt the Goldsmith and a man from Baxtergate who was a prominent baker. Behind them trailed other small tradesmen, all dressed in what appeared to be their best clothes, and conspicuously wearing badges, denoting their craft, on their sleeves.

"Looks like a deputation on their way to the castle," suggested Ernulf, "probably to protest that there is not enough being done to catch the murderer in our midst. The sheriff will not be pleased."

Bascot made no response. Soon they came to the small turning that held the shop of Thomas the Carpenter, and left their horses on Mikelgate, tied to a post put there for the purpose. Overhead the first hint of lightning appeared, a small tongued flash flickering momentarily before it vanished, making the horses skitter and pull at their fastenings.

Ernulf and Gianni went to the door of the carpenter's

shop and the serjeant rapped loudly. In a short time a woman appeared. She was slim and neatly dressed, her head tidily covered in a white coif, with a large apron covering her gown. Ernulf announced Bascot in a manner that made the Templar smile inwardly.

"Sir Bascot de Marins, Templar knight in the service of Lady Nicolaa de la Haye, come to question the woman, Agnes," he said in a strong voice.

The woman bobbed in deference, then stood aside to allow Bascot to enter. "I am Jennet, Tom Carpenter's wife, and Agnes' sister," she said. "I will get her for you directly, Sir Bascot."

She led them into the only room on the ground floor of the dwelling, where a table and chairs were standing in the middle of the room. On one side a few wooden eating utensils had been placed on top of a shallow chest, and baskets of onions and other root vegetables hung from the rafters. Directly in front of them at the back of the room a door looked as though it led out into the yard. Jennet disappeared up the narrow staircase to the room above, returning quickly with the alewife trailing reluctantly behind her.

Jennet bobbed again as Bascot seated himself in one of the chairs. Ernulf took up a position at the front door while Gianni placed himself behind his master's chair.

"Here is my sister, sir," Jennet said, pushing Agnes forward and down into the semblance of an obeisance. "She is still somewhat mazed from the loss of her husband, my lord. Earlier I gave her a potion with herbs to help her sleep. It is this that is making her so muddled in her steps."

The alewife did indeed look slightly disorientated but Bascot thought it was due more to his presence than her sister's herbal potion. "You told me this morning that you knew of nothing having been secreted in your brewing yard, mistress. That was not true, was it?"

His stern words and the import of them seemed to snap

Agnes back to clearheadedness. "Oh, yes, my lord. It was. Truly it was," she said, clutching her hands together in front of her, mouth quivering.

"Tell Sir Bascot what you told me, Agnes," Jennet interjected, then looked at Bascot. "I'm sorry to interrupt, sir, but my sister—well, she gets confused sometimes, especially now, finding her husband and those others dead and all. I was going to see Father Anselm in the morning and ask him if he would arrange for us to see you, Agnes and me, so she could tell you what she forgot to tell before."

Jennet said this deferentially and Bascot scrutinised her more carefully. There was only the faintest of physical resemblances between the two sisters, and he could see that, unlike the alewife, Jennet possessed an innate intelligence. Agnes, on the other hand, looked to be more sly than clever. That morning when he had questioned the alewife in the presence of the priest she had seemed so distraught that the answers he had received had been scarcely understandable. Now, he realised, this could have been merely a method of dissembling.

He gave the alewife a look of impatience and she responded by repeating, in a rush of words, what she had told her sister that morning. "I don't know anything of what Wat was doing, sir," she said finally. "He told me to keep myself upstairs and that's what I did, all night until it was time to come down in the morning."

As her sister looked at Bascot to see if he was impressed by the tale, the alewife hung her head, darting a glance from beneath her brows first at Bascot, then at her sister. Her wide face was blotchy, which could have been due to the tears she had shed that morning, or it could have been from fear. Throughout his long captivity Bascot had become well versed in the meaning of facial expressions—a sudden colour, or lack of it, in the skin; the quick glance of an eye or the tremble of a muscle. When one is a slave among other slaves and all subject to the whim of a master, it is well to be able to recognise the emotions behind another person's eyes. He instinctively knew that the alewife was not telling the truth.

"You are lying, mistress," Bascot said flatly. "You were not in your bed all night. If you had been, whoever murdered those three people and your husband would have killed you too. It is not likely he would have left so convenient a witness. Unless, of course, you were his accomplice." It was a wild guess he was making, that she had not been in her bed, but it seemed a reasonable one.

Agnes began to cry again, protesting her innocence and her sister, white and drawn, stood watching him. He stood up and said harshly, "My patience is at an end. Ernulf, take this woman to the castle. Perhaps a few days incarceration in a lonely cell will loosen her tongue. If not, there are other ways of making her tell us what she knows."

As he finished speaking there was a crack of thunder overhead, so loud that it seemed as though the very walls would split asunder. From the doorway to the yard two men appeared, one tall and thin with the leather apron of a carpenter over his rough smock, the other similarly clad but younger, with a sturdy frame and a shock of hair as red as Jennet's. When they caught sight of Bascot they stopped in the doorway and bobbed their heads deferentially. They were, presumably, Jennet's husband and son. The thunder continued to sound and then there was the heavy patter of falling rain, plopping loudly into the yard behind them. The noise lent weight to Bascot's words, seeming as though God himself was reinforcing the Templar's judgement.

Agnes had now fallen to her knees, imploring Bascot not to take her away and begging her sister to help her. Her wailing was interrupted by a loud knocking on the door of the small house. Ernulf opened it to find outside the man-at-arms he had left on guard at the alehouse. The soldier asked the serjeant if he could speak to him privately and Ernulf disappeared through the door, returning almost immediately.

"There's been a stabbing," he said in response to Bascot's questioning look. "The priest at St. Andrew's, Father Anselm. A parishioner found him behind the altar, lying in his own blood."

"How could that be? I just left him preparing to celebrate evening Mass," Bascot exclaimed.

"Must have happened after you left, and before anyone arrived for the service."

"Is he alive?" Bascot asked.

"Barely. Sheriff Camville's town guard is there, and a leech. My man thought you might want to know."

"He was right. We'll go at once." Bascot rose and added, "Bring the alewife with you, Ernulf. Perhaps the sight of the priest's blood will loosen her tongue. If not"—he shrugged—"the sheriff's guard can take her to the castle."

Bascot pushed out of the small house, Gianni behind him and Ernulf, with a loudly screeching Agnes in tow, following. They mounted their horses, dumping Agnes on the saddlebow in front of the man-at-arms, where she clung to the mane of his horse sobbing and calling out to her sister. Jennet, along with her husband and son, ran into the street after them, following Bascot as he spurred his reluctant horse forward into the drenching rain.

Eight

✝

A CROWD WAS GATHERED OUTSIDE THE DOOR OF ST. Andrew's church despite the heavy rainfall. They stood with
bowed heads, fear written large on their faces, keeping a
conspicuous space between themselves and the ring of the
sheriff's guard who stood in a phalanx of four, swords
drawn, outside the church door. To harm a priest, a man of
God, was a serious matter. His attacker would have damned
his immortal soul.

They fell back quietly as Bascot dismounted and made
for the door. The sheriff's guard parted to let him through,
their badges bearing Camville's emblem of a silver lion
glinting brightly through the mist of streaming rain. Ernulf
pulled Agnes roughly from her seat and, dragging her behind him, they followed Bascot into the church.

At the far end of the nave, beside the altar, a small group
of people were kneeling around the prone body of the
priest. Bascot recognised the burly figure of Roget, the
captain of Camville's guard. He and Roget had first met on
crusade when Roget had been a serjeant under Mercadier,

the commander of King Richard's mercenary forces. Roget was a brutal and vicious man, but he was extremely capable and usually loyal to his current paymaster, a trait not always found in hired soldiers. Tall, black-visaged and rangily built with the scar of an old sword slash running from brow to chin, he nodded to Bascot in recognition and moved back so that the Templar could see the body of the priest more clearly. Kneeling on the far side of Father Anselm was another priest, murmuring prayers and robed in readiness to give extreme unction. Beside him was a short rotund man, a fine gold chain strung with extracted human teeth hanging around his neck. This must be the leech that Ernulf had mentioned, a barber-surgeon. His neatly trimmed grey hair and clean-shaven chin gleamed with oil as he looked up at Bascot, round face shiny with excitement.

"I am sure he will live. And it is God's own hand twice over that has willed it so. Firstly, in that the saintly man was wearing a hair shirt beneath his garments, which served to deflect the blow, and secondly, in that it was I who found him. My skill in staunching blood was sore needed this night."

It was plain that the man spoke the truth for blood had spread in a dark viscous pool below the altar step on which Father Anselm was lying and his garments were soaked with it.

"Never in all my years of letting a patron's blood have I failed to stem it at the right moment," the barber said, displaying with pride where he had ripped apart the priest's robe and the inverted shirt of bull's hide, then wadded material from Father Anselm's own vestments over the lips of the wound. The priest, his body on one side and head cradled in the barber's lap, was unconscious and deathly pale but as the slow pulse at the side of his neck indicated, still breathing.

Bascot motioned to Roget and they moved aside. "I take it you did not catch the assailant?" he asked.

"No," Roget replied. "Nor was anyone seen or any weapon found. The barber and his wife, along with a couple of neighbours, came for Mass. They were a little early and the first to enter. They saw the priest's feet sticking out from behind the altar and the barber attended the wound. A few minutes more and the priest would have bled to death. No one else was about until the rest of the congregation began to arrive."

Roget glanced at Bascot shrewdly, the dim light in the church accentuating the hollows of puckered skin where the scar on his face pulled at the flesh around his eyes, and sending points of brilliance sparkling from the rings of gold threaded through his earlobes. "Nothing was stolen. The poor box is intact and nothing of value among the communion vessels appears to be missing. Do you think this assault is connected with the murders in the alehouse across the street?"

Bascot nodded. "It has to be. So near in time and so close in proximity. The priest must have been a threat to the murderer in some way. If Father Anselm recovers, and can identify his attacker, we may learn not only why the murders were committed, but who did them."

A few feet away Ernulf stood with Agnes, her arm firmly in the serjeant's grasp. She had ceased to sob and was watching Bascot and Roget with wide eyes, her body trembling with fear. Ernulf was leaning down, speaking to her, and suddenly she nodded, hands pressed to her lips.

The serjeant approached Bascot. "The alewife says she wishes to speak to you."

"The sight of the priest has shocked her into telling the truth, has it?" Bascot asked.

Ernulf gave a snort of laughter. "No. I told her that if she did not, we would give her over to Roget for questioning." He looked at the mercenary captain, eyes alight with mirth. "Seems the threat has loosened her tongue. Do you always have that effect on women?"

Roget threw his head back and laughed, showing teeth that were still strong and white but gapped in many places. "My mother was a scold, always berating me. I swore when I left her tender care at the age of nine that I would never let another woman lash me with her tongue. And I never have. Perhaps your Agnes can sense my remarkable intolerance with wailing women and has chosen the wiser course of tormenting you instead."

As Bascot took Agnes into a corner of the nave, Jennet, along with her husband and son, were admitted by the guard. They came hurriedly to the alewife's side. Agnes, shocked by the brutal attack on the priest and fearful of being handed over to the intimidating Roget, was now eager to talk. Her voice came rushing in a tumble as she told that she had not been in bed at all the night before, but had gone down into the yard while her husband was occupied elsewhere and had hidden behind the privy.

"I wanted to see what Wat was up to, sir," she said. "I thought maybe he was going to have a woman in there, or another of his dice games. So I hid and waited."

She looked up in earnest supplication at Bascot. "I didn't know them bodies was in the barrels until I saw Wat lifting them out. Truly I didn't. The barrels they were in were at the back, where I put ones waiting to be rinsed out and dried. I'd just made a new brew. Wat knew I wouldn't be using any of those for a day or two. I swear, sir, in the name of the Blessed Virgin, I didn't know those bodies were there."

"What else did you see?" Bascot asked impatiently.

Agnes' hands clutched nervously at the folds in the front of her gown as she answered him. "I saw a man—I think it was a man—at the door into the yard. He was standing there, watching, as Wat carried those poor dead souls inside. I couldn't see his face, he was wearing a cloak with a hood, and the candlelight was dim and behind him. There was little light from the moon. But it was him that shut the door after Wat had finished and then I didn't see either of them anymore."

"How long did you stay hidden?"

"Until the morning light came, sir." The tears on Agnes' face had dried, leaving her face flushed. "I waited all night watching for some sign that the stranger had left. He must have come in at the front and left the same way. It wasn't until it was light that I was bold enough to go inside and, then . . . you know what I found."

"There must have been some noise from inside—when your husband was killed."

"No, sir, there wasn't. Not that I heard anyway. The only other thing I saw was some candlelight from our bed chamber above. Just glimmed briefly at the open casement, then it was gone." She looked up at him hopefully. "You was right, sir. If I'd been up there, I'd of been dead, too. That was why I was frightened to tell the truth. I thought if the murderer knew I had been there, seen him—well, he might come back again and do me in to be along with my Wat."

"Did you tell the priest what you just told me?" Bascot asked.

"No, sir. I didn't tell anyone, not even Jennet. I didn't even show her this." She thrust a hand in the voluminous folds of her skirt and pulled out a small shiny object and handed it to him. "I found it, in the morning, just as the sun came up. I saw it glinting on the ground, beside one of the barrels that Wat took, took . . . one of them that had a body in it," she finished lamely.

Bascot examined the object she handed him. It was a small silver brooch, too tiny to be of use for a cloak, probably intended for pinning a woman's garment of light weight. It was fashioned in a circle, formed by a pair of clasping hands, and with the letter M—most likely for the Virgin Mary—scrolled on the top. The design was not unusual, betrothal rings were often made so, but uncommon in a brooch. The pin was bent, but still held in the clasp, as though it had been pulled from the material it held. It was not particularly valuable, but to Agnes it was worth quite a few of the pennies she charged for stoups of her ale. The fact that she had produced it meant that it was probable she was finally telling the truth.

He put the brooch into the purse at his belt, to keep company with the scrap of material Gianni had found. "Yesterday—you did your business as usual? You tended to your ale, served customers—all as on any other day?" Bascot asked Agnes.

She nodded. "It were busy, what with all the people come from other parts of the country for the fair. I served in the taproom. I barely had time to set out my malt for the next mash, or prepare my gruit." Bascot knew that gruit was the flavouring for the ale, and that Agnes would have used the herbs he had found in the cubbyhole upstairs in the alehouse. "I uses a special mixture for gruit that my mam taught me, bog myrtle and honey. That's what makes my ale so good."

"The Jew and the two strangers—they were never in the taproom?"

"No, sir," she denied positively. "I never have Jews in my house—and they wouldn't come in neither—and the other two I never saw before, before . . ." She faltered to a stop.

"Then they must have been brought to your yard and put in the barrels, or brought to the yard already inside them." Agnes looked at Bascot in confusion as he went on. "Your husband, Wat—did he leave the premises at all yesterday?"

"Only to do deliveries," Agnes said.

"What deliveries?" Bascot asked with more patience than he felt for the woman's slow thinking processes.

"There were three. Master Ivo the Goldsmith—he took two kegs; Mistress Downy, the widow—she took one 'cause she has her son and his wife coming to stay for the fair; and the steward of Sir Roger de Kyme, he took two for his master's house in town."

"And how did Wat go about these deliveries—what was his routine?"

At Agnes' look of bewilderment, her sister Jennet, who had seen the purpose of his questions, gave the answer. "He would put the kegs full of ale on the cart, get the cart-horse from its stable at the end of the lane and deliver them. If there were any old kegs that were empty, he would bring them back and put them aside for cleansing and reusing. That's how the bodies were brought back, sir. In the empty kegs."

"Thank you, mistress," Bascot said gratefully. "Then Wat must either have killed them himself, or have knowledge of who did."

"Oh no, sir," Agnes protested. "My Wat would never have killed anybody. I know he wouldn't."

"Seems he knew somebody else had, at least," Jennet remarked to her sister dryly. "If they had died natural-like he wouldn't have been stuffing them in ale kegs and lifting them out after dark, would he?"

Bascot felt satisfied that it was now known how the bodies had arrived at their final destination, and that Wat had been an accomplice in their deaths, if not the actual murderer. But he was already dead when the priest had been stabbed, so the person Agnes had seen in the yard last night must have been responsible for the attack in the church.

The noise of the rain pelting down outside was louder now, and Bascot looked to where the carpenter and young boy were respectfully standing a short distance away. He beckoned for them to come forward.

"This is your son?" he asked Jennet. She nodded and told Bascot his name was Will. He looked strong, with the big bones and wide frame of his aunt, rather than the slight ones of his mother and father. The boy stood uncertainly before Bascot, awed by his presence and that of the sheriff's guard, and looked anxious at being singled out for attention.

Bascot pointed to the hammer tucked into the belt of the lad's leather apron. "You know how to use that, Will, do you?"

"Aye, sir. I helps me da in the yard," the boy answered. Behind him his father nodded.

"Then keep it with you, and stay by your aunt for the next few days. If anyone threatens her, use it on them as you use it on the wood in your father's yard. Do you understand me?"

Will nodded his head in a determined fashion. "Aye, sir. I'll not let anyone harm her."

Bascot looked down at the drained face of the alewife. "If you recall any more of what you saw last night, send a message to Ernulf at the castle. He will see that I am informed."

Relieved that she was not to be taken to the castle for questioning, the alewife left the church with her sister and family. Bascot waited until the priest, still unconscious but with his wound now neatly bandaged by the barber with strips torn from an altar cloth, had been removed on a hastily constructed stretcher before he called to Gianni and Ernulf and they rode slowly back through the downpour of rain to the castle keep.

Nine

✛

"YOU BELIEVE, THEN, THAT THE VICTIMS WERE KILLED elsewhere and their bodies transported to the ale house in empty casks? The obvious question is: why?"

Bascot was once again ensconced with Nicolaa de la Haye and Gerard Camville in the small chamber where he had given his report earlier that day. Roget had reported the attack on the priest to the sheriff and Nicolaa had summoned Bascot, to listen to his account of the affair and any other information that he had uncovered.

Now, sitting at her table, she had carefully laid before her the scrap of material that Gianni had located and the little brooch that Agnes had found. Across from her stood Bascot, while her husband prowled restlessly about the room, his footfalls soft and sure despite the massive bulk of his body. From the hall below came the distant sounds of revelry as the multitude at the table enjoyed the entertainment of the tumblers and minstrels that their hosts had provided. Nicolaa and her husband had excused themselves from their guests to hear Bascot's report, and Gianni had been sent in the company of Ernulf to get some of whatever food still remained after the vast number of visitors had eaten their evening meal. The occasional flash of lightning could still be seen through the opening of the small arrow slit set high on the chamber wall, but the rumble of thunder was decreasing in strength and seemed to be moving away to the east. The rain, too, was lessening in intensity and already the fresh smell of its cleansing fall could be felt in the air.

"As to the first question, lady, I think that is the most likely explanation," Bascot confirmed. "Before being put into the barrels, they were probably put to death by means of poison or suffocation—although the latter is not likely unless they were given a potion that would have rendered them insensible beforehand. There was no sign of a struggle on their bodies, as would be the case with at least one of them, if they had been smothered while still in possession of all of their faculties. What the reason was—I am afraid I cannot even hazard a guess. If Father Anselm recovers, or regains consciousness, he may be able to tell us who his assailant was, or at least the reason why he was attacked. It seems plausible that the person who assaulted him also committed the other crimes."

"You still haven't found out who the two strangers are," Gerard interjected, irritation in his tone. "That's what I want to know. And if they have relatives who will come claiming compensation for their deaths."

"If Father Anselm is still unable to tell us what he knows by morning, then I will question the drapers and weavers in the town," Bascot replied. "The material is a fine cloth, too rich for a prostitute to wear, unless she was the leman of a patron of substantial means. If it can be determined where it was made, it might provide an answer to her identity."

"There are weavers and cloth mercers aplenty in Lincoln now, and will be for the next week," Nicolaa said. She picked up the scrap of material and held it in her hand. "It

looks like the red Greyne that is made here in Lincoln,
but . . ." She rubbed it gently between thumb and forefinger. "It seems a little too fine, too loosely woven." She
sighed and replaced it on the table. "I have no doubt Rolf
the Draper could tell you, although I fear his mood is somewhat truculent at the moment." She added this last with a
smile. "He and his fellow townsmen were not best pleased
with their reception tonight, or the rain that most probably
drenched them as they left in hasty retreat for their homes."

"Bloody merchants," Gerard said, stopping his pacing
to refill his goblet with wine from a leather bottle on the
table. "Whatever ails them they bleat and cry like lost lambs,
pleading poverty while they count their silver in secret."

Bascot made no remark; neither did the sheriff's wife.
Camville resumed his pacing. Bascot could not ever recall
him being still, except when he was eating. It was said the
old king, Henry, father to both Richard and John, had been
the same, forever moving. Gerard Camville had been *fa-
miliare* to King Henry, one of a coterie of young knights
that the old king had kept about him and to whom he had
shown much favour. Perhaps that was the key to the sheriff's fractiousness, the losing of a lord who had been a just
and fair monarch, as well as a friend. King Richard, against
whom Camville had rebelled while the king was in the Holy
Land on crusade, had fought with his father and, the rumour-
mongers said, had caused King Henry's death through heart-
break at his son's treachery. Even John, the present king,
had failed his father in the end, siding with his older
brother and King Louis of France to bring about Henry's
downfall. Now Camville was in the position of having to
trust his wife's friendship with one of Henry's traitorous
sons in order to retain the royal favour that he had once
held so firmly from the father. It was not surprising that he
was often in an ill temper.

"I will also ask about the brooch, lady," Bascot said, attempting to divert the sheriff from his train of thought. "It

is not valuable, but it may be remembered, if only because it is so small and the design unusual for a brooch, rather than a ring."

Nicolaa picked up the tiny piece of jewellery and held it against her clothes. "Too small to be of any use except for the flimsiest of gowns," she said, "almost as though it were to be worn under the outer clothing, hidden from view and unremarked except for the knowledge of the wearer. It looks familiar to me, but . . . it is probably only because it is a common design." She laid it back on the table.

"Are you sure the alewife has no part in this coil?" Camville asked suddenly. "If these people were given a sleeping potion first, then it could be that she did it. She would have a knowledge of the properties of herbs by reason of her trade, those both beneficial or poisonous."

"I think she is innocent of any complicity in the deaths," Bascot replied. "She has not the wits for such scheming and is of too hysterical a nature for her husband to have trusted her with any secrets. And I took the herbs I found in the alehouse to the castle cook. They are harmless. Mistress Agnes is nothing more than she appears to be—a competent brewer of ale."

"It might prove worthwhile to question the harlots in Butwerk," Nicolaa said. "They will know if one of their number is missing."

"I will do that," Bascot assured her, "but I have some doubts that the girl was a bawd. Rather, I think, she was made to look like one."

"What makes you think that?" Nicolaa asked.

"Her outer clothing was too big for her and was of cheap stuff, not like the undergarments from which I think that scrap was torn. Once I have all of the clothing from the nunnery, I will be sure of that assumption but, if I am right, it was put on her, along with the face paint, to give the impression that she was from the stewes in the lower part of town."

"And you say she was with child?" Nicolaa asked.

"So Sister Bridget told me."

"Another life for which damned compensation can be claimed," Camville said angrily.

A flicker of irritation crossed Nicolaa's face, so subtle that if Bascot had not been looking straight at her with his one good eye, he would have missed it.

"You have done well, de Marins," she said, rising from her seat. "Learn what you can about the cloth and the brooch. It may be the merchants of the town will be too busy to attend closely to your questions. You have permission to use my authority if you have need of it.

"We best return to our guests, husband," she said to Camville. "Tomorrow will be a busy day, even if this rain continues to fall."

As they prepared to depart Bascot thanked her and said, "I intend to visit the family of the dead Jew, as well."

Camville snorted. "At least I will not have to pay compensation for that death. Any property he owns will come to the crown, and I can claim a fee for collection. The shame is that all of the dead are not Jews. Then there would be no cause for concern, only profit."

This time Nicolaa did not veil her annoyance. "The king is careful of the Jewish community, as you well know, Gerard. He would rather have them alive and lending him money than being killed and losing silver they could bring to him in the future."

Camville made no reply and Bascot remembered that there had been some talk that it had been the sheriff who had instigated the raid on the Jewry of Stamford some years before. Now Gerard let his wife's words slide off him, and turned to the Templar.

"Bring me the murderer, de Marins, and I promise you I will hang him high enough that his feet will kick the heavens. If you can prove these people earned their death through their own fault rather than any lack of mine, I will be doubly grateful. You will not lack for a reward."

With that the sheriff left the room, his girth filling the door frame for a moment before he pushed through. Bascot followed Nicolaa out of the chamber and, once they were down the winding stairs of the tower, opened the door for her to pass through into the hall. As she returned to her place on the dais, he felt a sudden desire for a *candi* and, taking one from the scrip at his belt, put it in his mouth and savoured it as his eye searched the crowd for Gianni.

Nicolaa resumed her seat with a feeling of resignation. The hall was packed to its farthest walls tonight. With easy capacity for perhaps a hundred souls, now there were nearer two hundred crammed into its large space—visiting nobility and their servants, prominent merchants from outside Lincoln who needed to be shown a welcome from the castellan of the castle, a troupe of travelling musicians and acrobats, and the additional men Gerard had hired to swell the ranks of his guard. All sat in their various places, the nobility and knights above the salt, merchants a little lower, with the visiting nobles' servants and men-at-arms crowded against the rear wall. The storm-laden air was close in the press, with smoke from the myriad wall torches and candles making it into a murky eye-watering haze. Dogs barked, servants rushed and hurried with wine ewers and plates of sweetmeats and, in the midst of all this chattering humanity the musicians strolled, adding to the din with the screech of viol or rebec. The tumblers thrust their bodies through the aisles between the tables, turning somersaults and tossing brightly coloured balls as they whirled, the red and blue hues of their tunics and the spinning orbs making a kaleidoscopic pattern that hurt the eyes if one stared too long.

Nicolaa sighed and signalled for a page to refill her goblet. This was a feast that had been expected of her and Gerard, she owed it as a contribution to the success of the fair, but she would be glad when it was over. Once, long ago, when she had been but a girl and her father had still been alive, she had revelled in such gaiety, laughed at the antics of the acrobats, sang with the musicians, eaten marchpane until her stomach rebelled. Now, she thought, she was growing old, for she longed only for it all to be over and to escape for a week or two to her small manor house at Brattleby, relishing a stay in its quiet confines while Lincoln castle was cleansed of the collected rubbish of the year and prepared for the onset of winter.

The guest at her elbow made a remark and she turned to speak to him. Hugh Bardolf was, like herself, a vassal of King John and holder of much land in the area, some of it from her own fiefdom, most of it directly from the crown. He was a tall rangily built man with sharp clean features and a shock of light brown hair now liberally sprinkled with grey. About her own age, he had once been suggested, before her marriage to Gerard, as a candidate for her husband. She liked him, but was glad that in the end an alliance between the Hayes and Bardolfs had not been forthcoming. They were too much alike, she and Hugh, with a similar need for order and control. They would have battled constantly over the smallest decisions. Gerard she had never loved, or even liked very much, but he left her to run the Haye demesne as she wished, purely because he was too lazy to do so himself, preferring his hawks and hounds to the trivial details involved in the management of their lands.

And, she suspected, Hugh would have been more of a demanding partner in the marriage bed. He had five sons, as well as two daughters, and his wife was expecting another, the last baby she would have, Nicolaa surmised, before she became too old for childbearing. Hugh's need to control his surroundings would extend to ensuring his own blood would benefit from his industry, while Gerard, once their only child, Richard, had been born and was seen to thrive, had never again come to her bedchamber. She had never been sorry that this was so, although she would have liked more children. She supposed that it might be different to bed a man for whom you felt some affection but, for all that she and Gerard managed to maintain some degree of amiability on the rare occasions it was necessary to be in one another's company, it had been very apparent that neither of them had enjoyed the brief liaison that producing an heir had required. She did not think Gerard was a lusty man, for she had never heard of any leman or female servant that had attracted his attention, and thought rather that he expended all his energies on his enjoyment of the hunt and his duties as sheriff. Even though her husband had not liked King Richard, she reflected, they had been very much alike, both preferring the challenge of bloody conflict to the embrace of a woman.

"You haven't answered me, Nicolaa," Hugh complained softly, but without offence, beside her.

"I'm sorry, Hugh. My mind, I am afraid, is on other matters. Please forgive me and repeat your question for, truly, I did not hear it."

High gave her a mildly admonishing smile and leaned closer. "I am, as usual, asking if you have come to any decision about my Matilda and your Richard. It would be a good alliance, Nicolaa. One that should have been made between you and I, and was not. Now we should remedy it by uniting our lands through our children."

Nicolaa smiled in return and gave her usual reply. "As I told you, Hugh, Gerard wishes to give it more thought. And we would need to consult with the king. He may not relish such a union, especially now while he is trying to bring his vassals on the continent under control. I am sure he would not happily consider two such vast fiefdoms as ours being joined together. He has not a liking for his barons to have too much power in their own hands."

"He knows you would never betray him, Nicolaa. He has often spoken, not only to me but to others, of your father's loyalty, and your own." Hugh was being his most genial and persuasive but Nicolaa had known him too long for such tactics to work.

"He has no reason to doubt mine, Hugh, but every reason to doubt Gerard's. And Richard is Gerard's son. John is not a king to overlook past histories, or future possibilities. He has switched sides himself too often to be unaware of the propensities of others for doing the same. The question of marriage between my son and your daughter will have to wait. Neither Gerard or I will be offended if you should look elsewhere for a match for Matilda."

Hugh sat back, rebuffed, his smile disappearing. Nicolaa motioned for a server to refill his goblet. Her mind was too full of tiredness, the thought of the energy that would be required for tomorrow's festivities at the opening of the fair, and of the strange murders in the alehouse as well as Father Anselm's dire state, to be overly concerned about Bardolf's hurt feelings. There was not a lack of marriageable heiresses for her son, as Hugh well knew.

Her glance strayed down the table to where the eldest of Hugh's two daughters, Matilda, sat with her mother and younger sister. She was not an unpleasant girl to look at, moderately round with the promise of a pleasingly plump frame when she reached maturity, medium brown hair and a demure manner. However, Nicolaa suspected that her modesty was often a pose put on for the benefit of her elders. There had been a day, when Matilda had thought herself unobserved and was with people her own age, that Nicolaa had overheard her conversation with the others. Matilda's speech had been quick and racy, bordering on the lewd. From that moment Nicolaa had dismissed her as a possible wife for Richard, not because of her bawdiness, but because she hid her inclination for it so well. When she was finally presented with a grandchild, Nicolaa wanted it to be from her son's loins, not those of some carefully concealed lover.

Matilda's younger sister, Alaine, on the other hand, was far more to Nicolaa's taste, for she had an open merry face, with a ready laugh and quick wit. However, she was only eleven, some five years younger than her sister, and it was possible she would change as she grew older. The onset of womanhood was a difficult time for any girl and could often bring about radical changes in temperament. Her own sister, Ermingard, had become an entirely different person after the advent of her menses.

Nicolaa looked down the table to where Ermingard now sat, flanked by her husband, William de Rollos, on one side, and their dour-faced son, Ivo, on the other. De Rollos was a stolid Norman knight and had ostensibly brought his family from Normandy to attend the fair and to visit Ermingard's family, but in reality he was looking for support from Nicolaa and Gerard in regard to his claim over some disputed land in Normandy. Ermingard sat as though imprisoned between her husband and her son, her red gold hair dimmed with grey, as was Nicolaa's own, and her small heart-shaped face prematurely showing lines of age.

The placement between her two menfolk was not without reason on William's part, for his wife could, without warning, be subject to wild changes of mood, one moment unspeaking and the next spilling with laughter at some jest apparent to no one but herself. She had been subject to these startling lapses from lucidity ever since the day she had come running to Nicolaa in a state of fright, her clothing dishevelled, holding a bloodstained rag in her hand and screaming in fright at the gush of bright redness that had suddenly appeared between her legs. No explanations from Nicolaa or from the next eldest of the Haye daughters, Petronille, could alleviate Ermingard's distress and she stayed in a state of shock for days until her cycle had ended, only to get into a similar condition a month later when it happened all over again. Never since the day their mother died had Nicolaa felt her loss so heavily.

Her gaze strayed over to her other sister, Petronille, a plump motherly figure who had inherited the dark hair and eyes of their mother. She was sitting at the far end of the long table on the dais, between an elderly priest and another vassal of King John's, Philip de Kyme. De Kyme was a grizzled and truculent baron about the same age as Gerard. He had rheumy dark eyes, a sallow expression and could be extremely argumentative when he had taken too much wine. Seating Petronille beside him had been a diplomatic decision on Nicolaa's part. Her middle sister had a very calm nature, capable of listening to another's speech without showing impatience or the need to thrust her own conversation forward. She was at ease with her table companions even though the old cleric was mumbling almost constantly as he ate meat from the trencher in front of him, and Philip de Kyme, as usual, was complaining about his son-by-marriage and lamenting the lack of an heir from his own seed. Petronille, deftly passing more food to the priest and murmuring an assent to his disjointed phrases, still managed to be able to listen to de Kyme and give the correct response in the right place.

Nicolaa hoped Petronille would be able to stay for longer than the few days she had said was all she could afford to be absent from her husband and household in Stamford. Petronille was a balm that Nicolaa sorely needed at the moment, especially with difficult guests like Philip de Kyme, who was, at that moment, casting angry glances about him.

The object of his disgruntlement, his stepson Conal, stood laughing and drinking a cup of wine a short distance away in the company of her own son, Richard. The pair had finished eating and had strolled over to watch a trio of tumblers who were cleverly balancing on each other's shoulders and dropping down and back in almost constant motion, all within the confines of a tiny patch of floor. One of the tumblers was female, her legs encased, for modesty's sake, in thin woollen stockings under her skirt. But for all the covering, her shapeliness could be seen as she flew up and down between the hands of her two partners and Nicolaa saw that Richard's eyes were fixed in an avid stare on her antics while Conal, son of de Kyme's wife from her first marriage, watched Richard, amusement on his face.

They made a handsome pair, the two young friends, so recently dubbed into knighthood. Richard had hair that was almost as bright a red as her own had once been, with a genial manner and a strength of limb and shoulder that promised to soon equal his father's. Beside him Conal looked slim, but his tall lanky build was deceiving, for Nicolaa had seen him best larger and more experienced men on the practice field. He was fair, like his mother, and his features were finely drawn, giving his full mouth and bright grey eyes an almost feminine look.

Nicolaa shook her head. Richard, she knew, was a lecher, just as her father had been. Somehow it was more disturbing in an offspring than a parent, but she gave thanks that his inclinations were not like Conal's who, although it was never spoken of openly, was suspected of liking members of his own sex in preference to females. This conjecture stemmed from the fact that he seemed to show none of a young man's usual interest in women. To be fair, neither did he seem attracted to any of the young pages or squires with whom he came into daily contact and Nicolaa was sure that Richard would not have befriended Conal if there was any suspicion of an aberration in his sexual proclivities. The hint of sodomy was ever apparent in de Kyme's complaints of his stepson, however, and in his bewailing of no heir to carry on his line. There were de Kyme's aplenty in Lincoln, he would moan, but not one of them his own true son. Then he would look pointedly at the long-suffering woman to whom he was married and shake his head. It was fortunate that tonight his wife, Sybil, had asked to be excused from the feast, pleading illness as an excuse to keep to her bed.

Nicolaa shrugged. It was nothing to do with her. She re-

membered vaguely from her own youth that there had been
some ruckus at the time of de Kyme's marriage to Sybil,
who was older than he and a widow with a young son.
Philip had apparently wanted to wed another, but the girl
had been of low birth and dowerless and Philip's father had
threatened his son with the loss of his inheritance if he did
not wed Conal's mother. Recently, he had taken to constantly referring mysteriously to the fact that, had he been
allowed his own inclinations in the matter of his marriage,
he would have heirs aplenty and it was not too late to rec-
tify the matter. So repetitive were his complaints that no
one took much notice of them anymore, not even Gerard,
who was closest to de Kyme in that they often shared the
pleasure of the hunt or the sampling of some new wine
from Poitou.

Nicolaa gave herself a mental shake. That morning the
castle chaplain had spoken at Mass of the dangers of the
seven deadly sins, no doubt aiming to warn his flock against
indulgence while the fair, with its atmosphere of freedom
and gaiety, took over the more sober routine of Lincoln for
the next few days. Each of us, the priest had said, is guilty
of at least one of the deadly sins at some time, and often of
two or more. Nicolaa ran through them in her mind—Lust,
Pride, Avarice, Envy, Sloth, Anger and Covetousness. She
looked around at her companions at the high table. Yes, she
thought, the priest was right—we are all guilty of at least
one of those sins. Hugh of covetousness, de Kyme of anger,
Gerard of sloth, Richard, her son, of lust—just in such a
short space she could pick these out and, she admitted,
there was her own sin of pride, which she excused to herself
by naming it a strong sense of duty. We are all sinners, she
thought, even if only in the secrecy of our own hearts. But
the priest had also reminded his flock of the seven
virtues—Faith, Hope, Charity, Justice, Prudence, Temper-
ance and Fortitude—and told them that at least one of these

also was possessed by each man or woman, and that by prayer these virtues could be strengthened to overcome the temptation of the seven deadly sins.

Judging by the raucous laughter and drunken merriment of the crowd in the hall tonight, Nicolaa thought it certainly seemed true that the virtues were harder to find than the sins. Her gaze fell on the Templar, Bascot de Marins. He was an enigma to her, seeming to be completely self-contained except in his relationship with his young servant. It had been on impulse that she had given him the task of trying to discover the identity of the murderer of the four people in the alehouse. He had proved himself a valuable addition to her retinue, but she had the feeling that he had talents beyond those required for a simple clerk and she had wanted to bring them out. The rule that the Templars who left their Order could only do so on condition they join a monastic order stricter than their own was a loose one, and Nicolaa was sure that if she brought pressure to bear on the Grand Master of the Temple in London he would agree to overlook this stipulation with regard to Bascot. Since she hoped the Templar would wish to leave the Order and accept an offer to remain in her household, she wondered if giving him additional responsibility might not defeat her own purpose. It may just drive him into making the very decision she least wanted, that of returning to the Order that he had become, at least temporarily, disenchanted with. Ah well, she thought, as her father had often said, a metal must be well tempered to ring true. And, as with metal, so it was with men. That was a lesson she had learned too well to ignore.

Ten

✦

Bᴀsᴄᴏᴛ ᴀɴᴅ Gɪᴀɴɴɪ ʟᴇꜰᴛ ᴛʜᴇ ɢʀᴇᴀᴛ ʜᴀʟʟ ᴅɪʀᴇᴄᴛʟʏ after Nicolaa de la Haye stood and announced that she was retiring. Her husband, Gerard, stayed in his seat, motioning for the servers to refill his wine cup and that of Philip de Kyme, who had moved to sit beside him. Most of the ladies who were staying within the precincts of the castle followed their hostess' example, leaving the men folk to their wine and talk of old battles, while the visiting merchants and their wives, with lodgings hired in the town, also left. But the bulk of the barons and lesser lords stayed where they were, settling themselves in to enjoy the Haye largesse for as long as it was proffered. There would be sore heads aplenty in the morning but since they were there for pleasure and not for work, as the merchants were, none cared.

When Bascot and Gianni reached their tiny chamber the boy, finally full of food, slumped onto his pallet and within moments was fast asleep. Bascot left the boy to his slumbers and walked up the few steps to the battlements of the tower. The walkway faced south, so that he could see out over the curtain wall to the town spread out below and to where the streets drifted down the hill to the River Witham at the lower end. The night air was fresh from the rain and a small wind was blowing. Above was a canopy of stars, washed with the faint light that never seems to leave the sky at the high point of summer. In the semidarkness a few bats flitted. He removed his eye patch and felt a rush of air cool the withered socket beneath.

As always when up high, the loss of half his sight made him feel slightly dizzy, but long years of practice had made him accustomed to it and he gripped the solid stone of the battlements to steady himself. The light of torches could be seen bobbing here and there as the merchants and their families made their way to their various lodgings. Even within some of the dwellings a light could be seen, though it was long past *couvre feu* or, as the English speaking population pronounced it, curfew. There would be no fines tonight for those who broke the law and stayed late abroad since the advent of the fair in the morning was considered a valid enough excuse to do so.

His dizziness under control, Bascot leaned onto the stone of the crenellations and let his thoughts drift, planning how he would set about fulfilling the task that Nicolaa de la Haye had given him. The scrap of cloth that Gianni had found he could show to the drapers and weavers gathered for the festivities. It might be worthwhile to visit a few silversmiths and ask about the brooch, to see if they could determine its origin. He would need to visit the Jews and ask if the whereabouts of Samuel in the day or two before he met his death were known. It would also be advisable to visit the three places where the alekeeper had made his deliveries and try to discover if he had been seen at any house other than those at which he was known to have stopped. Of course, if the priest recovered and could identify his assailant, Bascot's task might be made easier.

Bascot shook his head to clear it. Tomorrow there would be so much activity within the town he would have difficulty getting anyone's attention for long enough to gain a coherent answer to his questions. The other side to that problem would be that people would be off their guard and he would be able to move comparatively unnoticed through the throng. The scrap of material was, although slight, his best indication of the young woman's identity. If he could find out who she had been, perhaps then he might also discover the identity of her companion, if the young man had been such, that is. He pondered on that for a moment. Had the boy been her husband? Or a stranger, their only link the manner of their death? There had to be a common thread weaving all of the dead people together and binding them to the murderer. It seemed only fitting that he should start his enquiries with the scrap of material.

Before he went inside to his pallet, the Templar replaced his eye patch, and looked up again at the canopy of stars overhead. Into the peace of the heavens he murmured a prayer for assistance and aid in successfully bringing the murderer to justice.

The next morning the day dawned with as fair a promise of sunshine as any of the townspeople could wish. Before first light there was movement as people gathered in knots of two, three or more, full of anticipation for the festivities. At midmorning there was to be a procession, starting at the principal gate of Stonebow in the lower town and winding its way up Mikelgate and Steep Hill through Bailgate to the Minster where the cathedral was situated. Every guild in the town would be represented, some by a delegation of its members marching in their finest clothes, others by a cart decorated with a scene to display their wares, all accompanied by the same strolling musicians and tumblers that had entertained in the castle hall the night before. The townspeople were already beginning to line the streets, some sitting on stools or benches they had brought with them for the purpose, others claiming an advantageous corner by planting themselves firmly in possession, and for those who were lucky enough to either have a house on the main street or to know someone who had, viewing the procession from the comfort of an open casement in the top storey of the dwelling.

Bascot knew it would be pointless to embark on his queries until the pageant had finished and, since Gianni was all agog to watch it, they climbed to the walkway of the outer wall of the castle bail and got a good vantage point from the battlements. They would see the procession just as it finished the trek up Steep Hill and turned into the grounds of the Minster. Gianni had come prepared for the entertainment by begging some pieces of bread and cheese from the castle cook, which he had carefully wrapped in a square of clean linen, and Bascot carried a flask of watered wine at his belt.

They were not alone in their chosen spot. Many of the soldiers from the garrison clustered beside them as well as those of the castle servants who had finished their duties in time to scamper up to the walkway. But in deference to Bascot's rank and, he suspected, out of consideration for his physical infirmities, he and Gianni were right at the front, and could see the street beneath them clearly through one of the gaps in the crenellations.

The cobblestones below them were thick with people and the hum of conversation. Excited laughter could be heard long before the strains of the musicians accompanying the procession were audible. Finally the leaders of the parade came into view as they passed through the huge arch of Bailgate. An exultant shout went up from the crowd as the most prominent members of the Draper's guild stepped out from under the arch, their faces red with perspiration as they sweated under the weight of the fine clothes they had donned for the occasion. The sun struck bright on the materials they wore—short summer cloaks in lustrous velvets of blue or green, silken tunics of red, yellow and ivory, and close-fitting caps of softest amber decorated with feathers dyed to match. There was embroidery on every hem and sleeve, and jewels as well, pinned to cap and cloak. They made a magnificent display and the crowd gasped and called out their admiration. Cloth was the main staple of the fair and, as such, deserved pride of place at the head of the procession.

Behind the drapers came the other guilds, first the ones associated with cloth-making such as the weavers, dyers and tailors, then the gold and silversmiths, the parchment makers, the barbers—a wooden pole painted with stripes of red and white carried aloft in front of them—the soap makers and salters, the bakers and carpenters. Many had a cart in their midst, decorated with flowers and strips of cloth, with one or more of the guild members standing inside and displaying samples of their produce or, where possible, actually plying their trade as the carts moved slowly along. Beside and among them the musicians strolled, piping and playing, while the tumblers threaded their way cleverly through the procession and the crowd, deftly catching any pennies that might be thrown their way.

At strategic intervals, Bascot saw, there were pairs of Gerard's guard, eyes darting amongst the throng, on the lookout for cutpurses. Occasionally one of the soldiers would swoop into the crowd and grab some mean-looking fellow, shake him roughly and issue a warning before letting him go. The sheriff was determined that there would be no charge of laxness against his authority.

When the last of the procession, a few members of the butcher's guild, passed into the Minster, the crowd flooded behind, laughter and merriment cresting like waves in the wake of a boat. As the last of the revelers disappeared, Bascot and Gianni left the walkway and descended into the bail.

The huge open space was almost empty, only the shrill cries of a goose girl shooing her errant flock back into their pen breaking the unusual stillness. A faint clanging could be heard from the blacksmith's forge but it was halfhearted and stopped as the Templar and Gianni walked towards the main gate. Down the wooden walkway of the keep's forebuilding, a party of nobles was descending. Bascot recognised Richard Camville, Nicolaa and Gerard's son, in the lead, walking beside Conal, Philip de Kyme's son-by-marriage. Conal was looking straight ahead, his bright fair hair riffling in the breeze and a sullen look on his handsome face, lips pursed and chin high. Richard kept pace with him, slicing a glance at his companion now and then, but saying nothing. Behind them came Gerard and Philip de Kyme, the latter red faced and angry, shouting words lost by distance to Bascot at the descending back of his stepson, while Camville laid a restraining hand on the arm of his friend.

Suddenly de Kyme stopped and turned on the stair. Behind him and Camville were Lady Nicolaa and another woman that Bascot recognised as Sybil, de Kyme's wife, a tall thin woman with a long face and sad eyes. She was watching her husband and son with an expression that was a combination of anger and grief. De Kyme mouthed something at her and she flinched visibly, then straightened as Lady Nicolaa, copying her husband, laid a hand warningly on her shoulder.

At the bottom of the stairs, which Conal and Richard had just reached, Sybil de Kyme's son turned and, his hand at his sword, started to run back up the steps towards his mother's husband. As if with one accord, Richard Camville grabbed his companion forcefully about the shoulders and Gerard, his hand dropping to the blade at his belt, stepped in front of de Kyme. For a moment it was like a tableau as the four men, two young and two middle-aged, glared at each other. Then de Kyme tried to push Gerard aside and

scrabbled at his own blade, shouting as he did so. Smaller
and slighter, he had no chance of moving the sheriff, who
stood like a rock barring his passage. Suddenly Conal
shook himself loose of Richard's grasp and marched back
down the steps and across the bail in the direction of the
stables. Richard, after a glance at his parents, shook his
head and followed him. Camville released his sword hilt,
laughed, and then flung an arm about de Kyme and led him
off across the bail to the armoury, while Nicolaa and her
companion slowly descended the stairs, Sybil de Kyme
with faltering steps and an unsteady hand on the rail. Behind them came a group of other ladies, veils and sleeves
fluttering, heads together as they spoke in whispers and
gave covert glances at the back of Sybil de Kyme.

As the group moved slowly towards the main gate and
went through it, trailed by a few younger squires and
pages, Ernulf appeared at the top of the forecastle steps, a
linen-wrapped bundle under his arm. He saw Bascot and
hailed him, signalling him to wait, then trotted down the
stairs and over to where he stood.

"A monk from the priory came while the procession was
passing," he said. "Brought the two dead youngsters' clothing. Seems the nuns got 'em cleaned as best they could and
dried 'em in yesterday's sun before the storm came. Also
said that Father Anselm is still alive, but only just. Seems
none of his vital organs were damaged, as far as can be
told, but he is very weak. Brother Jehan is dosing him with
a potion to keep him asleep. Give the wound a chance to
start mending."

Bascot digested the news and took the bundle from Ernulf. "I'm glad the nuns were so swift with the clothing,"
he said. "Since it seems that Father Anselm will not be able
to communicate with anyone just yet, I shall visit some of
the drapers today and see if they can identify the cloth."

"Even if they do, it might have travelled far and wide

before it was made into the clothes those two were wearing," Ernulf opined.

"I know, but it's a logical place to start." Bascot looked at the serjeant with a raised eyebrow. "What was the ruckus between the de Kyme's?"

Ernulf shrugged, his seamed face set into disgruntled lines. "De Kyme woke with a head mazed with wine. Decided to ease the ache by blaming his wife for some imagined thing or other. Conal said some hard words about the treatment of his mother—quite right, too, by my way of thinking, the lady is ill-used by her husband most of the time—and de Kyme turned on him, like he usually does. Told the lad he was a sorry excuse for a man, let alone a knight, and said he wished that both he and his mother had never come into his sight. Said he had the hammer to make more sons, but Sybil's anvil could produce only the like of Conal or nothing at all and he was going to set the matter straight. The boy took offence—as who wouldn't?—and it was only by young Richard and Sir Gerard intervening that there wasn't more than hard words said. From the way de Kyme spoke," Ernulf added musingly, "it wouldn't surprise me if he's sent off to the archbishop for licence to have his marriage dissolved. He and Conal's mother are cousins of a sort, even if distant. Could be grounds for consanguinity."

The serjeant rubbed his face with a distracted hand as he finished speaking. "Well, nothing to do with us and these murders, is it? Lady Nicolaa said as I was under your orders until the matter got sorted out. Do you want me to accompany you today, or have you another errand? I could take a walk down to Butwerk; ask among the prostitutes about the dead girl, if you like. Might help if I had her clothing, though. Someone might recognise it."

Bascot considered a moment. "Let's go together, Ernulf. The drapers might be more content to answer my questions once they have assured themselves there are profits in the offing."

"And the harlots will be less busy this morning than tonight," Ernulf agreed with a grin. "But it's a fair piece for you to walk with that ankle, what with the crowds and all. If we get mounts, we can ride outside the walls down to the lower town. Be easier on all of us."

Bascot agreed and they walked towards the stables. Just before they reached the open gates, a large black stallion shot out, Conal on its back, kicking hard with his spurs. Behind him thundered another mount, a heavy bay ridden by Richard Camville, who was calling to his friend to slow his pace. Conal paid no attention, but galloped headlong across the bailey, scattering the goose girl's flock once more, and rode through the west gate, across the drawbridge and out into the open countryside, Richard behind him. They left a cloud of dust and goose feathers in their wake.

"Let's hope there's not more blood spilled before sunset," Ernulf said sadly. "Lady Nicolaa's trencher is already as full as it needs to be without de Kyme and the results of his bad temper adding to it."

"At least if there's murder done amongst the de Kymes we won't have to look far for the culprit," said Bascot, not realising, as he spoke, that he would soon have cause to remember the careless words.

Once mounted they left by the same gate as the two young men but at a more sedate pace. Dust whirls still lingered along the track that Conal and Richard had taken. Bascot, with Gianni riding pillion and the serjeant's mount behind, descended the hill, hard under the lee of the castle wall to start with, then beside the stone boundaries of the city as they descended still farther, finally reaching the lower part of Lincoln town and the banks of the River Witham.

Along the riverside a path led, beside which barges laden with goods lifted gently in the tide, and fishing boats and small coracles were moored. The water in this part of the river had been turned a muddy brownish grey colour by the effluence discharged from the vats of the dyers, most of whom had premises in nearby Walkergate. A few mangy curs patrolled the docks, snarling at each other and engaging in the occasional fight. The air was filled with the furious shrieks of scavenging birds as they swooped to pick up a dead fish or eel, vying for their prey with the rats that scurried under the wharves, black eyes and sleek fur flashing as they darted out of reach of the birds' sharp beaks.

The path along the bank led to High Bridge and the trio turned and entered the lower town through Briggate, horses at a slow walk, and made their way past Saltergate and Baxtergate towards Stonebow, the principal gate into the city. Once through its impressive arch, they bore east until they came to Butwerk, a poor suburb of Lincoln situated across the expanse of the Werkdyke, a huge ditch into which most of the filth from the surrounding area was thrown. Here, in Butwerk, were the stewes where the harlots of Lincoln lived and offered their charms for sale.

Ernulf led the way to Whore's Alley, the main street of the district. The buildings, like those in most of Lincoln, were of three stories, but these were more cheaply built and the top floors sloped inwards towards each other across the street, so close in some places that they seemed in imminent danger of collapse. Most of the casement shutters were closed, even though the day was well advanced, and the walls of the buildings were shabby, cracked in places and buttressed by timber that was warped and split. Except for a couple of bedraggled cats, there was no sign of life, just a sour smell from the rubbish overflowing the open drain that ran down the middle of the street.

"Who holds the fee for these properties?" Bascot asked Ernulf. "I have not seen any of Butwerk listed among the Haye lands."

"There were a couple in the days of Sir Richard," Ernulf answered, "but when her father died, Lady Nicolaa got rid of them." The serjeant smiled. "He was a rare lecher, Sir Richard, although he didn't have need to come to such whores as live here. But Lady Nicolaa didn't want to have rents earned by prostitutes in her coffers, so she sold off all the properties here when she came into her inheritance."

He looked up the street to where it ended in a wall that had been built to contain the area. "Most of the houses belong to whatever stewe-keeper lives in 'em. Bought with money loaned by the Jews, of course. Usual arrangement, you know, the Jews loan the money for the purchase, then whoever has borrowed it pays it back, plus interest. Most of 'em manage to keep going and make a profit. The Jews are happy to have the property as surety for their silver and are satisfied if they only get the interest each year. But if trade slacks off and a stewe-holder can't pay the interest then he has to sell and pay the Jew his money. Not too many have to do that, though. Whoring can be profitable if the girls are toothsome."

As he finished speaking, they turned into Whore's Alley and Ernulf stopped his mount at the first door. He and Bascot slid down from their saddles and gave the reins of the horses to Gianni to hold. The serjeant banged on the wood in front of him, saying as he did so, "Probably all still asleep. I expect trade will be brisk tonight and they'll need to have taken some rest. There'll be customers aplenty once the daylight is gone."

His knocking finally brought a response. The door in front of them was pulled open, but just a cautious crack. Behind it was a shabbily attired individual with a face that closely resembled a ferret. His dark dirty hair fell down cheeks shadowed with week-old stubble, and his few remaining teeth were black with rot. Eyes sliding nervously from Ernulf to the Templar and back again, he asked, with a feeble attempt at heartiness, "What are you doing here, serjeant? Come to sample one of my beauties, have you?"

"Not likely, Verlain. I don't need a dose of the pox at my age."

"My wenches are all clean," the stewe-keeper protested. "You know they are. The bailiff inspects them every week, just as he's supposed to. I keeps the king's ordinances, I do. And the town's as well. No victuals or ale on the premises, no woman kept against her will, and I don't charge any of the girls' more than four pence for her room. If that's why you're here, then . . ."

Ernulf stopped the man, whose voice had dropped into a whine. "If you're such a saint, Verlain, how is it the city bailiff tells me he has to fine you regularly for breaking the very ordinances you've just told me you keep?"

"Only once or twice, serjeant, only once or twice, when bad times was on me and I had need to pay my money to the Jew. I wouldn't have broken the injunctions otherwise, I swear." The stewe-keeper's voice now had a grovelling tinge. "If you've come to check up on me, you must know that with the fair on . . ."

Again Ernulf stopped him. "That you've got more wenches in your house than you're supposed to have and that I might just find a pot or two of ale about the place. Well, if you have and if I do, then I might just let the bailiff know about it. Unless, of course, you answer my questions, and any Sir Bascot has to ask you."

Bowing, and unctuously assuring them of his willingness to comply with any wishes they might have, the stewe-keeper let his visitors into the premises, and they walked across an entryway lit only by the light of a guttering rush lamp and into a large room. Pushed against the walls were a number of stools and, in the farthest corner, stood a plain wooden table with a scarred and stained surface. On it were some empty tumblers and an unstoppered jack of ale.

Ernulf raised an eyebrow as he looked at the forbidden liquor and Verlain hastily assured him it was only for his own and the harlots' consumption. The serjeant nodded, then said, "Your women, all asleep, are they?"

"Upstairs, resting," the stewe-keeper confirmed.

"Well, wake 'em up and tell 'em to get down here. We want to ask if they know of any doxy from round here that's disappeared in the last couple of days, and to look at some clothes and see if they recognise them."

"Is this about that whore found murdered in the ale-house, serjeant?" Verlain asked. "It weren't no girl of mine, that I promise you. I don't have to wake 'em up for you to ask 'em. I can vouch for their answer."

"Can you?" Ernulf said sarcastically. "Well, unless I hear their answers myself—and without you prompting their replies—I might think as how you know more about that murder than you're telling. And if I think that, then I might consider that maybe I should drag you by the heels and hand you over to one of Sheriff Camville's men and let him ask the questions."

No more threat was needed. The stewe-keeper almost ran from the room in his haste to acquiesce with Ernulf's request. Within moments half a dozen sleepy-eyed harlots were standing in the room before them. They were in vary-ing stages of undress, ranging in age from young to old. Some had a jaded prettiness, but most looked haggard and, without exception, wore an expression of irritation at being disturbed from their rest. Once the bawds heard the reason for which they had been summoned, however, they all will-ingly examined the clothing and listened carefully to Er-nulf's description of the girl who had worn it. But even so, none could remember any girl of their acquaintance that was missing nor, they claimed, had they ever before seen the clothes held out for their inspection. Bascot did not interrupt Ernulf as the serjeant spoke to them, merely watched the women's reactions closely. As far as he could tell, none of them seemed to be lying and when Ernulf looked at him to see if he wished to ask anything further, Bascot shook his head.

As they left the stewe, the keeper's voice rasped gratingly in their ears as he wished them good fortune with their quest and, with obvious relief, shut the door behind them.

Eleven

✛

Through a chink in the shutter of an upper storey casement, a stewe-keeper in a house at the far end of Whore's Alley watched Ernulf and Bascot as they knocked at each door on the street in turn. The watcher was a man of middle years, with thin straggly hair that had once been yellow and was now stained by dirt and time to the colour of greasy pewter. He had a face much like a loaf of unbaked bread, soft and lumpy, but his eyes were sharp and almost as black as currants. His name was Bernard, but because when he was younger he had been called Le Brun on account of the darkness of his eyes, Bernard had been corrupted into Brunner and it was as such that he was known.

He waited nervously as the serjeant and the Templar made their slow progress down the street. He knew that they would soon arrive at his own door and he waited with indecision, uncertain as to whether to take refuge in flight over the wall or to stay and do as he had promised Wat the day before the alekeeper had been found dead. Brunner had never thought matters would come to such a pass. Wat had merely told him there was a goodly pile of silver to be had if he gave the alekeeper one of his harlot's old gowns and was to tell anyone, if asked, that the girl who would be wearing it was known to him as a prostitute.

Never had he thought that murder would be involved. Nor had Wat apparently, since he had not foreseen his own death. The alekeeper had hinted that the money would be forthcoming from someone of high birth and Brunner had assumed that the whole charade was designed to compromise some girl who was, perhaps, dunning a young lord to marry her. It wouldn't be the first time hot blood had led to rash promises which were later regretted. During his time as a stewe-holder he had seen more than one young buck get heartsick over a fresh little doxy. A few beddings were usually all that was needed to make the ardour disappear.

When Brunner had heard of Wat's death, and that there had also been a dead female dressed as a harlot along with him, he had felt the sharp taste of dread rise on the back of his tongue. To dispel it he had reminded himself that only Wat had known of Brunner's involvement and, if any enquiries were made, he could simply deny knowledge of the dead woman or her dress. The gown had only been an old shabby one, after all, belonging to a harlot that had died the year before. That thought had comforted him until yesterday night when, after all his wenches were tucked up in their rooms with customers, he had found a scrap of parchment lying on the bed in his room. Brunner couldn't read, but it wasn't necessary to be literate to understand the drawings that had been limned on the paper. In black ink two prostrate figures had been sketched, one with a broken head and the other with a knife stuck in his heart. It was easy to identify the man with the crushed skull for he had a huge belly just like Wat and a barrel of ale had been pictured standing beside him. The other, blood pouring from the wound in its chest, had black eyes inked in, just like his own. He knew it for a warning that he must keep to the story Wat had told him to tell and, if he didn't, he would be as dead as the alekeeper now was. The sour taste of fear had quickly returned.

Brunner had slept not at all, but had lain tossing on his pallet until dawn. He had been up and drinking a cup of wine to steady his nerves as, one by one, the customers his women had been entertaining had left. Then he had heard of a priest being stabbed and his fear intensified. Anyone who would try to kill a priest would think nothing of murdering a lowly stewe-keeper. And now the very thing he had been dreading was about to take place. He was about to be questioned by someone in authority. Thinking furiously he began to pace, then he left his room and ran up the stairs to the landing above. Along the narrow passageway dirty leather curtains hung, shielding the entry to a number of small closets, each one only big enough for a pallet and stool, where the doxies carried on their trade. He went to the curtain at the farthest end and pulled it aside. On a straw mattress lay a young girl. She was buxom and fresh faced, with long blond hair loose and spread on her pillow. She was not asleep, however, even though her eyes were closed, for her hands were pressed hard against her mouth to stifle the sobs that were shaking her.

Brunner went inside and grabbed her by the arm. "Up, you. Now. I want you downstairs."

She pulled away from him, but there was no way to escape. He stood at the door and watched her as she crouched against the wall. "I want to leave," she snivelled. "'Tis against the ordinances for you to keep me here against my will. You said you wanted me for a servant, not to be a harlot. If you don't let me go, I'll find the bailiff and tell him."

Brunner leaned over her and gave her a sharp kick in the belly. She doubled up and began to moan. "You knew what it was all about when you came here, my girl. Don't pretend the innocent with me. Not so keen now you find that you have to lay with whoever wants to pay for you instead of being able to pick and choose your customers, are you? Well, you say one word to the bloody bailiff and I'll fix you up so no man, not even an old and ugly one, will ever want you to pleasure him again. Now get up and go downstairs, before I take a paddle to your bare arse."

He flung the leather curtain aside and strode out into the passage. The girl rose and crept after him, her hands to her stomach where he had kicked her. She followed Brunner downstairs and into his room, and he shut the door behind her. Then, with more threats of physical injury, he primed her in what she was to say when Ernulf and the Templar arrived.

Twelve

✛

As they approached Brunner's door, Ernulf hawked and spat. "If I find any ordinances broken in here, I'll take the fine out of the stewe-holder's hide. Nothing would give me greater pleasure."

Bascot looked at the serjeant and smiled. "I take it you have no liking for the man," he said.

"None at all. Most of the stewe-holders we've just seen are not too bad. They treat their wenches passably well and don't take too many liberties with the regulations. But this one . . . I've been tempted more than once to take my fist to his pasty face."

"Has he given you a personal offence?" Bascot asked while Gianni, still holding the horses, looked in surprise at Ernulf's grim face.

"No, but we fished a young girl out of the river once. One of the rat-catchers down on the docks saw her as she jumped in, but she drowned before anyone could get to her. About two year ago now, it were. She was just a little bit of a maid, not much more than a child. Drowned herself she had, but before she jumped into the river someone had taken a birch rod to her back and legs. She was cut from neck to ankle. Been one of Brunner's wenches we were told, but he swore he hadn't seen her for a week or more before we found her and, although we tried, we couldn't prove different. But I know he did it. Beat her so badly she committed the sin of killing herself rather than face him again. Poor soul was probably too afraid to go to the bailiff, so she took the only way out left to her."

"What did you say his name is?" Bascot asked. "Brunner?"

"That's right, but he should be named Devil's Backside, for that's what he is."

When Ernulf knocked on the door and the stewe-holder opened it, the serjeant did not enter into any good-natured banter the way he had at the other stewes. He pushed Brunner roughly aside and told him to call his women down, and to be quick about it. When the harlots were all roused and standing downstairs, Ernulf asked them the same questions he had asked at all the other houses along the street. Did they recognise the clothes? Did they know of any harlot that had pale brown hair, was about midway in her term with an unborn child and had not been seen lately?

Most of the women shook their head but one of them, a blond-haired wench who called herself Gillie, had looked startled when Ernulf had said they were looking for a woman who was pregnant. She had then hesitantly said she had met a girl like that the week before, when she was travelling the road to Lincoln.

"Where were you coming from?" Bascot asked, the first question he had personally put to any of the prostitutes.

"From near Nottingham, sir," she said. "But I'll not tell you the name of my village. I run away and I don't want my kinfolk to find me. Especially here."

She kept looking nervously at Brunner until Ernulf, a scowl on his face, said to her, "If you want to leave, you have only to walk out of that door with us when we go. No one shall stop you."

For a moment the girl faltered, then she glanced once more at Brunner and, curling her arm so that it crossed her stomach, murmured, "I thank you, sir, for your offer. But there's no need. I'll stay where I am."

"Are you free born?" Bascot asked. If she was a villein and tied to the land, she was committing a crime against her family's lord by running away.

"I am, sir. That I promise you. I ran away because my mam died and my father married again. His new wife don't like me and she beats me all the time. A week ago when she took a rod to me, I struck back at her and when my father came home he gave me the brunt of his fist for giving her an injury. So I left and joined up with a party of travellers coming to Lincoln for the fair."

The girl's attitude throughout had been one of extreme nervousness, but this last sounded like the truth and Bascot let it go. "This girl you met on the way here, was she with the other travellers?" The girl nodded. "Did she tell you her name or say where she was from?"

"No, sir, she did not. She said she was coming to meet her husband, that he was a mason and had sent for her to come and enjoy the fair with him. But I didn't believe her. She didn't look like a goodwife."

"Why?" Bascot asked.

The girl looked down. "It were her clothes, sir," she said, her voice so low Bascot had to ask her to repeat herself. "It were her gown, sir. That one you've got there. She had a light summer cloak over it, but I seen it plain and clear. No decent man would want his wife dressed in colours like those. It looks like a harlot's gown and I reckon that's what she was. Like I am now." She lifted her shoulders and dropped them as though she had been defeated.

"When was the last time you saw her?" Bascot asked.

"The day we got to Lincoln, sir. About a week ago now. We all came through Stonebow gate, then each of us that were in the party went their own ways. The last I saw of her she was going up Mikelgate towards the upper part of the city."

"Did she mention to you the name of anyone she knew? What her husband was called, perhaps, or on what building he was working?" The story could be true. Masonry was an itinerant trade and those who plied it had to travel to whatever town had need of them.

"No, sir. Like I said, I didn't believe her anyway, so if she did say his name I didn't hear it for I wasn't paying much attention. I didn't talk to her much. I fell into company with another girl who was more to my liking."

"And you're sure she didn't say where she was from?" Bascot asked again.

Gillie shook her head. "I'm sure, sir."

Bascot looked at the other girls, who had been listening to Gillie's story with curiosity and awe. Even though she didn't look very happy as she had spun her tale, this new girl in their midst would now enjoy the fame that went with having actually spoken to the young woman who had been found murdered. It might even earn her a few extra pennies from customers who had a grisly interest in her tale.

The Templar nodded to Ernulf, and they started to leave. Before they went through the door, however, the serjeant turned and spoke to the girl again. "If you find yourself ill-treated here or"—he paused to gaze at each of the harlots in turn—"if any of you others have cause to complain, send for me at the castle. My name is Ernulf."

Turning towards Brunner he said, "And I'll be telling the bailiff to have an extra sharp inspection here next week, so there better not be anything amiss, either with your premises, or your wenches."

Brunner made no reply but once the Templar and Ernulf had disappeared through the door, he sank onto a stool and called to one of the women to bring him a full measure of wine.

Thirteen

✛

THE PEOPLE OF LINCOLN TOWN WERE ENJOYING THE
entertainments of the fair to the full, and trade was brisk in
the cloth markets, on the stalls and outside the walls where
sheep and cattle were being sold. Pedlars of pies, bread rolls
and savoury jellied meats were everywhere, their boards balanced on top of their heads or held in front of them by means
of a strap around their necks. Women sold trinkets and ribbons from baskets held on their hip, tinkers offered cheap
pots and mended spoons from the selections dangled about
their bodies on lengths of twine, and beggars covered with
sores or having some disability such as a withered arm
or a crippled leg—some real, some faked—importuned pass-
ersby for alms. Among the throng walked the sheriff's
guards, while town officials bustled to-and-fro, checking that
every stallholder had paid the fee for keeping it and watching to see that no unwary customer was cheated by short
weight or measure. There were bearbaitings and dog fights,
wrestling matches and strolling players, each contending

with the others to win a fourthing or half-part of the silver penny pieces thrown by the spectators. Near the end of the afternoon, the prostitutes joined the crowd; green sleeves attached to their gowns and dyed horsehair wigs on their heads.

As day drew into evening, the selling halls and vendor's stalls closed, but still the fair went on, the entertainment now of a different nature. Mugs of ale purchased at the packed alehouses were carried into the streets and young men and women danced to the music of wandering troubadours, the girls' skirts twirling in gay abandon and hair tumbling unheeded from discarded coifs. Their partners lifted them high and swung them about, faces sweating from exertion and excitement. Tonight, and for all the next ten nights of the fair, there would be no curfew, and torches would be kept burning all night along the main thoroughfares so that the revellers could enjoy themselves in safety.

In the keep of Lincoln castle, there were far fewer to sit down to the evening meal than there had been the night before. Only those members of the castle garrison who would be on duty that evening were eating the cold viands and cheeses that had been laid out by a depleted staff of servants and, at the high table, the company was diminished to the relatives and personal guests of the sheriff and his wife.

Bascot sat at a lower table, alone except for an older knight who was attacking his trencher with vigour. Below the salt sat a few clerics and a couple of squires. Gianni, after serving his master, had retired with his own food to his favourite spot in a corner of the hall with the dogs, and Ernulf had gone to ensure that the castle had been made secure for the night.

As he ate, Bascot ruminated on his visit to Brunner's establishment and the tour he had made of the cloth halls afterwards. What he had learned had not aided him much and, as to the young harlot's protestation that she had seen the dead girl on the way to Lincoln, he was uncertain as to how truthful she had been. The elderly knight beside him kept up a steady flow of conversation, mostly about previous fairs that had been held in Lincoln and of the various troublesome incidents that had plagued them. Bascot listened with only half his attention.

At the table on the dais he could see that Philip de Kyme was seated next to Lady Nicolaa, on his other side Hugh Bardolf's daughter, Matilda. Both of the women were engaging him in conversation and he seemed both flattered and animated. At the far end, beside Nicolaa's sister Petronille, sat de Kyme's wife, quietly eating her food and nodding occasionally as her companion sought to draw her into speech. A judicious arrangement, Bascot decided. Distract the husband and placate the wife and perhaps there will be no more arguments. He could not see Conal anywhere, or Richard Camville either. Perhaps the two had not returned from their headlong flight out of the west gate that morning.

"And there's more trouble at this fair, too, so I understand. Murder done—four of 'em killed in one night—and a priest attacked." Bascot's companion was still talking and the Templar brought himself back to the conversation with an effort. "Always trouble at these fairs. Common people get too excited and don't know how to behave, that's the trouble."

The knight, who was wearing what surely must be his best tunic, a knee-length garment of bright yellow over a handsome undergown of dark blue with an embroidered cap of matching colours on his straggly white hair, gave Bascot a direct look, finished chewing his mouthful of cheese and apple and said, "Lady Nicolaa set you to find the villain who did it, didn't she? Have you got him yet?"

As Bascot started to explain he was merely trying to discover the identity of the unknown couple found on the taproom floor, he was interrupted by the arrival of the young man who acted as *secretarius* to Philip de Kyme, a fresh-faced fellow named William of Scothern. He had come into the hall while the old knight had been speaking and had made his way at once to where Bascot sat, standing quietly until a pause came in the conversation.

"Sir Bascot. I have seen you about the castle, but have never yet had speech with you. I hope you will excuse my interruption, but I have just spoken with Ernulf and we both thought I should bring a concern I have to you."

His manner was deferential, even though Bascot had heard a tale that he was a grandson of Nicolaa de la Haye's father, Richard, son of an illegitimate daughter born to one of the baron's lemans, a woman who had been kin to one of the more prosperous merchants of the town. The leman, Scothern's grandmother, had died in birthing the child, and Richard de la Haye had provided for the girl, marrying her off to one of his retainers. In due course she had produced William and, Bascot seemed to recall it being said, another child, a girl. They were both now in de Kyme's household. William, although eligible for a knight's rank because of his father's status, had chosen instead to be educated and now fulfilled the role of personal clerk to de Kyme. The girl was one of Lady de Kyme's attendants. Scothern was a fair-looking lad of about twenty years, with a touch of the Haye red in his brown hair and serious green eyes. He seemed extremely edgy and Bascot noted that his ink-stained fingernails had been bitten to the quick.

Bascot gave him permission to speak and the clerk said that Ernulf had told him that the cloth merchants he and the Templar had spoken to had been of the opinion that the clothing they had been shown had come from Maine, in particular from the town of La Lune where there was a weaver of great skill. The cloth was easily recognised by its individuality among merchants accustomed to trade with those parts of the Angevin empire which lay on the borders of France.

Bascot, wondering at Scothern's interest, gave no reply

beyond agreement with the statement, and waited for the clerk to continue.

Scothern glanced at the elderly knight, who was listening to their conversation with interest, and said, "I do not wish to interrupt your meal, Sir Bascot. Perhaps you will give me a few moments of your time when you are finished. I do not think you will find it wasted."

Bascot nodded and said he would meet with the clerk in his room in the old tower in an hour's time. As Scothern left, Bascot's companion leaned forward. "Bright young spark that. De Kyme wouldn't know what to do without him, so I'm told. Old Richard de la Haye would be proud of his grandson, I'll warrant. Too bad William's mother hadn't been born male for, even though illegitimate, a boy child might have been made Richard's heir, since his wife only gave him daughters. Then it would have been young Scothern's destiny to sit up there on the dais instead of Lady Nicolaa. Not that he'd have made a better castellan, of course, for Lady Nicolaa fills the office just as well as any man. But a man's parts are easier in the saddle than a woman's, if you know what I mean."

Bascot let the knight ramble on while he finished his meal, then excused himself and, calling Gianni, made his way to his chamber.

Scothern was waiting on the steps outside the door to Bascot's room when the Templar arrived. They went inside and Gianni poured a cup of ale for both of them then, at Bascot's signal, made himself comfortable on his pallet in the corner. The room was so small that Scothern had to sit on a stool beside Bascot's bed in order to speak to him, but what he had to say soon drove the closeness of their proximity out of the Templar's notice.

"A couple of months ago, Sir Philip bade me write to a lady who lives in Maine," the clerk said. "It was a letter he told me to hold in the closest of confidence, but in view of the knowledge I had from Ernulf tonight, I am in a quandary as to whether to inform Sir Philip of my suspicions, or to just let the matter rest. It is really your advice I have come for, Sir Bascot. I know you will keep what I have to tell you as private as I have myself."

Scothern took a swallow of ale and waited for Bascot's nod of agreement before he continued. "As you are probably aware, for most of Lincoln is, Sir de Kyme is not happy that he has only Conal, his son-by-marriage, for an heir. If he should pass Conal by there is a nephew, Roger de Kyme, who at least has a son to follow him, but my master would rather have an heir of his own issue, if at all possible."

Here the clerk looked down at his ale, seemingly embarrassed. "It appears that early in his youth Sir Philip was enamoured of a young lady of the town and planned to make her his wife. His family stopped the marriage and a contract was arranged with his present wife, who was then a widow with a young son. However, even though the marriage of his choice was stopped, and the young girl who held his affections was sent away, it seems she was already with child by Sir Philip, a circumstance known only to him and to her. She later had the child, a boy, and wrote to Sir Philip of the birth. He was not then in a position to help her and, besides, he had hopes that the wife chosen for him would present him with a son. But many years have now passed and he despairs of any issue from his present wife so he decided to contact the woman he was in love with in his youth by sending her a letter and asking if his child by her still thrived."

"And you wrote this letter for him?" Bascot asked.

"I did, sir, and the one that followed her reply. When Sir Philip found that the boy had grown up hale and hearty, he offered a place for the lad here and I know, if the lad pleased him, it was his intention to formally acknowledge him and make him his heir. He intimated as much to the boy's mother when he wrote."

Scothern now leaned forward in earnestness. "This last letter was written a scant two months ago and a response was made indicating that Sir Philip's son, Hugo by name, would leave almost immediately, and that he would bring with him his wife, Ernestine. She was with child, the letter said, which made Sir Philip overjoyed, for he thought not only to have a son of his own, but perhaps a grandson, too, into the bargain. Do you see my dilemma, Sir Bascot? All the circumstances—the age of the two murdered strangers, the woman being enceinte, the origin of the cloth that was part of her apparel—all point to them being this same son and his wife. But if I should tell Sir Philip and I am wrong, then I give him grief for nothing, while if I am right . . . then he should know at once."

"I take it that Sir Philip has never seen this illegitimate son?"

"No."

"And the messenger who took the letters to Maine, did he meet with the boy?"

Scothern sighed. "They were sent in the usual way, by one of the de Kyme retainers to the south coast via London, then in the charge of a captain on a boat crossing the Narrow Sea, and by hired messenger on the other side. The replies were brought back in like manner. The situation in Maine and neighbouring Brittany and Anjou is volatile at the moment, what with King Richard's death and his brother John ascending the throne. As you will be aware, there are many who hate the English there, thinking that Arthur, son of King John's dead older brother Geoffrey, should have the crown. Sir Philip thought it best if no attention was drawn to his former love by the arrival of a messenger from England. And he wished to keep the matter secret. It is quite likely that Conal or his mother would have noticed if one of Sir Philip's servants was gone for any length of time and they might have asked questions."

"Well, if it is this Hugo and his wife that have been murdered, Lady de Kyme and Conal will soon know of it, whether Sir Philip wills it or no. But how are we to prove the dead couple's identity? By the time the boy's mother could journey from Maine to Lincoln, her son would be no more than an unrecognisable rotting corpse. And from what you have said, it sounds unlikely that there is anyone in England that would know him, dead or alive."

Gianni came forward at this point and respectfully tapped Bascot on the shoulder. When the Templar looked at his servant, Gianni drew his finger down the side of his neck, then pointed to the pouch at Bascot's belt.

"Yes, Gianni. The scar—and the trinket we found. They may help, if one is known of and the other familiar." He stood up. "I think it best, William, if we take this matter to the sheriff and Lady Nicolaa. Let them decide what should be done. The weight of the matter will then be taken from your shoulders, and mine."

A short time later Gerard Camville had Philip de Kyme brought to a private room in the castle and there, in front of Lady Nicolaa, Bascot and William Scothern, told his friend what the clerk suspected.

"It is possible that they may be some other travellers, Philip," the sheriff said, "but if we can, we must be sure. Do you know the general description of the boy, if he had any scars or marks on his body? Is this"—he placed the tiny brooch on the surface of the table at which de Kyme was seated—"familiar to you? Although it may not have belonged to the girl, but have been dropped by another some time before the murders occurred," he added.

De Kyme sat as though mazed when he had been told what Scothern had revealed to Bascot. It was some moments before he could take in the possibility that his illegitimate son and the boy's wife had been murdered. At first he had shaken his head, denying the thought, then he dropped his head into his hands. "My last hope," he muttered. "Am I never to have a son of my own? Why does God always deny me what he gives freely to other men?"

Gerard Camville poured a cup of wine and handed it to his friend. "It may be that these two are not your son and his wife," he said with compassion in his usually surly voice. "That is the need now, to identify them. Have you any way to do that, Phillip?"

"No, I have not, not unless his mother is sent for. Poor Eleanor. Again she has suffered through my hand, however much I wanted to do her good." He looked up at Camville and shrugged. "If I see the boy I might perhaps recognise a likeness to myself or his mother—but that is tenuous at best. As for scars, or the like, I do not know if he had any. How am I to tell . . . ?"

He stopped speaking as he belatedly caught sight of the tiny brooch and reached forward quickly to pick it up and examine it closely. His face turned grey as he looked at Bascot. "This . . . this . . . it was found on the boy?"

"On the premises," Bascot answered. "The alewife said it was lying on the ground near where one of the bodies had been hidden. Do you recognise it?"

De Kyme nodded slowly, his face now drawn with lines of certainty and renewed grief as he turned the brooch over, revealing a small circle of two strands of twisted silver wire set on the back. "I gave it to his mother all those years ago," he said. "It was a pledge between us, for her to wear next to her heart, hidden under her clothing. I had the metal entwined together to symbolise our love, that we should never be parted. How I wish I had kept my bargain with her, and not given in to my father's demand that I wed his choice of wife instead of my own."

De Kyme jumped up, anger contorting his features. "And now my son—the only son I have—has been murdered.

There can only be one person foul enough to do such a deed. My wife. Her and that prancing hellhound she has for a son. Somehow she must have found out my intention to put my own true blood in place of Conal and has had him killed, along with the wife who bore another of my line. I know it as surely as I breathe my life's breath, for I know her for the bitch that she is."

Hand on sword he strode towards the door but Camville was there before him, speaking softly and advising caution. If his friend truly believed Sybil and Conal were guilty of secret murder, he said, than a charge must be made against them. This was the lawful procedure and much preferable to resolving the matter with violence. Philip calmed somewhat at the sheriff's words and listened as Camville went on persuasively, reminding his fellow baron that proof of their culpability must be found else any accusation would be too weak to merit their being brought before the king's judges.

"I will lay the charge for you, Philip," Camville said, "and then let us find out, if we can, where Conal was during the day when the killing must have taken place. Also your wife. Someone must have seen your son as he travelled up from the south. Then let us see if we can ascertain where the deed was done and if it is reasonable for Conal to have done it himself or have hired some wolf's-head to do it for him. That is the best course if you would see them brought to the king's justice."

"Gerard is right," Lady Nicolaa added. "There must be some proof to set before the king's judges, as you well know. Leave the matter with us for now, and keep private counsel before others until we can act."

De Kyme's temper flared again at her words. "By God," he shouted, "that is all well enough, but not only do you ask me to keep my sword from that bitch and her spawn, you also ask me to stomach their company and keep silent. I cannot do it, I tell you. I cannot."

Nicolaa looked at her husband with raised eyebrows and he nodded. "Then I think, Philip, it would be best if you returned to your own demesne. I will ensure Sybil stays here and, with my son Richard's help, Conal also. We will keep them close and away from your presence until the truth is known."

Reluctantly de Kyme agreed, saying only that first he would stop at the priory to see the remains of the lad who had been his son. "For," he said morosely, "although I had no opportunity to honour him in life that does not mean I cannot do so in death. He will be buried in the station I would have raised him to, and his wife and the unborn child beside him. That you will not deny me, will you, Gerard?" he asked of the sheriff roughly.

"No, only that you wait a space. Once you have seen them, the bodies can be sealed in their coffins for the time being. Give us a few days only, Philip, we will get to the bottom of this soon enough, I promise you."

With that, Philip de Kyme nodded his agreement and, calling to Scothern to accompany him, left the chamber.

Nicolaa looked at Bascot. "Find out if Conal did this thing, Templar, if you can. And if he did not, who did. I have today received a message from King John. He will be here in just a short time hence, in November. I want him to find that justice has been employed in this matter, not mayhem. And mayhem we will have if de Kyme lets his sword loose. Sybil's family, and that of her long dead husband, are not without influence. If they find she and Conal have been unjustly accused we will have a local war on our hands. I doubt that would please the king, since it is just such turbulence he is trying to forestall in his territory on the continent. Let him find that England, at least, gives him no such grievance."

Fourteen

✦

IN THE CHAMBER NICOLAA USED FOR HER SOLAR Bascot sat facing Sybil de Kyme and her attendant, Isobel, who was sister to William Scothern. The room was a comfortable one at the top of the new keep. A number of padded settles and stools scattered around the perimeter of the chamber marked it as one used by women, as well as the embroidered tapestries that hung upon the walls. A large fireplace, now unlit, dominated the far side of the room, and an array of comfits and containers of honeyed wine were set out on a table near the door.

Conal stood by his mother, his handsome face weary and drawn, but solicitous of his dam as he laid a hand gently on her shoulder now and then to reassure her. Nearby Richard Camville paced, angry strides carrying him the length of the chamber and back in a manner reminiscent of his father's restless movements. He and Conal had returned to Lincoln just before dawn and had been told of the charge laid by Philip de Kyme against his wife and stepson. The accusation and any plea in defence would be placed before the royal justices when their circuit of the kingdom reached Lincoln later in the summer, near the end of July.

"This whole matter is absurd," Richard expostulated as Bascot was asking Sybil de Kyme if she had known of the existence of her husband's illegitimate son. "Why would Conal want to kill this Hugo? He was a bastard. The justices would never give claim to an illegitimate heir over a lawful one."

"If it was proven that the child was the result of a union before Sir Philip contracted his marriage with Lady Sybil, then it could be considered that the liaison with the boy's mother constituted a prior contract, and the later marriage was unlawful," Bascot said. Remembering that Ernulf had voiced the opinion that Philip de Kyme was in the process of finding some means of releasing himself from his marriage the Templar had sought out the view of Nicolaa de la Haye's *secretarius*, an older clerk who was well versed in the law. "They are difficult circumstances to prove, but it has been done."

"Neither my mother or I knew of this Hugo. Nor did we know that he was coming to Lincoln," Conal said quietly. "As for de Kyme's inheritance, I have no interest in it. My own father left me a small manor near Scunthorpe. It is enough for me."

Lady Sybil reached up and laid her hand over her son's. "The justices will not see it that way, Conal. They will see only that there was the prospect of a rich fief, and this illegitimate boy stood in your way of it."

Bascot glanced at Isobel Scothern, who had sat silent and with downcast eyes throughout this exchange. A strange position she and her brother were in, one the servant of the master, the other of the mistress, and these two at odds with one another. "Did your brother tell you of the letters that had been exchanged with the boy's mother?" Bascot asked her.

"No, he did not," she answered. "My brother is scrupulous

about the confidentiality of his post as *secretarius* to Sir Philip. He tells me nothing of his work."

Bascot considered the answer, and the girl. She was a striking contrast to Lady Sybil, and not only for the twenty-some years difference in their ages. Where Conal's mother was a tall angular woman, fair of hair and face, and dressed in a gown of cool colours that set off the whiteness of her complexion, Isobel was petite and dark, the Haye red showing only in glints of auburn in her glossy brown hair, and her eyes, heavy lidded, were a rich deep hazel. Her dress was of mossy green, reflecting the lustre of her colouring in an undergown and sleeves of tawny yellow. Her manner was restrained and polite, but there was a latent sensuousness about her person, hinted at in the graceful angle in which she held her head and in the easy movement of her small delicate hands as she smoothed the folds of her gown. Even Richard Camville, preoccupied with his anger, still found time to give her an occasional appreciative glance when his pacing took him near to where she sat.

"I do not wish to belabour the point, demoiselle," Bascot said to her, "but are you sure that you knew nothing of this matter? It will be part of the accusation that Lady Sybil or Conal knew of Sir Philips' intentions and were thus provided with a motive for murder. Even if you did not see the letters, did your brother perhaps let something slip about the business in a conversation with you? Something you may have, albeit innocently, mentioned to your mistress?"

Isobel regarded him with eyes of amber. "I am sure. How could I have done so when I had no knowledge of the matter myself until this morning? It is impossible." With a small smile she dropped her gaze downwards.

Bascot nodded in acceptance of her words as Conal burst out, "Sir Bascot, if I had wanted to kill anyone and not be found to have done so, I would have murdered them in the greenwood and left them for the wolves to devour, not pushed them into barrels and dumped them on the floor of an alehouse."

"Exactly," interjected Richard. "It would have been far better for Conal, if he had done this deed, that this bastard son had just disappeared without a trace, would it not?"

Bascot sighed. Always it came back to the same question—why had the young couple and the Jew been murdered as they had? Why had they been stabbed after death? Why had Wat been involved in leaving them on his premises?

"I agree with you," Bascot replied. "This is a coil that there seems no way to unwind."

He spoke once again to Lady Sybil and her son. "It is believed that Hugo and his wife, along with the Jew, had been dead for some hours before they were left in the alehouse. This puts the time of their deaths as during the second day before the fair began, that is three days ago. Can you both tell me where you were then?"

"We all—my husband, Conal and myself—came to Lincoln a few days before that," Sybil answered. "We stayed at the house of my husband's nephew, Roger de Kyme. Roger was not there himself, but his steward was, stocking up with victuals for when his master and mistress should arrive. On the day about which you ask my husband went on a hunt with Gerard Camville and later that same day—in the evening—I, on Lady Nicolaa's invitation, took up guest's lodging, with my husband, at the castle. Conal stayed on alone at Roger's until the day before the fair. He left when Roger and his wife arrived since they had guests with them and the chamber Conal had been using would be needed. He then came to the castle and Richard was kind enough to share his quarters with him."

"Then on the second day *before* the fair, both of you were at Roger de Kyme's house?" Bascot asked, feeling a chill start to creep at the back of his neck. "What were your movements on that day?"

Sybil looked up at her son, a little frown drawing her delicate brows together. "My mother was unwell, Sir Bascot," Conal answered for her. "She believed she had eaten something that had been turned sour by the heat, and so she kept to her bed until she went to the castle. I rode to Newark and was gone most of the day."

"Did either of you have servants in attendance? Lady Sybil, did Isobel keep you company in your sickness? Conal, did you travel with a friend, or perhaps take a groom with you?" Bascot almost felt their answers before they were made, so great was his sense of foreboding.

"I sent Isobel away," Sybil said. "There was much to see around the town and since my husband would not be wanting her brother to attend him while he was hunting, I gave her permission to keep him company for a few hours of pleasure. I had no other companions or servants with me. Roger's steward was gone also, fetching fresh eels for his master's table, a delicacy Roger enjoys and prefers to be obtained from an area just south of Lincoln. The house, I believe, was empty. The rest of the household staff, except for the steward, had not yet arrived. With the aid of a nostrum Isobel prepared for me I slept most of the time and felt much better when I awoke."

"And you, Conal?" Bascot asked.

Conal shook his head. "I went to Newark alone. I wanted to think. I stopped for a sup of ale and food at a tavern in the town, but there was no one there I knew."

"Why did you go to Newark?"

Conal's face flushed, but he didn't answer. Lady Sybil did instead, with an upward glance at her son and a tightening of her fingers on his hand. "My son and my husband exchanged heated words early that morning. When Conal is . . . distressed, he prefers no company but his own. He has been that way ever since he was a small boy. Riding to Newark helped him exhaust his temper, just as it did yesterday."

"Richard Camville was with you yesterday. Would that he had been with you on the previous occasion," Bascot replied heavily. "Although Hugo, his wife and the Jew were all found a day later, it is almost certain that they had been dead for longer than a few hours, and were killed on the very day that neither of you had witnesses to your movements. Moreover, Roger de Kyme's house was one scheduled for a delivery from Walter, the alekeeper. It would have been very convenient, Conal, for you to have done the deed and then, aided by your mother, have stowed the bodies in barrels which were then passed to the alekeeper when he called, under the guise of empties being sent for return."

Richard Camville erupted again, almost before Bascot finished speaking. "This is ridiculous. Conal, you must . . ."

Whatever he had been about to say was cut short by the entrance into the solar of Nicolaa de la Haye's two sisters, Petronille and Ermingard. With them was Hugh Bardolf's daughter, Matilda. The chatter of their conversation stilled as they entered the room and saw the group seated near the fireplace.

"Your pardon," Petronille said, her eyes singling out Bascot as she apologised for the interruption. "We had not thought to find anyone here and my sister is in need of a small respite from the crowds below."

Ermingard did indeed look flustered. Her face was flushed and tendrils of hair escaped from under the linen coif she wore on her head. Her gaze was confused, darting sideways and back, then down at the floor. As Petronille spoke, Ermingard pushed up a hand to rub her eyes, staring to where Sybil and Isobel sat.

Bascot rose. "There is no need for apologies, lady," he said. "Our speech here is finished. We will leave you ladies to your own company."

Bascot rose as he spoke, as did Isobel, who moved to stand behind Sybil de Kyme's chair. As she did so, Ermingard's confused gaze moved with her and she started to cry.

"It is the wrong colour, Petronille. I tell you, it is the wrong colour." She became very agitated, pulling at the stuff of her sleeve as though she would tear it, and sobbing as she repeated the words over and over again.

Petronille moved close to her and encircled her with her arm, while Matilda looked to where Ermingard had been staring. "It is the tapestry," Matilda said, pointing to a large wall hanging which depicted the Three Wise Men bringing their gifts to the Christ child. All of the figures were picked out in threads of gold and silver, with garments of deep blue and green against a background of a deep dark red, the colour of ripe cherries.

"It reminds her of blood," Matilda added. "She does not like blood."

"Hush, Matilda," Petronille's habitually benign expression flashed with a look of annoyance at the girl's words, quickly reverting back again as she tried to comfort her sister, whose sobbing and moaning had increased. "Come, Mina," she said, using a sister's privileged soubriquet, "have a cup of Nicolaa's honeyed wine. It will cool your head."

Petronille led Ermingard over to a window at the far end and sat her down on a settle, then poured a tumbler of wine and pressed it into her sister's hands, murmuring quietly to her. Ermingard gradually subsided, but she continued to shake her head and mutter about the wrongness of the colour.

Bascot, whose blinded right side was towards the offending tapestry, turned full around to see the object of Matilda's words. As he did so, he caught a flare of irritation on Isobel's face. It seemed to be mixed with something else—loathing, perhaps—but he was not sure if it was directed at the weakness of Lady Nicolaa's sister or the offensiveness of Matilda's outspoken words. He glanced back at Hugh Bardolf's oldest daughter. Her eyes were fixed on Conal, and there was a little smile curled at the corner of her lips as though she had scored some small triumph. Conal and his mother's attention were fixed on Petronille and her disturbed sister, but Richard's face had resumed it's angry look, with a different target this time, as he gave Matilda a look of fury.

"If you are to keep my aunt company, Matilda, I suggest you refrain from upsetting her with careless speech," he said icily.

"I am sorry, Richard," Matilda murmured apologetically. "I did not think."

Despite the words, her tone did not sound contrite and Richard said no more. As the men rose to leave, Bascot was aware of undercurrents of emotion in the room, and not all caused by Ermingard's unfortunate outburst. It was clear that Matilda and Isobel did not have any affection for each other, and also, from the sidelong glance of impatience that Isobel threw at Conal, that he was somehow involved in their enmity.

When they reached the door, Bascot motioned for the two younger men to precede him down the winding stone stairway, pleading that the enforced slowness caused by his unsound ankle would impede their descent. As they clattered down and disappeared round a turn in the tower, he could hear their voices echo back to him, Richard's importunate and Conal's blunt in refusal. Bascot heard his own name mentioned, then the voices drifted farther away before they were stilled by the slam of the door at the bottom of the stairway. When Bascot reached the base of the tower there was no sign of either of the two young men. Only Gianni, patiently awaiting his master's return, was in sight, sitting in the shade of the stairway up to the forebuilding, passing the time by repeatedly tossing three stones from the back of his hand to the palm in an age-old children's game.

Fifteen

+⫞+

From the entryway into the great hall Nicolaa de la Haye stood and surveyed her guests. The company had thinned out since the eve of the fair, but there was still a fairly large number to be accommodated at mealtime. She fingered the chatelaine at her waist, and the keys hanging from it, mentally running through the supplies of wine, flour, meat, vegetables and fruit that were held in store in the huge room at the bottom of the keep. There was still plenty, and the coolness of the lower floor should keep most of it fresh enough for consumption. She was pleased that the intensity of the summer heat had abated a little. It was still hot, but not as oppressive as it had been before the storm had cleared the air. She shrugged irritably in the gown she had donned for today. It was one she had ordered newly made for the festivities and the neckline was stiff and scratchy. Then she smiled at herself. It was not really the discomfort of the gown that was bothering her, but the murders in the alehouse and the attack on Father Anselm. She was no stranger to death. The conflict of battle, accident, sickness—all took their toll, and often. It was rather the mystery of these murders that she did not like, and mystery there was even if de Kyme's wife and stepson were responsible. She had no affection for Sybil beyond that of distant courtesy between two women whose husbands were friends, and Conal was only well known to her because of the amity between him and Richard. Still, the accusation did not lie easily on her mind. It had about it an untidiness that she did not like, and that offended her.

Her glance flicked to where her husband was seated. Gerard was in a mood of rare good humour this morning due to the fact that, as far as he was concerned at least, the charges laid by de Kyme had relieved him of looking further for a culprit to bring before the justices. The silver in his coffers was safe, for the moment.

Farther down the hall she saw Petronille take Ermingard, who was beginning to rock back and forth in her seat, by the arm and persuade her to leave the table where they had been breaking their fast. Matilda Bardolf rose with them and positioned herself on Ermingard's other side. It was probable they would take her up to Nicolaa's solar away from the curious eyes of the other guests. Ermingard's husband and son stayed where they were, Ivo looking with concern at his mother's retreating back and then turning to speak low in his father's ear. William de Rollos shook his head briefly, placing another morsel of cold meat in his mouth and chewing with determination, eyes straight ahead. Ivo made to rise, then changed his mind and sat back down, toying with a piece of bread and staring into space. Nicolaa frowned. Ermingard had been unusually difficult these last two days. De Rollos said she had seemed better during the previous months and so he had decided to bring her with him on the long journey from Normandy. Even the summer storm that had caught them while crossing the Narrow Sea had not given her undue stress, he had told Nicolaa. It had not been until after they had arrived in

Lincoln that Ermingard had become unsettled. Perhaps it was the press of so many people and the discomfort of the unseasonable heat that had disturbed her, Nicolaa thought. Or, she reasoned grimly, it was the murders that were maz-ing Ermingard's senses, with gossip running rampant of poisonings, stab wounds and dead pregnant women. If so, Nicolaa could feel some affinity for her sister's discontent.

Agnes stood in the yard behind the alehouse waiting for her cauldron of water to boil. Across the yard her nephew, Will, was crushing dried husks of barley to make the malt that would be added to the water once it was ready. Her own special gruit was waiting for when it was time to make the mash. It would take a full day for the mash to settle be-fore it was ready for straining, then a few more hours to wait for it to be strained a second and a third time. If she was lucky, she would be able to serve ale to her customers by tomorrow night.

Wat had been buried early that morning. Jennet and her husband, Tom, along with Will, had accompanied her to the funeral Mass. She had come straight back to the alehouse afterwards for she could not afford to let her yard stand idle while she made a show of grief. Tears would not turn into silver, but her good ale would, and she needed to take ad-vantage of the influx of visitors to the fair. She shivered as she watched Will finish his task of grinding the barley and turn to cleansing the ale barrels so they would be ready for her brew. Agnes did not know which ones had held the dead bodies of the two young people and the Jew, and she had not tried very hard to find out. A good scrub would take the contamination away, she reasoned, and she could al-ways tell her customers, if they asked, that she had de-stroyed the barrels that had held the dead bodies.

The gate into the back lane opened and Agnes saw the tubby figure of her neighbour, Goscelin, come into the yard. He was a baker who had his premises on the same street as her own. She smiled to herself as he came forward and deferentially asked how she was faring. Goscelin had always been friendly—theirs were reciprocal crafts after all, with his grain and her ale-brewed yeast—but he had shown a rare concern as soon as he had learned that Wat was dead, even offering one of his sons to spell Will in giving her protection. He was a prosperous man, was Goscelin, and a widower for some twelve months since the death of his wife from a fever. Agnes murmured a prayer under her breath asking God for forgiveness for her flightiness, then set her most winsome smile on her face as she returned the baker's greeting.

Jennet had been right. Wat had been no good husband to her. Agnes had realised that on the last day that Wat had been alive when he had kicked her for pestering him with questions about why she had to stay clear of the yard. Surreptitiously she rubbed the spot on her thigh where his boot had made a great purple bruise. Well, there would be no more of that now, thanks be to God.

She told Goscelin that she was feeling much better and regarded the baker closely under cover of what she hoped was a demure glance. He had a kind face, ruddy with the heat from his ovens, and a mouth that curved easily when he smiled. It was reputed he had treated his wife well while she was alive and had himself cared for her most tenderly when she had been taken ill. He also had three strong young sons, one of whom he was now offering once again as company and protection. There would be no shortage of hands to do the heavy work in any household of his. Yes, Goscelin would make a much better husband than Wat and it was plain that, once her bereavement was over, he would not cease his attentions to her. If she wanted the baker, she could have him. It was a thought which had comforted her often in the last two days.

· · ·

Ernulf did not bother to knock on the door of Brunner's stewe-house; he kicked it in instead. As the door crashed wide on its hinges the serjeant told the two men-at-arms he had brought with him to wait outside while he went in to find his quarry.

At the top of the stairs Ernulf could hear the rustling of the leather curtains that covered the entrances to the girls' cubicles and a muttered oath or two amongst the customers as the noise of his arrival disturbed the business of the bawdy house. Drawing his sword, Ernulf next put his foot to the door that led into Brunner's private chamber. The door swung open to reveal an empty room, the bed rumpled and filthy covers askew. A leather jack of wine lay on its side amongst the dirty rushes on the floor, drained of its contents. There were no clothes hanging from the peg behind the door, and the small ironbound chest that he had noticed in a corner when he and Bascot had last been here stood with the lid flung back to reveal an empty interior. Ernulf went back into the hallway and, taking the steps two at a time, roared out a question at the harlots now gathered in a fearful group at the top.

"Where is Brunner?" he demanded, directing his words at the oldest of the bawds, a woman of some probable thirty years, although she looked a score more.

"He isn't here," the harlot replied, trying to frame her words with some degree of dignity despite clutching desperately at the soiled and stained wrap which was all that covered her skinny frame. Behind her Ernulf could see her customer's alarmed eyes, peeking from behind the curtain of her cubicle.

"That isn't what I asked you," Ernulf said patiently, "I asked you *where* he was. I can see he isn't here for myself."

"I don't know, serjeant, and that's the truth. Nor do any of us," the bawd replied, looking to the other harlots for confirmation, which they all gave with much nodding of their heads. "He was here early this morning—showing his usual cheery face," she added with a sneer. "Then he left. Took young Gillie with him, though I reckon she didn't want to go from the argument we heard between them, but she went just the same. He yelled up to me that he'd be back for any silver we owed him for last night's work and that he'd have the hide off of any of us that tried to cheat him, then slammed out the door. Looked worried, I'm glad to say, God rot his soul."

Again there was more nodding of heads from the other bawds as they agreed with her words, especially the last.

"Are you sure he didn't give any indication of where he was going?" Ernulf persisted.

"None," said the older bawd, then she gave a sly giggle. "Perhaps he knew you was coming, serjeant. Didn't fancy your company maybe, although, speaking for myself, I'd be right pleased to see you here anytime." She winked at him. "For as long as you like," she added with a knowing grin. "Just ask for Maud."

The other harlots tittered and Ernulf threw a smile back to the one who had made the invitation. "I might find it on my way to pass here again," he said easily, "but it'll have to wait until I find Brunner. If he comes back, I want to know. Is that lass your servant?" He pointed to a slip of a girl about nine or ten years of age who was cowering at the edge of the group.

"That's my daughter," Maud replied. "She's too young yet to earn her keep with the rest of us, so she clears out the slops and cooks our meals."

"Then send her to the castle if you have word of Brunner. Just come to the gate, lass," he said to the girl, "and tell the sentry that Ernulf sent you. Can you remember that?"

The girl nodded, her eyes stretched wide with awe at being entrusted with such an important task.

"What's Brunner done, serjeant?" called out one of the bawds. "Enticed a castle wench away from your bed, has he?"

Again there was laughter, but Ernulf did not join in. "No, he hasn't. This time he's gone too far with his lies. I want him, and I'll have him. And I'll be just as hard on any that help him. Remember that if any of you are tempted not to do as I ask if, and when, he comes back."

The harlots fell silent as they saw the gravity of Ernulf's expression. They were still quiet as he went out the door and closed it behind him. One of the men-at-arms looked at Ernulf hopefully. "Any luck, serjeant?"

"No. He's gone. And taken the girl with him. But I'll find him if I have to search every ramshackle hovel in Butwerk. We know the tale the young bawd told of meeting the dead girl on the road was a lie. The girl was the wife of Philip de Kyme's illegitimate son and was travelling with her husband, who was most definitely not a mason here in Lincoln. And it was Brunner put the bawd up to telling such a falsehood, I'll warrant. When I find him he'll tell me the reason why." He flexed the strong fingers of his right hand into a fist. "I hope he'll be reluctant to talk. It would give me great pleasure if there was a need to persuade him."

Father Anselm was still in the throes of fever. His wound had suppurated despite Brother Jehan's application of a marigold poultice and it looked as though the poison would kill him. The injured man had never regained full consciousness since they had brought him to the priory nor, even in his delirium, had he uttered any word that would give a hint as to his attacker. All he had said, over and over again, was one word—"Unclean." The brothers who were looking after him were not sure what he meant. It could have referred to his wound, or perhaps the hair shirt he had been wearing. There was even a possibility that he felt, deep in his delirium, the imminence of his death and was concerned that he was not able to be shriven and his soul cleansed of sin. He was never left alone, and prayers importuning for his recovery were said at every Mass. As the heat of the day grew Brother Jehan ordered his patient bathed with water cooled in the deep recesses of the priory's buttery. "It is all we can do for him now," Jehan said to the novice who was his assistant. "His fate is in the hands of God."

Sixteen

✦━✦

Bascot's thoughts were scattered and unsettled
after he left the solar. And he was angry. Questioning Sybil
de Kyme and Conal had been humiliating for them, embar-
rassing for him. He knew he was ill-suited to the role of in-
quisitor. All those years of being subjected to the will of his
Saracen captors had made him very reluctant to expose any
other person to an invasion of their privacy, even if such
an intrusion was sanctioned by the sheriff and his wife. But
such interrogations were justified, a necessary task that
must be performed in order to try and find the murderer of
those innocents in the alehouse, especially the unborn babe.
It seemed to him that their souls were crying out for ven-
geance. His discomfiture—and that of Sybil and Conal—
was of little measure when set beside the heinous act that
had been perpetrated.

He motioned for Gianni to accompany him and walked

across the bailey in the direction of the stables. Earlier, it had been his intention to ride out to Philip de Kyme's manor and talk to both the baron and his *secretarius*, William Scothern, and perhaps have a look at the letters from the dead boy's mother. Now, instead, he felt a need to be away from the whole question of who had murdered the victims in the alehouse, and for a brief space put aside the task which Nicolaa de la Haye had given him so that he might perhaps be able to bring a semblance of order to the disquiet of his mind.

Crossing the crowded bailey he stopped briefly at the barracks to enquire if Ernulf had been successful in his trip to Butwerk to bring in the stewe-holder, Brunner. Relieved at being told that the serjeant had not yet returned, he walked through the huge gate that was the eastern entry into the castle grounds and crossed the wooden bridge leading down to street level.

Lincoln had resumed the frenzied activity that had begun during the opening parade as the business of the fair entered its second day. Across from the castle the crowds were thick in the precincts of the cathedral and as Bascot passed through Bailgate and started to walk down Steep Hill, he was hard-pressed to push through the crowds of people gathered about stalls and the open fronts of shops. There were entertainers everywhere; strolling players, performing dogs, jugglers, even a shambling old bear being baited by two or three mangy dogs in front of St. Michael's church. The bear, its muzzle haltered by a leather snaffle, was lackadaisical in its response to the wary bravado of its attackers, ignoring the snapping and snarling of its tormentors and raising a paw only when one of the dogs would overcome fear and make a dash towards him. The crowd was heckling the bearward, offering to find him a pig or a goat as replacement for his bear, yelling that even a goose would be superior as an adversary for the dogs. Bascot edged past the throng while Gianni, as usual, kept pace at his right hand. The boy knew his master's blindness on that side could make him unaware of an imminent collision with a passerby or the encroachment of a nimble-handed thief. He had also noticed Bascot's dark mood and wanted to prevent any such upset from deepening it.

As they pushed their way down the sharp incline Bascot cursed his ankle, which had begun to ache. The air was filled with the cries of vendors, the raucous hum of voices raised to be heard above the din and the acrid aroma of human sweat, animal dung and fish guts. This last was from High Market on Spring Hill, a winding street that led off Steep Hill where the fishmongers of Lincoln kept their stalls. In an attempt to escape the press of people Bascot veered off the main thoroughfare, going past the Drapery where the cloth merchants and their customers milled like bees around a hive, and across the top of Parchmingate into the comparative quiet of Hungate. This street led to an intersection with Brancegate, a larger street that crossed the main road of Mikelgate. Since Hungate was nearer the city wall and the residents were mainly merchants selling less expensive items such as household implements, blankets and napery, it was not as congested as the streets they had left behind. Most of the items here would not attract those with a lot of silver to spend and so there were fewer street hawkers and the shop owners had, in the main part, put up the shutters over the casements of the bottom floor of their houses and were displaying their wares by spreading them over a counter just inside the opening. To guard against thieving, the merchant would usually stand outside on the street while a member of his family watched from within.

Many of the shops had a variety of goods for sale since most of the houses were of three stories and occupied on each level by a different family, or two or three, engaged in varying occupations. Such houses had combined their wares, laying them out carefully side by side, and took turns at guarding and selling. The customers meandering down this street were of a less pretentious sort, clothed in sober garments of russet brown or dark green, the women with plain white coifs covering their hair and the men with simple leather caps on their heads. They inspected the goods carefully, the women judiciously fingering small cloths for wrapping cheese or making swaddling bands while their husbands carefully examined the iron that had been used in making nails or carpentry tools for flaws.

To ease the ache in his ankle, Bascot stopped underneath the cloth awning of a leather worker. There were several pairs of soft shoes laid out on the counter along with a few purses and belts. Nearby, a young man clad in a leather apron was punching holes in pieces of leather with an awl. When Bascot approached, he shoved his work into a large pocket in the front of his apron and gave his prospective customer a smile. His long yellow teeth and narrow face gave him a horselike appearance and his voice, when he spoke, was also similar to the high-pitched neighing of a steed, rising and falling in quavering tones. Bascot would not have been surprised if he had whinnied in accompaniment.

"Some fine pieces I've got here, sir," he said deferentially, glancing obliquely at Bascot's Templar badge. "And belts and wrist-guards made to your order, if you wish."

Bascot gave him a nod in response, then picked up a pair of shoes and idly examined them. Behind the counter stood a woman, older, with teeth curved in the same equine smile as the young man's. She bobbed her head at Bascot in courtesy, then spoke in a voice that was surprisingly sweet in contrast to the lad's. "We make good boots, too, sir. My husband could make you a pair that would serve you far better than those you're wearing. Could even pad the left one to ease your pain."

Surprised at the quickness of her observation, for he must only have been in her view for a few limping paces, Bascot laughed amiably and asked her the cost.

"One mark," she replied promptly, "with an extra ten pence for the padding."

Bascot grimaced at the price. Since he had agreed to carry out some duties for Lady Nicolaa she had insisted on paying him the rate her household knights received, ten pence a day, but except for a few pieces of silver he kept about him for immediate expenses he had not touched the money, leaving it with the Haye steward against the time he might return to the Templar Order and, in accordance with his vow of poverty, pay it into their coffers. The amount the shoemaker's wife had mentioned represented more than a month of his earnings. Could he truly justify spending such a sum for his own comfort?

The shoemaker's wife saw his hesitation and added quickly, "They would be well worth the cost. My husband is an expert at his trade."

She turned and gestured behind her to the back of the long low-ceilinged room that comprised the first floor of the house, to where an elderly man sat at his workbench. He had a small hammer in his hand which he was using to soften a piece of leather stretched over a last held between his knees. "If you will come through, sir," the woman said, "my husband will show you a sample of his work."

Attracted by her promise and feeling the need to rest his leg for a moment, Bascot accepted the invitation. Gianni trailed behind him to where the cobbler sat. The shoemaker immediately got up and put his work aside as soon as he saw them come in, pushing forward a chair for Bascot. The cobbler was a small man with clear blue eyes and legs permanently crooked to the shape of his stool. His pate was bald, covered with skin the colour of nutmeg, but he had arms that were strong and wiry beneath the short sleeves of his tunic, with corded muscles roping his forearms.

Once Bascot was seated, the cobbler knelt in front of him and, with surprising gentleness, removed the Templar's left boot and placed the bared foot on his own curved thigh. As Gianni looked on curiously, he ran his fingers over Bascot's injured ankle, and nodded his head in a knowing manner.

"That was a nasty injury, sir."

"It is mended as well as ever it will be, I think," Bascot replied. "Sometimes I bind it with strips of linen, but that does not seem to be much help."

"No, linen will not do any good," the cobbler said. "It firms but does not strengthen. It is here and here you need support." He placed his fingers one on each side of Bascot's ankle and pushed lightly with a soft pressure. Bascot could feel the benefit almost immediately.

"Can you make me a boot that will do what your fingers have just done?" he asked.

"I can, sir. Small pads, one on each side, made from the soft underbelly of a calf. You will not even know they are there, except that your pain will be lessened."

"For that, shoemaker, I would be most grateful." The lure of relief from the almost constant ache was too great a temptation to resist. He decided to purchase the boots. "How long would it take you to make them?"

The cobbler glanced at his Templar badge. "For you, sir, I will do them straight away. They will be ready in two days' time."

Bascot nodded his acceptance and, while the cobbler took the measurements of his feet with the aid of a long piece of leather marked with notches at regular intervals, looked to where Gianni had been distracted by a pair of shoes that were lying on the cobbler's workbench. They were about the boy's size and had been decorated with a row of red beads sewn along the seam at the front of the shoe. Gianni was turning one of the shoes around and around between his fingers, touching the beads gently in admiration. Bascot smiled in amusement at the boy's interest. The shoes Gianni was wearing were the only ones he had and, albeit still sturdy, had soles that were wearing thin.

"How much for the shoes the boy has there?" he asked the cobbler. If he was going to indulge himself, it might ease his conscience if he gave his servant a similar pleasure. Gianni's head snapped up as Bascot spoke.

The shoemaker glanced over his shoulder and then called to his wife. "I only do the work," he said apologetically, "my wife sets the prices."

"You are a wise man, shoemaker," Bascot said with a grin as the cobbler's wife came bustling from her place at the front counter after giving the young man, who was obviously their son, instructions to keep his eyes sharp in looking after her wares.

Gianni listened anxiously as the cobbler's wife examined the shoes in question. "They were made for another customer," she explained to Bascot, "but have not been called for. If these fit your servant, I will let you have them for five silver pennies. If my husband has to make new ones, then it will be another half-penny on top."

"Agreed," Bascot said, and watched with stifled laughter as Gianni grabbed the shoes and, kicking off his old scuffed ones, pushed his feet into the pair decorated with the red beads. Delighted, he danced around the room, his mouth stretched wide into a grin and his fingers snapping loudly while the black curls on his head bobbed from side to side with his movements. Both the cobbler and his wife watched in amazement, and the wife asked, "He does not speak, sir. Is it that he cannot?"

"He is a mute," Bascot confirmed.

The wife clucked her tongue in sympathy and the cobbler gave a sad shake of his bald head. "He is a handsome lad, sir," he said. "And fortunate to have such a kind master as yourself. I am glad the shoes fit him."

"So am I," Bascot replied as he dug in his purse for the money with which to pay the cobbler for Gianni's shoes and a small deposit to show good faith for the commission of his boots.

As he and Gianni left the shop Bascot felt a release of the tension that had gripped him earlier. But he was not yet ready to visit Philip de Kyme and decided instead, since it was nearing the time for the midday meal, to walk down to Brancegate where Lincoln's butchers sold their wares. There would be pies and pasties for sale and hopefully a baker's stall with some good white manchet bread to go with them.

Gianni capered along all the way, kicking out his feet to admire his new shoes, even turning a somersault at one point, which made a couple of young maidens passing by giggle into cupped hands as his tunic flew up and exposed the baggy linen drawers he wore underneath. As they approached the market, however, the boy's interest turned to food. The butchers had erected more tables than usual to accommodate the influx of additional trade, and their apprentices were darting everywhere, engaged in filling orders for delivery, waving leafy branches to keep flies from their master's work, or strutting with importance as they proffered live caged birds for the scrutiny of a prospective buyer. The noise here was as deafening as it had been earlier on the upper stretch of Steep Hill, this time with the squawking of ducks and geese, the squealing of piglets and the bleating of a dozen lambs shut up in a pen. Stray dogs yelped and snarled at one another as they vied for any gobbet of meat that was accidentally dropped and half-wild cats prowled around the edge, keeping a wary eye on the dogs and the apprentices as they, too, searched for food. Over it all hung the smell of blood, pungent in the summer heat, emanating not only from the butcher's stalls but also from the malodorous mixture of discarded feathers and offal that was clogging the refuse channel running down the middle of the street. Stepping carefully over the rank mess Bascot headed for a stall that was crowded with people buying pastry coffins filled with meat and gravy. He also bought, from a young serving maid with bright eyes and heat-flushed cheeks, some pease pudding that had been rolled into balls and skewered on splinters of wood. A loaf of fine manchet bread purchased from the wicker basket of a roving baker's apprentice completed the makings for their meal and it remained only to find a quiet spot in which to eat it.

It was just as they had found an empty space by the wall of St. Martin's church that Bascot heard his name called.

"*Hola*, de Marins," the voice roared over the din of the crowd. Bascot turned to see the captain of Gerard Camville's guard, Roget, coming towards him, the crowd parting like melting cheese before his tall, thickset figure and badge of office. Roget had a girl hanging on his arm whom Bascot recognised as one of the serving wenches from the castle. She was young, no more than fifteen, and pretty in a full-blown way that would, with maturity, turn to obesity. She was gazing up at Roget with admiring eyes, simpering when he looked at her, and swinging her body in a way that showed she relished the company of such a prize.

"I have been looking for you, de Marins," Roget said. "Ernulf asked me to give you a message. The stewe-holder Brunner has flown from his perch and taken the harlot, Gillie, with him. Ernulf has taken some of my men to aid him in a search for the pair." He threw back his head and grinned, amusement sparking in his eyes. "I think it will give Ernulf great pleasure to take hold of Brunner. Although I do not believe that the stewe-holder will get any enjoyment from the meeting."

"I think you are right," Bascot replied. "Ernulf has an intense dislike of the man."

Roget dropped down onto the ground beside Bascot, leaning his back against one of the barrels of water that had been placed along the base of the church wall as they were in other convenient places about the town, for use in case of fire. After taking a long pull from the wine skin he was carrying, he passed it to the Templar who took a drink and passed it back. The serving wench, impatient at Roget's ignoring her for the moment, pulled at his arm.

"Here, *ma belle*," he said, giving her the wine skin. "Drink deep, my pretty one. You will need to keep your spirits up for later." He put his arm around her shoulders and gave her a great squeeze, then pushed her to her feet, patting her on the rump as he did so. Pressing some coins into her hand, he said, "Now, go and amuse yourself for a space. Wait for me at the alehouse on the corner. And see that you do not find any gawky lads to keep you company. I do not take kindly to having another enjoy a morsel I want for myself."

The girl gave him an uncertain look, then glanced at Bascot and Gianni and decided to do as she was told. She walked away with hips swaying under the folds of her kirtle.

"A toothsome piece," Roget said, "but her company is tedious. Still," he shrugged saying, "there are few women whose conversation interests me. It is only their bodies I find enjoyable."

Bascot made no reply. Besides the vow of poverty he had taken when he had joined the Templars he had also taken one of obedience and another of chastity. The purchase of the boots had been the cause of breaking the first and his vow of obedience had been broken when he had voiced his doubts about his fitness for the Templar Order. So far, the vow of chastity remained unsoiled. That he had kept these ten long years, although he had to admit that his capture and subsequent imprisonment had made the vow easier to keep. He still remembered the feel of the lambskin girdle and sheepskin drawers a Templar donned when he took his oath. They were never to be taken off, not even for washing either the garments or the body, so that an initiate would not be tempted by their absence into the sin of lust. At first, Bascot had felt proud to be part of such a strict ethic, but as the weeks and months wore on and he travelled to the Holy Land in the blazing heat, the stench of his own sweat mingled with the rancid smell of sheep oil had finally overcome him and he had been taken with a vomiting fever which had lasted for seven days. He had to admit that the only enjoyable aspect of his imprisonment had been when the Saracens had stripped him of his Christian clothes, including the girdle and drawers. And he had never donned those two particular items of Templar apparel again, not even when he had arrived in England and had been welcomed back by the Order. Now, Roget's remark had reminded him of the stir he had felt in his loins when Scothern's sister, Isobel, had gazed at him with her heavy-lidded amber eyes. Inwardly, he mumbled a prayer for strength.

Roget was measuring him in amusement, the scar on his face creasing as he rolled his eyes upwards in mock resignation. "Ah, de Marins, you Templars are a chaste crew. But me, I am a libertine, and pleased to admit it."

Bascot joined in his good humour and they finished the wine in Roget's skin while he and Gianni ate their meal. Across the street from where they sat, a wooden stand had been set up, the top covered with rough sacking threaded on a string that could be pulled back to reveal a tiny shelf. Inside the stand, a poppet maker had secreted himself and, with the aid of two of his dolls, was manipulating them on the shelf in a parody of real life. One poppet was attired as a middle-aged matron, with a plump stomach and wobbling jowls, the other was her husband, a long stringy doll with a downcast expression and sad eyes painted on his wooden face. The poppet maker provided their voices, high-pitched for the wife, low and plaintive for the husband. The matron was berating her spouse for his shortcomings, citing everything from parsimony and incivility to lasciviousness with a neighbour's daughter. Attached to the woman's hand was a tiny broom made of twigs. At every protestation of innocence from her husband, the wife, propelled by the movement of the poppet maker's fingers inside the sleeves of her gown, beat him severely about the head and shoulders with her broom. The husband cowered and covered his head with his hands—again with the help of the poppet maker's fingers in his sleeves—moaning all the while about his misfortune in choosing a wife, which opinion caused his beating to be mightily increased. The people that had gathered to watch were howling with laughter, as was Roget, doubled over with mirth at Bascot's side.

"*Ma foi*, de Marins, what a spectacle. That is why I have never taken a wife. Marriage brings a man only a lifelong imprisonment that he can never escape, except in death."

Thinking of Sybil de Kyme, Bascot said, "Not only a man, Roget, but a woman also sometimes." As he said the words the glimmer of an intruding thought impinged on his consciousness. The distraction of the poppet maker's show had caused him to remember something he had heard someone say, a remark that had submerged below the surface of his thoughts as being of no importance. He tried to retrieve it and could not. Was it to do with the alehouse, or perhaps the injured priest? Vainly he struggled with the memory but still it escaped him. He sighed. It was no use, he thought; he could not dismiss the matter of the murders from his mind. They kept floating back. He pushed himself to his feet, awkward on his aching ankle, but decisive all the same. He had had a short space of pleasure, now he must resume his task.

"I must leave you, Roget," he said to the mercenary. "I have a matter to attend to."

"Are you going to see if Ernulf has found Brunner?" Roget asked, looking up lazily from his comfortable position leaning against the water barrel, his interest in the poppet play momentarily diverted.

"No. I am going to see Isaac, the Jew."

Seventeen

✛

Bascot sat across from Isaac in the chamber where the usurer carried out his business transactions. It was richly, but not ostentatiously, furnished. In one corner stood an empty brazier and on the floor beside it was a stout wooden chest, intricately carved on the front and side panels and securely banded with strips of iron. In a wall niche was an incense holder. It was lit, and emitted a wispy stream of smoke, filling the room with a pleasant musky smell. The aroma reminded Bascot of the Holy Land, where the spicy gum was used in abundance.

Wine was brought by a servant and, once the man had left the room, the Jew spoke. "You said you wished to have speech with me about my cousin, Samuel, who was found dead with the two Christians. How may I be of assistance?" Isaac's words were formal, but there was no obsequiousness in his tone.

Bascot took a sip of wine before he answered. It was good, dark red and laced with sweet spices. "Are you aware that a charge has been made against Lady Sybil de Kyme and her son, Conal, in connection with the deaths of the two Christians found in the alehouse?" he asked. "It is being claimed that the two dead strangers were the illegitimate son of Sir Philip de Kyme and the son's wife."

Isaac nodded. His face was heavily fleshed above a robe that was loose sleeved and made of finely woven cloth, as was the close-fitting cap that held back the curling mass of his hair. On both hands he wore thumb rings of gold. He regarded Bascot with a solemn air, but his dark Semitic eyes were wary.

"It is said that Lady Sybil feared for her own son's disinheritance in favour of Sir Philip's bastard," Bascot continued, "and, with the connivance of Conal, removed that threat by killing the son and his wife. I have been given the duty of finding out the truth of that charge. If it is proved, or if I cannot disprove it, then Lady Sybil and her son will stand to answer it before the king's justices at the assizes in July."

Bascot paused, picking his words carefully. "Since your cousin, Samuel, was found slain along with the two Christians, it would seem that whoever murdered them also killed him."

Isaac said nothing, merely kept his watchful silence, and Bascot went on. "Wherever all three were killed, it was not the alehouse. They had all been dead some hours, we believe, brought to the alehouse later from some other place, perhaps a house in the town. The two Christians were from Maine, and must have come to Lincoln recently. I am trying to determine where it was that they came to be in company with your cousin. If I can find that out, I may also be able to determine if Conal or Lady Sybil had the opportunity to kill all three of them. Can you tell me Samuel's whereabouts on that day?"

Isaac leaned forward and picked up his wine cup, not drinking but merely holding it between his hands. When he spoke, it was softly. "Will Lady Sybil and her son, or any other Christian you may find guilty, also be charged with the death of my cousin?"

Bascot answered him straightly. "You know the answer to that question as well as I. They will not. The death of a Jew at Christian hands will not be considered of sufficient import. Whoever, if anyone, is found guilty of the Christian deaths will, I presume, also be found guilty of the death of your cousin. In that case a fine may be levied concerning his loss—which will go into the king's coffers—but that is all."

"Then, why, Templar, should I help you?" The question was couched in the same low tones Isaac had used before.

Bascot tried to answer with honesty. "I had hoped you would want to find out the truth of the matter. Who it was that brought about the death of a member of your family."

"It will not bring Samuel back, and any information that I give you may be held against me by the kin of whatever Christian is found guilty. Indeed, if my cousin had not been found along with the Christians, I have no doubt that their murders would have been found to have been carried out by a Jew. We are usually blamed in such matters, whether implicated or not."

Bascot took a breath and leaned back in his chair. He had expected such a response and hoped that he could circumvent it. "It was said in my hearing that such would be the case. It was also said that a hue and cry after the Jews of Lincoln would be bad for trade during the fair. That is the reason I am here. If it is disproved that Lady Sybil and Conal are guilty, do you think it will take long for suspicion to be cast in the direction of you and your brethren? It will be said that your cousin was killed by one of his own race merely to cast the blame elsewhere. Are you willing to take that chance?"

For the first time Isaac smiled. "You speak with a strange directness for a Christian. Especially one"—he gestured with his wine cup in the direction of Bascot's Templar

badge—"who has dedicated his life to the slaying of the enemies of Christ. How do I know that you will not use any information I give you against one of my own kind?"

"You do not," Bascot replied. "But unless a member of
the Jewish community is guilty, I give you my pledge, in
Christ's holy name, that I will keep in the strictest confidence anything you may tell me."

The usurer stared at Bascot for a moment, then took a
sip from his wine cup. Finally, he seemed to reach a decision. "Since that oath is one that I know means much to
you, I must assume your promise is made with integrity.
Very well, Templar, I will help you as much as I can. What
is it you wish to know?"

"As I said, where your cousin was on the day that he was
killed. Would he have had occasion to visit any of the
Christian houses in the town and, if so, which ones?"

Bascot waited for the answer with held breath. If Isaac
named the house of Roger de Kyme it would, with the lack
of either Lady Sybil or Conal being able to provide a witness to their activities on that day, press the finger of guilt
on them as surely as if they had been caught stuffing the
bodies into the barrels. Isaac's reply, however, was not one
that Bascot had expected.

"My cousin was not in Lincoln on that day. He left early,
to visit a client who has his manor to the northwest of Lincoln, off the Torksey road. The last time he was seen was
when he left to fulfill that task."

Bascot took in the information with surprise. How had
Samuel, if he had left Lincoln alive, come to be back there
after he was dead?

"You are sure he did not return? Perhaps later in the
day?" he asked Isaac.

"I am sure," Isaac replied. "Samuel was seen leaving by
the warden on the western gate and was never seen to come
back. We have asked both shifts of the guards, who all knew

my cousin well, and have also enquired at the other access points into the town. He did not return. Alive, that is."

"What was the name of your client? Have you spoken to him? Did Samuel complete his errand?"

Isaac sighed, the curls in his beard bobbing slightly with the movement. "I cannot tell you the name of our client because, as you know, it would be a breach of the confidence placed in us and might lead not only to loss of the customers we have, but could also involve unpleasant recriminations for our lack of discretion. But this much I may tell you. Samuel was on his way to deliver a small quantity of silver to a borrower and to bring back a signed note of the debt. The client has been contacted and insists that Samuel did not arrive as arranged, but . . ." Isaac lifted his shoulders in an eloquent shrug of dismissal.

Bascot finished the sentence for him. ". . . the client would say that was the case even if Samuel did deliver the silver as promised. Without the note of debt you cannot prove that any money was borrowed from you."

Isaac nodded. "Exactly."

"The Torksey road—that leads in the direction of Philip de Kyme's demesne, does it not?"

"It does," Isaac confirmed, "and also passes by many other, smaller fiefs. I will tell you that it was not to Sir Philip's manor that my cousin was bound."

"Was he carrying a large sum?" Bascot asked.

"No. Samuel was allowed to deal only in some of the smaller transactions of my business. My cousin was . . . a simple man, Sir Bascot. He did not have great intelligence, but he was willing and honest. I cannot think why anyone would want to kill him."

"But someone did," Bascot replied, "and there must be a reason why." He pondered for a moment. "If the two young people were making their way to de Kyme's manor, it may be that they travelled on the same route, and at the same

time, as your cousin. The Torksey road is not the only way
to de Kyme's demesne, but it would be the most direct for
travellers coming from the south. I suppose the boy and his
wife could have been abducted as they neared their destination but there are no marks on either of their bodies that
would indicate a struggle and, if they were taken against
their will, it is most certain that they would have made
some resistance. And how did your cousin come to be with
them when they met their deaths? It is most unlikely that he
knew them."

"I would not have thought so," Isaac agreed. "Neither I
nor any member of my family has any connection with
Maine and, to the best of my knowledge, Samuel had never
been farther from Lincoln than a solitary trip to London
many years ago. But it is unlikely that they met with abduc-
tion on the Torksey road. It is well travelled and patrolled
by the sheriff's guard. Samuel would never have been sent
on his errand alone if there had been any danger to his
safety."

"It is thought that poison was the means of death for
both the Christian couple and your cousin."

"So I have been told," Isaac informed him. "Our own
physician has examined Samuel's body and he agrees with
that opinion and also that the stab wounds were made after
death."

The usurer gave Bascot an oblique look. "I have also
been informed that the bodies were secreted in ale barrels
before being placed on the taproom floor. I presume that
the alehouse keeper must have been in collusion with the
murderer?"

"It would seem so," Bascot answered. "It is possible that
the bodies were kept, for a few hours at least, at the house
of Roger de Kyme in Lincoln. Both Lady Sybil and Conal
were staying there for a time and neither can prove their
actions on that day. Lady Sybil says that she was in bed
suffering from sickness and Conal claims he was in New-

ark. Both were alone and have no one to vouch for their honesty."

Both men fell silent for a moment, each collecting his thoughts. Then Isaac said, "If Samuel was persuaded by another party to accompany the couple from Maine, it would have to have been by someone he knew. A Jew does not lightly fall into the company of Christians, especially strangers."

"Did he know either Lady de Kyme or her son?" Bascot asked.

"Yes," Isaac replied solemnly. "Since you have assured me you will hold any knowledge I may have in confidence and since the debt is in the past, I can tell you that Sybil de Kyme had occasion to borrow money from me once, using some of her personal jewellery as surety. She paid the debt promptly. It was her son who handled the transaction. The sum was not large and it was Samuel who was entrusted with the commission of picking up the payment of the loan."

And Newark, where Conal had professed to spend the day, was to the southwest of Lincoln. A destination that was reached by leaving through the same gate as dead Samuel. Had Conal turned north onto the Torksey road instead of turning south to Newark, as he had said? Had he known Hugo and his wife were near to arriving at their destination and had set out to forestall them, perhaps under the guise of welcoming them in his stepfather's stead, then luring them into the forest where he offered his wine flask with a vintage that was deadly? Had the Jew seen and recognised him when he was in their company so that it was necessary to include him among the victims? But even if this were so, the one main question still remained—why had Conal not simply left the bodies in the greenwood? It was the question Richard Camville had asked, and also Conal himself, and it was a valid one. There could be no advantage to having the bodies discovered in Lincoln and run the risk, as had happened, of their being identified. In the summer heat, and with the help of foraging wild animals, the bodies would most probably have either decomposed or been devoured. Surely a conclusion a murderer would see as preferable, enabling the crime to remain hidden and not brought out into the light of investigation.

"My information has confused rather than enlightened you, has it not, Templar?" Isaac asked softly.

"Yes. It helps to bolster the sheriff's charge against Lady Sybil and Conal, but it still does not convince me of their guilt and I do not doubt it will fail to convince the justices either. There are still too many questions without an answer."

Isaac leaned back in his chair, taking a sip of his wine. He gave Bascot a wry glance. "The answers must surely be there. It remains only to find them."

Eighteen

BASCOT SET OUT EARLY THE NEXT MORNING ALONG the Torksey road, to carry out his intention to visit Philip de Kyme at his fortified manor house near Stow. Accompanying the Templar were Ernulf and two men-at-arms from the castle garrison. All were armed and Bascot wore a hip-length coat of mail over a lightly padded gambeson. The frustration the Templar had felt the morning before had returned during a long night in which he had slept badly. He recognised the cause as being rooted in the disillusionments he had experienced from a very young age but, even so, could not eradicate it.

His thoughts roved back to his childhood. The youngest of three sons, his father had decided to give him as an oblate—an offering—to the church, where he would be trained for life as a monk. At first he had been frightened, had felt all the aloneness of a seven-year-old boy amongst strangers. But the kindness of the monks and serenity of the abbey soon caused this strangeness to pass and he had come to enjoy the regularity of his day and the security of the stout walls that surrounded the enclave. He had excelled at his lessons and been praised for his industry. He had been happy. Then, a few short years later, the brother next to him in age had died in a hunting accident and his father had come to remove him from his new life, citing the need for the security of a younger son against the chance that some mishap should befall his eldest. That was when Bascot's deep-seated anger had begun. He had resented his father's decision but, cautioned by the monk who had been his tutor that duty to a parent was an obligation he must not deny, he had done as he was bidden and taken up training for arms. Translating his anger into energy he quickly learned how to wield a sword and mace and was barely eighteen when he won the spurs of knighthood at his father's side in battle.

That had been in the last days of the reign of King Henry, during one of the many skirmishes that the king had engaged in with his recalcitrant son, Richard. But throughout all the glory of battle and the attendant dangers of injury or death, Bascot had still yearned for his boyhood days in the cloister. When Henry had died and Richard had succeeded to the throne, the new king's obsession to mount a Crusade to the Holy Land had seemed to Bascot to provide a way to satisfy both his own desires and those of his father. With his eldest brother now married and a new heir on the way, Bascot had begged to be allowed to combine his yearning for the life of a monk with his military skills and join the Knights Templar.

For Bascot, his first months as a warrior monk had lived up to his expectations. He had been attached to a Templar contingent that had accompanied King Richard to the Holy Land, and the battles along the way, at Sicily and Cyprus, had satisfied his conviction of the rightness of his decision. He had still felt this way when the army had reached their destination and had begun the tremendous task of trying to retrieve Jerusalem from the infidels. This ebullience had carried him along until the siege of Acre. There, on a hot August day, on the plains outside the conquered city, he had watched in horrified amazement as King Richard had ordered the slaughter of nearly three thousand prisoners taken as hostage. Bascot had felt his stomach churn with a sickness that had never before assailed him, not even on the day he had first plied his sword and drawn the life's blood of an armed enemy. Amongst the prisoners were many women and children and they were slain as mercilessly as their men folk. He had finally fled the bloody scene when the lifeless bodies were being methodically gutted in a search for gold that the victims may have swallowed in an attempt to hide it. Others in the Templar contingent had been as shocked as he but, although the Templars were not under the king's command and were answerable only to the head of their own order, their master, Robert de Sable, was a friend of King Richard's and they had continued, despite the stigma of the massacre, to accompany the king on his mission. It was about that time that Bascot had begun to question the depth of his devotion to the Order, and his subsequent capture and imprisonment had done nothing to help him find any answers.

Now he was confronted by a different kind of riddle and, in order to solve it, needed to fathom the machinations of a mind that would secretly plot the killing of four people. A spark of his old anger at being manipulated by the intrigues of others rose within him and he encouraged it, making a firm resolution that he would not let any obstacle deter him from being the victor in this battle to apprehend the assassin. And he would fortify himself for the fray ahead with the best weapons he had, the mail and sword of a knight of Christ.

Attempting to dismiss the gloomy and introspective thoughts from his mind, Bascot distracted himself by noting the terrain that bordered the road upon which they were travelling. After crossing the Fossdyke they followed the

course of the Trent river, on the western side of which a
fringe of forest began, sweeping away in a sporadic growth
of trees to become the northern tip of Sherwood Forest.
They passed a few hamlets with the open spaces of tilled
fields around them, but there were many places where alder
and oak grew, as well as the drooping branches of willow at
the river's bank, and there was dense undergrowth that
would provide perfect concealment from the road. Had it
been in one of these spots that the murderer had waited,
hidden, until his victims should come into view? It would
be easy to appear behind them, as though travelling the
same route, and engage them in conversation. But where
had they then been taken? As Isaac had said, the road was
well patrolled by the sheriff's guard. Bascot and his escort
had already passed a pair of Roget's men, and he could see
two more ahead, riding slowly north in a circuit that would
no doubt end at Torksey.

The day was hot and Bascot did not press the pace out of
deference to their mounts. About an hour after they had
passed through Torksey they approached Philip de Kyme's
demesne. Outside the palisade that surrounded his manor
house an orderly and prosperous looking village was spread.
The cottages were sturdily built of wattle and daub and a
meeting hall of reasonable size stood in the center, two stories high and constructed of timber. There was a quantity of
pigs, geese and some penned sheep which all looked fat and
healthy, as did the inhabitants, who doffed their caps respectfully as the group of horsemen cantered past.

Bascot rode down the track of packed earth that led
through the village and up to the gates of the manor, Ernulf
at his right hand and the two men-at-arms behind. The
gateward let them through, once they had identified themselves and stated their business, giving one blast on a signal horn to announce their arrival. Inside the bailey de
Kyme's steward met them and called a groom to see to the
stabling of their horses. The manor house itself was im-

pressive, with corner turrets built of stone, a central hall of timber and a massive oak door reinforced with iron plates. The steward led the way into the hall which, since it was not yet mealtime, was bare of tables except for a large one that sat on the dais and was a permanent fixture. Directing the serjeant and two men-at-arms to a corner where there was a keg of ale, the steward led Bascot to the other end of the hall. There a group of men were seated around an unlit fireplace, drinking wine. A chessboard lay nearby, its pieces set ready for a game.

At the center of the group sat de Kyme, richly dressed and, to judge by his high colour, already blown with wine. His greying locks hung lankly and his mouth was slack. Next to him sat a man Bascot did not recognise. He had a wide fleshy face and hatchet-shaped nose below a thatch of black hair cropped in a haphazard fashion. Next to him was a lad of perhaps fourteen years, enough alike in appearance, especially about the nose, to be his son. On de Kyme's left sat another stranger, this one above middle height and with red hair and a foxy expression. Sitting beside this stranger Bascot was surprised to see Hugh Bardolf and, next to him, William de Rollos, husband to Nicolaa de la Haye's sister, Ermingard. Bardolf's loose-limbed body was sprawled neatly in his seat, and with more than a glimmer of interest in his eyes he watched Bascot approach, while de Rollos gave the Templar only a curt nod of greeting and flicked his eyes away, as though embarrassed at being found in de Kyme's hall.

"You are well come, Templar," de Kyme said, his speech slurring slightly. Calling to a servant to bring more wine and another cup for his guest, he then introduced Bascot to his companions. The burly man on his left was, he said, his nephew Roger de Kyme and the boy his son Arthur, while the red-haired individual was a cousin, Alan de Kyme. "Bardolf and de Rollos you will already know," he added, lifting his cup in a salutary gesture in their direction.

He looked up at Bascot. "I hope you have come to tell me that proof has been found of my wife's guilt. Even now, the son of mine that she killed lies in my chapel awaiting burial. That bitch, to take from me the one thing above all that I desire. It shouldn't be too hard to find a witness to Sybil's perfidy, or that of her hellhound son. They are a devilish pair, as anyone here will tell you."

Roger de Kyme and his son both nodded in agreement, as did Alan de Kyme. Hugh Bardolf held himself aloof from committal to the baron's opinion, keeping his expression pleasant but devoid of emotion while de Rollos stared into his wine cup.

"I have found no proof of their complicity as yet," Bascot replied carefully. "It seems likely, however, that Hugo was on the Torksey road when he and his wife were detracted from their journey, possibly near your manor."

De Kyme banged his cup down on the carved wooden arm of his chair, spilling wine as he did so. "I knew it, by God. The boy was nearly here when that she-devil got hold of him. Ah, did ever a man have such misfortune as I? Once here he would have been safe, I would have seen to that. That bitch . . ."

Here de Kyme trailed off as self-pity and wine fumes robbed him of speech. His nephew, Roger, spoke to him consolingly. "Do not distress yourself, Uncle. Soon you will be free of her, and Conal. Time enough then to think of the future."

"Roger is right, Philip," Hugh Bardolf drawled. "You have heirs aplenty—two right here in the persons of Roger and Alan. Both of them have sons, although Alan's boy is young still. And you are not old, man. You may yet have one of your own. If you marry again."

As Bardolf spoke Roger swung an angry face in his direction. Bascot remembered that Bardolf was seeking a suitable husband for his daughter, Matilda.

"Whether Sybil and her brat are found guilty or not, it

will still be a lengthy business for my uncle to rid himself of his wife," Roger spat. "He must needs think of his estates. They would be held in wardship by the king if aught should happen to him and there is no heir declared."

"A deplorable state." Hugh Bardolf chuckled as he spoke. "But your uncle is in good health yet. He has time aplenty to spawn sons, especially if the new wife is young, and comes from a family known for its fecundity." Since the size of Bardolf's brood of children was well known, this was a pointed remark and not taken well by de Kyme's nephew.

De Rollos looked increasingly uncomfortable as Roger turned his angry face away from Bardolf and took another pull at his wine cup. De Kyme's cousin, Alan, kept his silence, his pale brown eyes sly and cunning as they darted back and forth from his host to the rest of the company. Roger's son Arthur looked defiantly ahead of him, hatchet nose high in the air in imitation of his father.

Philip de Kyme looked blearily up at Bascot. "If you haven't come to tell me you have proof of my wife's guilt, Templar, then why are you here?"

Tired of the baron's maudlin attitude and still feeling remnants of his earlier irritation, Bascot answered him with little patience. "I have come to see the letters written by Hugo's mother. It is possible they will give some hint of how Lady Sybil or Conal could have found out about your illegitimate son's existence."

De Kyme nodded drunkenly. "Yes. A common acquaintance here in Lincoln, perhaps. Some merchant the boy was to travel with that had a loose tongue. I will send for Scothern. He has the letters in his safekeeping."

As a servant was sent scurrying for the *secretarius*, Bardolf gave Bascot a lazy smile. "You are assiduous in your task, Templar. I wish you joy of it."

"There is no joy in murder, Bardolf," Bascot said shortly, "and still less for those who profit from the deed."

The pretence of amiability dropped from Bardolf's

expression as he pushed himself up straighter in the chair, seeking whether the Templar's answer was directed at himself or not. De Rollos put a hand on his companion's arm as Bascot's own hand dropped casually to the sword at his belt. Just then William Scothern appeared and Bardolf, thinking better of testing the strength of the insult that might have been contained in Bascot's remark, relaxed as the *secretarius* came to stand behind his master's chair.

"Sir Bascot has come to see the correspondence you exchanged with Hugo's mother, William," de Kyme said, his mazed senses momentarily sobered by the imminent clash between one of his guests and the Templar. "Take him to my chamber and show her letters to him."

Bascot was not loath to leave the group behind him. They reminded him of the vultures that had gathered over the corpses on the plains outside Acre. With the exception, perhaps, of William de Rollos who, as far as Bascot could determine, would have little to gain from the death of de Kyme's bastard son or the imminent disposal of his wife and stepson. His presence here was puzzling.

Scothern led Bascot to an upper chamber in one of the manor house's corner turrets. The room was well appointed, with a large bed and bolster covered in good linen and sweet-scented rushes strewn on the floor. The *secretarius* went to a locked coffer standing on the floor against the far wall. Opening it with a key taken from the scrip at his belt, Scothern removed a small number of parchment rolls and placed them on a nearby table. Beside them he laid several sheaves of parchment covered in writing and tapped them with a forefinger.

"These are the copies of the letters that Sir Philip sent to Hugo's mother, Eleanor. The others are her replies. You will find they are in the order of their dating."

Bascot motioned to the coffer. "These have been kept locked away all the time Sir Philip was in correspondence with the boy's mother?"

"They have," he affirmed. "Only Sir Philip and myself had access to them." Scothern's genial freckled face was drawn in lines of tautness and there was a fine sheen of perspiration on his upper lip.

"Is Sir Philip literate?" Bascot asked.

Scothern shook his head. "He can sign his name, and scan the tallies of some of his holdings, but not much more."

"Then you will have written all of his letters and read the replies for his benefit?" The *secretarius* nodded. "How did your master locate the boy's mother? It would seem she had been gone many years from Lincoln."

"Her father was a perfume maker, and Sir Philip knew that he had relations in Maine and also believed that was where she was sent when . . . her condition . . . became obvious. I made enquiries among the merchants of Lincoln and, from the information I garnered, we discovered that it was most likely she was in the town of La Lune. Sir Philip directed that a letter be sent there—to the provost of the town—asking that he make an attempt to locate the lady he was looking for. Not much later we had a reply from a priest—the lady apparently lived in his parish—and Sir Philip sent a letter, written at his direction by myself, for the priest to forward to her."

"I see." Bascot picked up one of the scrolls. It was neatly dated on the outside with the inscription of a day in early April. "This is the first one received from her?"

Scothern nodded and Bascot unrolled the letter and scanned the contents. The scribing was neat, probably written by a clerk or priest. It was in formal language, thanking her former lover for his interest in their son and telling how she had, with the help of relatives, been able to follow her father's trade of perfume maker. She went on to say that she had never married, that her whole existence had revolved around Hugo and that she had never let him forget that his father was of the English nobility. He was a fine boy, she had appended, whom she had managed to have educated and who had repaid her efforts by being hardworking and honest. The letter closed by saying that she hoped one day Philip would want to meet his son and that they looked forward to further communications from him.

In all, it was a letter written with almost fawning politeness and hinted at the underlying hope of some gain from the resumption of de Kyme's interest. Philip's reply was enthusiastic, expressing a desire to see his son and offering to pay the expenses of the boy's trip to England. Eleanor's reply to this letter was effusive, as was the next, and last, one. She told him the boy would journey as soon as he could to Lincoln and would bring his pregnant wife with him. She thanked him for his generosity and said that, once Hugo was safely on his way, she would be going on a pilgrimage to the shrine of St. James in Compostella to thank God for her boy's good fortune in being reunited with his father.

"That Hugo's mother was going on a journey was not mentioned when Sir Philip learned that it was his son who had been murdered," Bascot said to Scothern.

"I believe he had forgotten," the *secretarius* replied. "He was so distraught, I think he gave little thought to how much Hugo's mother would be grieved."

"Has any attempt been made to inform her?" Bascot asked, noting again the clerk's seeming nervousness as he replied.

"Sir Philip bade me write a letter to the priest at La Lune. When she returns I have no doubt he will tell her the sad news."

Scothern busied himself rerolling Eleanor's letters and started a little when Bascot told him that he would take them back with him to Lincoln for it was probable they would be needed when the charge was brought against Lady Sybil and Conal at the assizes. The clerk's edginess irritated Bascot and finally he said, "What is it, Scothern?

You quiver like a deer that has scented the hounds. Is there something you are not telling me?"

The clerk shook his head vigorously. "No. No, Sir Bascot. It is only . . ."

"Out with it," Bascot prompted.

"It is only that I wonder if I did the right thing in telling you my suspicions about the identity of the two murdered young people. Perhaps it would have been better had they been left unknown. When the boy did not turn up Sir Philip would perhaps have thought he had not come after all, or that he had perished somewhere on the journey long before he reached Lincoln."

"Why do you say that?" Bascot asked.

Scothern shook his head again, and his reply, when it came, was hesitant. "I never thought that Sir Philip would think Lady Sybil and Conal had anything to do with the boy's death. And now, Roger and Alan de Kyme, they . . ."

As his voice trailed off, Bascot felt empathy for the clerk. "All and sundry gather like beggars at a funeral feast, do they not? You fear that whichever way this turns out, those who are not satisfied with the result will turn on you as being the instigator of their misfortune?"

"In the days before heralds were honoured for their craft, it was not unusual for a lord to have the bearer of bad tidings put to death," Scothern replied, his full mouth drawn into a tight line.

Before Bascot could make any response there was a light footfall at the door. The Templar swung on his heel, cursing the stab of pain in his ankle as he did so, turning the sighted side of his face towards the person that had entered. It was Isobel Scothern. She had a trail of gowns over one arm and a clutch of ribbons in the other. She gave Bascot a cool look.

"My sister is here to gather some clothing for Lady Sybil," Scothern explained. "Her mistress did not take many garments with her on the journey to Lincoln."

"Neither did I, brother. We did not expect to make such a long stay."

With barely concealed contempt she gave Bascot an aloof nod of acknowledgement, then spoke again to Scothern. "I have nearly completed my task, but Lady Sybil instructed me to also bring some jewellery that she left here. It would seem to have been taken from the casket where it is usually kept. Do you know where it is?"

"I do, Bella. It is locked away and Sir Philip has ordered that it remain so. He said that most of it was his gift to her on their wedding day and, since she has not proved a true wife, he does not feel any obligation to leave it in her possession." Scothern stammered over the words.

"I see. So your most puissant lord intends not only to strip his lady of her good name, but also of the few paltry trinkets he gave her as a bride gift." The scorn in Isobel's voice was like ice. "I will tell Lady Sybil your words, Will. I wish you well of your master."

With her parting remark she left the room, a trace of honeysuckle perfume lingering after her. Scothern turned to the Templar. "That is another problem with my revelation to you, Sir Bascot. My sister and I have become estranged over it."

"Are you surprised at that?" Bascot asked.

"Not really," Scothern replied miserably. "Females are ever capricious."

Nineteen

✦

GIANNI SAT IN HIS PLACE AMONGST THE CASTLE hounds and peered out from behind one of the shaggy heads to stare at the people seated with Lady Nicolaa at the table on the dais. The midday meal had already been served and the castellan was lingering over wine and sweetmeats with the newly come guests. Gianni had never seen any of these people in Lincoln before. They were two men of middle age, both tall and fair-haired, and an elderly woman who was almost as tall as the men but, unlike them, was thin and fond of punctuating her speech by thumping on the floor with the short staff she carried as an aid in walking. The cane was mounted on top with the head of a raven fashioned in silver. Gianni watched as her fingers clenched and unclenched in frustration around the sharp pointed beak as she spoke.

As far as Gianni could tell, Lady Nicolaa was trying to placate the two men, who looked enough alike to be brothers. Gianni knew they were speaking about the murder of the people in the alehouse and, since his master was concerned in the affair, he strained his ears to try and hear what was being said over the scratchings and grunts of the dogs.

Bascot had left early that morning, before these new visitors had come. Gianni did not like it when the Templar was away from him, even for a short space, and he almost always took refuge with the hounds until his master returned or went to sit by himself in their tiny room at the top of the old keep. Even now, after he had been with the Templar for almost a year, he mistrusted any other human companion. He had too many memories from his childhood of the blows and curses that had rained on him when he had begged for scraps of food, and happenings far worse from some of those who had at first seemed inclined to be generous, to ever feel entirely comfortable with any other person.

He had even distrusted the Templar at first, although he had snatched the loaf of bread that Bascot had held out to him before running away to eat it. It was only when the Templar had come again the next day, this time with some cooked meat wrapped in a cloth, that Gianni had begun to feel that the one-eyed limping stranger meant him no harm. Bascot had laid the food down in the middle of the wharf among the pilings where Gianni spent his nights, then had moved a distance away, keeping at bay the other beggars clamouring for his largesse, until Gianni had crept from his hiding place and taken the bundle. With an amused grin, Bascot had watched while Gianni, his eyes flicking warily back and forth from the Templar to the hungry gaze of the other beggars, had wolfed down the contents of the parcel until there was none left. Still the Templar had not made a move that was threatening. He had just nodded his head and turned away. At a safe distance, Gianni had followed his benefactor and seen him turn into an inn near the docks. All night the boy had sat, waiting, until in the morning the Templar had reappeared and handed him a pear and some cheese.

From that day on, Gianni had never left the Templar's

side. He had been fed and clothed, taught to read and write, and had willingly clambered up behind his new master to travel on horseback the many days and nights it had taken to reach this strange land across the Narrow Sea. To Gianni, with only memories of pain and hunger throughout the duration of his young life, the Templar was a combination of the father he could not remember and the God he had never been able to find. Now, when de Marins went away from his company, the Palermo urchin was always uneasy until he returned.

Up on the dais, the old woman was again banging her stick and this time her voice carried clearly to Gianni. She was speaking to one of the two men who had come with her and seemed to be berating him.

"You Danish! Always the same, hold fast with one hand and reach to take more with the other. Sybil and Conal did not commit this crime, I tell you. If it is her dower property you are concerned with, then know that it will never be returned if she is found guilty. How can you think of oak trees when it is the honour of your family you should be defending?" The old lady banged the floor with her stick again. "She would have had short shrift at your board, Magnus. Neither you or Ailwin are known for your generosity."

With this last riposte she threw back her head, causing the white linen of her old-fashioned headdress to flutter around her thin shoulders as she added another insult. "But what else can you expect from Danish stock? The people of Norway know that to their cost."

Ailwin spoke again. "*Tante* Hilde, your family and mine have all lived in England for many generations now. Let us forget these old feuds of our ancestors."

"To forget one's heritage is to take away the meaning of life," the old woman expostulated. "I am the only member left of Conal's father's family, and he is the one that will carry on our name. For him I will fight with all the strength I have left."

On saying this, the old woman pushed herself to her feet, using her cane as a lever. A woman servant of middle age rushed to her side from below the dais, but Hilde brushed her away and stood proudly erect. As she turned to leave, there was the sound of voices at the entrance to the hall and Conal and his mother came in, followed by Bascot and Ernulf.

Conal strode immediately to Hilde's side, taking her in his arms and embracing her. "*Tante*, I am pleased to see you."

"And I you," Hilde said as she reached up a gnarled hand and stroked his cheek. "You grow more like your father every day."

Gently he led her back to her seat, then greeted his uncles. Sybil did the same, then both she and Conal sat down beside Hilde.

Gianni crept forward now, closer to where Bascot and Ernulf stood. Nicolaa de la Haye beckoned to the Templar and introduced him to her guests.

"These are Lady Sybil's brothers, Ailwin and Magnus Redwison. Lady Hilde is great-aunt to Conal. His father was her nephew, her brother's son." She explained Bascot's role in the matter of the crime with which Conal and his mother were charged. "Sir Bascot is gathering evidence to place before the judges at the assizes. It is to be hoped he will find some information that will prove your sister's innocence, my lords," she said to Magnus and Ailwin, "but so far, none has been forthcoming." She looked at Bascot. "Unless, de Marins, there is something new since last we spoke . . ."

"Nothing, lady," Bascot replied, "but neither is there anything to prove their guilt."

"Exactly," burst out Hilde, leaning forward and thumping her cane to emphasize her point. "That is because they have none. Tell me, Templar, have you found any indication of someone else's involvement? Another party who would profit by this boy's death? There are other heirs to de

Kyme's estates, are there not? A nephew and some cousins? Where were they when this deed was done? Does he have a leman who hopes to become his wife if he is free of Sybil?"

Bascot smiled at the old woman. He liked her forthrightness and, since his visit to de Kyme that morning, her thoughts echoed his own. There were others beside Conal for whom the inheritance of the baron could provide a strong enough lure to tempt them to commit murder. But to interrogate persons of the status of de Kyme's nephew and cousin might result in harsh complaints from them at such treatment, and needed to have the direct authority of the sheriff, not just that of Nicolaa de la Haye. In answering Lady Hilde, he chose his words carefully, in order not to offend the woman who had so generously given him a place in her retinue.

"So far, lady, my commission has been only to determine if your great-nephew and his mother could or could not have had the opportunity to commit the murders. But perhaps you are right, it may be worthwhile to look for another likely culprit. But to do so, I will need a warrant whose power will not be questioned. Many who are touched by this affair will not take kindly to my intervention otherwise."

Lady Hilde immediately understood the delicacy of his words and swung her piercing gaze on Nicolaa. "The truth must be found, and it is the duty of the sheriff to ensure that it is. And your's also, Lady Nicolaa, as keeper of the king's castle and his peace. Will you persuade your husband to this course?"

Nicolaa considered the suggestion, not taking offence at the imperiousness in the older woman's tone and the unnecessary reminder of the obligations of her office. Finally she nodded in agreement. "There is sense in what you say, de Marins. And, since Conal is of knight's rank, there should be no complaint if those of equal status are questioned. I have no doubt Gerard will agree. He is as anxious as I to have this matter resolved. I pledge the warrant in his stead, and those here are witness to my words. May God give you His divine assistance."

So saying, she rose from her seat, tired of the subject and the wrangling that had accompanied it, but conscious also of the courtesy due her guests. "I have no doubt we can all do with a brief rest before the evening meal. There are chambers above that you may consider your own while you are in Lincoln and my servants are at your bidding."

Ailwin and Magnus sighed with relief at the dismissal, and Conal assisted his great-aunt to her feet and helped her down the two shallow stairs to the floor of the hall. As they passed Bascot, the old lady paused. "You are a man of honour, Templar, I think. It would please me if, when you have finished your duties for the day, you would attend me. It might prove profitable for us to have speech together on this matter."

Bascot had been amused by the manner in which Hilde had spoken to the others for, although haughty, she had comported herself with courage and a keen perception. And, he surmised, she was driven by an honest intent that was laudable. Her request to him had been couched in a more conciliatory fashion and he was intrigued by her wish to speak to him privately. He decided to humour her and nodded politely; assuring her he would do as she wished. Gianni, now standing beside him, stared with fascination at the silver raven's head on the top of her cane as, leaning heavily on Conal's arm, Hilde went slowly from the hall.

It was late in the evening before Bascot began the ascent up the stairs to the chamber where Lady Hilde awaited him. The Templar was tired and his leg ached from the riding he had done that morning, and also from his walk to the priory that afternoon after he had left the company in the hall. The purpose of his visit had been to see if the priest, Father Anselm, was showing any signs of recovery. Brother Jehan led him to the injured man's bed, explaining that his patient had still not regained consciousness and from lack of any sustenance except for a few mouthfuls of honeyed wine dribbled into his mouth, was likely to remain so until death should take him.

"It is a strange irony that his wound has finally begun to heal," the infirmarian said. "It is almost as though he remains unconscious of his own choosing."

Bascot looked down on the face of the priest. It was peaceful, smooth and unlined in repose. The Templar had judged him to be a man just a few years older than himself, but lack of food had brought a gauntness to his features that made Anselm seem closer to middle age. His hands lay one on either side of him, resting on the thick woollen blanket that served as a cover, the fingers long and sensitive. On the priest's brow dark hair curled thickly, but his eye sockets were sunken in deep shadows. Beneath the blanket his chest rose and fell in shallow movement. What hidden failing, Bascot wondered, had prompted Anselm to don a hair shirt beneath his vestments? Was it a penance for the commission of a sin or for the pleasure of an imaginary one? Had it anything to do with the murders in the alehouse?

"Were you acquainted with Father Anselm before this incident?" Bascot asked Brother Jehan.

The infirmarian shook his head slightly. "I have spoken with him but twice, and that is all," he said. "He is only recently come to Lincoln, arriving here some two years ago. Before that he was in Canterbury, I believe."

"And the times that you saw him, did he make mention of anything that was troubling him? Any problems he was having in his new parish, perhaps?"

Brother Jehan gave him an uncertain look, as though asking the reason for the Templar's questions. "I am searching for an explanation as to why he was stabbed, Brother," Bascot said. "I had thought it to be connected to the murders in the alehouse near the church where he officiated. But I could be wrong. It might be completely unrelated, the cause instead to be found in some personal matter, even something from his past. But his injury and his death, if it comes, are just as deserving of inquiry as those of the unfortunates found on the alehouse floor. I would discover the identity of the culprit, if I can. But to do that, I need to know more about Anselm. Can you help me?"

Jehan gave the matter a few moments thought before he answered. "It is not likely that I can for, as I said, I was not often in his company. But I will tell you the little that I know." The infirmarian cast a brief look at his patient before he continued. "The first occasion that I met Anselm was not long after he arrived in Lincoln. A fellow cleric had advised him to enquire of me if I had a remedy for a persistent rash that had appeared on his lower extremities. He seemed to me, at that time, to be a man who was distracted, as though his thoughts were far away from his surroundings. I did not pay his demeanour much mind. It is not unusual for removal to a new parish, especially one so far from a place he might have come to regard as his home, to be unsettling for a priest. I gave him a salve to use on the rash and he left. I did not see him again until some time later."

Bascot noted that a frown had appeared on the infirmarian's careworn face as he had spoken the last words, as though the second meeting had not been as unremarkable as the first. "And when was that, Brother?" he prompted.

As Bascot spoke, Anselm stirred on the cot. He was still deep in unconsciousness, but his limbs had suddenly become restless, and his fingers began to twitch with movement. Brother Jehan immediately leaned over him, taking a moistened cloth from a bowl of water on a nearby stool and gently dabbing Anselm's forehead, murmuring soothing words as he did so. Suddenly Anselm's eyes flickered open, just for the briefest space, and he stared unseeingly past the two men at his bedside, seeming to focus his attention on a point beyond them. Then his eyelids closed, and he began to mutter. "Unclean. Unclean. Forever unclean."

Jehan continued his ministrations and Anselm slowly subsided back into his heavy sleep and the murmuring ceased. Finally the infirmarian placed the cloth back in its receptacle and straightened the covering over his patient. When he had done, he leaned back from the bed and heaved a deep sigh.

"Always he is thus. Continually speaking of something, or someone, that is 'Unclean.' It is clear that his mind is greatly disturbed but there is no way of determining the cause of his anguish," Jehan said heavily.

Bascot let a few brief moments of silence pass before he urged the elderly monk back to his recollections of the times he had met Anselm. "You were telling me, Brother, of the second time you met Father Anselm."

Jehan nodded his head, unwilling to distract his attention from his patient. "Yes, I was," he said finally. "The next occasion that I was in his company was just a few weeks before he was attacked. The rash on his legs had reappeared, more virulently this time. I suggested he try an unguent that I prepare from a plant commonly called Bee-Bread, which is red clover. He thanked me for it and went away. I never saw him again."

"And the second time he came, did he still seem distracted?"

"No, he was more . . . how shall I put it . . . intense. As though a great matter was on his mind. Because of that it seemed to me that his blood might be out of balance with the other humours in his body, possibly overheating. It is often the cause of an eruption on the skin. I suggested he go to a leech for bleeding, but he did not seem of a mind to take my advice. Barely paid it heed, in fact."

"And you had no inkling of what was troubling him?"

Jehan shrugged. "I might be in error—that there was something amiss with him, I mean. Perhaps he had always been so. Or he may have been in the throes of an internal struggle with his conscience." The infirmarian flicked a glance at Bascot. "You must be aware that many of us who take up the pledge to serve Christ often find the way long and hard. Thanks be to God that I have never found it so, but it is not uncommon."

Bascot nodded his acknowledgement of the truth of the brother's words, thinking of his own struggles as the infirmarian continued. "But I am not in a position to judge Anselm for I hardly knew him. Except . . ."

After a long pause, Bascot again had to prompt Jehan into speech and it was with reluctance that he explained the reason for his reticence. "What I am about to tell you is only hearsay, told to me by one of the more garrulous monks of our house. I know not of its veracity, or even if I should repeat it." He smiled ruefully. "I berated the monk who told me, scolding him for the looseness of his tongue."

"Unless the matter is pertinent to the attack on Anselm, or the murders in the alehouse, you have my assurance that it shall be kept between us two," Bascot told him.

Jehan nodded. "Very well. It is only a small thing, but if it will help you in your quest, then it is my duty to relate it, I suppose." He reached over and once more straightened Anselm's cover before speaking. The stricken priest made no movement at his touch, still deep in senselessness. "It was said that Anselm was sent to Lincoln because some grave matter necessitated his removal from Canterbury. It was implied that he was in a disgrace of some sort, but for what, I do not know. The fact that he was wearing a hair shirt when he was stabbed is an indication that he was undergoing a heavy penance, but whether it was self-imposed or laid on him by his confessor . . . again, I do not know."

Bascot thanked the infirmarian for his help, even though the information he had given brought little aid in discovering if the attack on Anselm was connected to the alehouse murders. Perhaps Bascot would never find the answers to the questions he was asking. If the priest died without regaining consciousness, it was quite possible his secrets would be taken with him into heaven.

Bascot ruminated on those secrets, if there were any, as he knocked on the door of the chamber that had been assigned to Lady Hilde.

The room was a small one, a narrow bed encircled with hangings set against one wall, a tiny clothespress and a low polished oak table. Hilde sat by the table in the one chair the chamber possessed. The elderly maidservant that had been in the hall was perched on a stool in the corner, sewing a rent in one of her mistress' garments by the light of a thick candle. Beside her a straw pallet was neatly rolled, ready to be spread and used when her mistress should retire.

"You are well come, Templar," Hilde said. "I have only a stool to offer for a seat, but there is a good wine I brought from home, if you will take a cup."

Bascot accepted her offer and seated himself on the stool. The servant brought him wine. It was thin, but sweet, and he drank it gratefully, feeling its warmth drain some of the tiredness from his body.

"It is good, eh?" Hilde said, motioning for her servant to refill his cup. "It is made from damsons grown on the land left to Conal by his father. It is a small holding, but the soil is good and produces enough for the needs of the household."

Conal's great-aunt had discarded the close-fitting coif she had worn earlier that day, allowing her white hair to rest on her shoulder in one thick braid with only a light head-cloth for covering. She wore a loose gown of plain material, and no ornamentation of any kind. The open collar of the garment revealed her thin neck, the flesh softly wrinkled. But although her body seemed frail, there was still much strength of purpose in the straightness of her back and the gleam in her eyes.

Against the arm of her chair rested her cane, the silver

raven's head gleaming dully in the dim light. Hilde saw Bascot glance at it and smoothed the great beak with her finger. "This staff is all the wealth I have ever had. It belonged to my father, commissioned by him when a battle wound made walking difficult." Her eyes misted at the remembrance. "My father had only two children, my brother and myself. My brother was a sickly youth, but gentle natured and I loved him. He lived just long enough to sire a son, Conal's father Leif, before he died. And then Leif was taken too, leaving only one small boy to carry on our family name. The grief of his losses killed my father, and I vowed on his deathbed that I would look after Conal as he would have done if he had lived."

She gave Bascot a direct look. "I have never married, Templar. I was neither comely enough nor had sufficient dower to interest any but the most niggardly of suitors. But I was never sorry, for I had Conal. And he has more than justified my love for him. I hope I will not fail him now."

With her customary directness, she turned the conversation away from herself and to the reason she had asked Bascot to come to her chamber. "This is a sad business, Templar, and I hope it will be handled with dispatch. That is why I have asked you to come here tonight. Whoever killed those people, I am convinced—nay, I know—it was not Conal, nor Sybil. It seems to me that the quickest way to prove their innocence is to find out who is guilty. If the deed were done to pave a clear way to Philip de Kyme's inheritance, then the killer has rid himself of both the baseborn heir and Conal by his actions. I have a feeling that is where the search should be made, among those who will profit by these deaths, and I would like to offer you my assistance, if you will have it. I have lived near Lincoln all my life and have knowledge of most of the members of de Kyme's family and their history. If you would be willing to tell me what evidence you have gathered, it may be that I can give you some insight into who would have the motive, and the opportunity, to have committed this cowardly act."

Lady Hilde spoke, as she had in the hall, in a blunt fashion. Bascot considered her offer. She had a sharp mind, of that Bascot was sure, and she also had what he did not, knowledge of the background and character of each of the people involved. He was also confident that, apart from her conviction that Conal was innocent, she would give him what information she possessed in an unbiased manner, a pleasant prospect after the frustrating attempts at extracting details from the alewife and Isaac, the Jew. He signalled for his wine cup to be refilled and ruminated for a few moments before making a decision.

"I think your opinions might be useful, lady," he said at last. "And a recounting of the facts that have been discovered thus far may assist me in marshalling my own thoughts into a more coherent order." Taking a deep draught from his wine cup he then told her all that had happened since that morning just a scant few days before when he and Ernulf had gone to examine the bodies on the alehouse floor.

Lady Hilde heard him through without interruption as he told of his difficulties with Agnes, of Gianni finding the scrap of material in the alehouse yard and how he had become convinced that the bodies had been taken there in empty ale barrels and how, through Philip de Kyme's *secretarius*, William Scothern, the identity of the two strangers had been determined. He also told her of his visit to Isaac and how he was convinced that all three of the victims had been somehow abducted while travelling along the Torksey road. Finally he told her of the attack on Father Anselm and his rather tenuous suspicion that it might somehow be linked to the alehouse murders and of the lies that had been told by the prostitute Gillie and of her subsequent disappearance along with Brunner, the stewe-holder.

As Bascot's words came to a halt, Hilde picked up her

cane and rose from her chair, waving away his offer of assistance and motioning for her maid, who had jumped up to help, to remain where she was. "I think better on my feet, poor creatures that they are. A few paces will suffice to order my mind."

She trod slowly the short distance to the far end of the room and back, then stopped in front of Bascot. "You have met the nephew, Roger de Kyme?"

"This morning, lady. He had his son, Arthur, with him. There was also a cousin, Alan de Kyme, in the company."

"A poxy crew, all of them," Hilde said. "Roger more than most, along with that whey-faced son of his. Alan is little better. They all of them fawn on Philip to gain his favour and he, self-pitying wretch that he is, responds in kind, lapping up their commiserations for his sorrows as though they were sincere. I am sure either Roger or Alan would be more than capable of murder if they foresaw future benefits."

She thought for a moment, standing motionless. "I believe that Roger is in debt to the Jews. And Alan could be also. They both have good reason for not wishing the promise of a wealthy inheritance to pass to another."

"And if de Kyme should proclaim one of them his heir—it would be a collateral of enough strength to enable more to be borrowed," Bascot said, agreeing with her reasoning. He had formed similar opinions himself that morning in de Kyme's manor house. "Their whereabouts that day must be looked into."

"Yes," Hilde agreed, "but it could be they used hired minions. There are many such about Lincoln these days, just as there are in the rest of England." She shook her head. "The lawful days of King Henry are long past. Since his death first Richard, and now John, have not kept the order that their father did."

"I do not think underlings were used to commit these murders," Bascot said thoughtfully. "If I am correct and the victims were taken—either with willingness or by coercion—on the Torksey road, then it must have been by someone who would not arouse the suspicions of the sheriff's guard. Patrols are carried out regularly, and often. Anyone seeming to be on unlawful business would have been noticed by them and challenged."

"Unless it was one of their servants, claiming to be on a legitimate errand for their master."

Bascot shook his head. "Possibly, but secret murder is a dangerous undertaking to entrust to a servant. If caught they could implicate their master and, if successful, such knowledge could be used as a threat to gain preferential treatment."

He paused for a moment. "There is also one aspect of this murder that has bothered me from the beginning. Why were the bodies taken into Lincoln and left in the alehouse? Surely it would have been far better to have left them in the greenwood. They may or may not have been discovered eventually, but the purpose of eliminating Sir Philip's heir would have been accomplished. It speaks of a need for them to be found, and found quickly. But, if that is so, then why remove all identification from the corpses?"

Lady Hilde sat down, obviously tired from the long day and her few brief moments of pacing. After ruminating a space she said, "Your questions are the very same ones to which I gave much thought while I was waiting for you. There are two other persons besides Roger and Alan de Kyme who may hope to gain by these deaths. One is obvious, the other not." She gave Bascot a challenging stare. "The first is Philip de Kyme himself," she said.

"But it is he who has laid the charge against Conal and Lady Sybil," Bascot protested.

"Yes. And what better way to rid yourself of an unwanted wife and stepson? Much quicker than trying to dissolve the marriage through a weak claim of consanguinity. Such a process can take years. If he has the prospect of another wife in mind, he might be in haste to formalize the marriage. Lust is a powerful goad, especially to a man who is past his prime."

"But to kill his own son, illegitimate or not—well, at the very least, is it not a rather drastic method of obtaining freedom from a wife?"

"If the boy actually was his son," Hilde replied shrewdly. "We have only his word for that, and it was a nebulous identification at best. That may, or may not, be the answer to your second question. From what you tell me, he claimed the boy to be his own through the recognition of a cheap silver brooch. And you yourself helped to confirm it by identifying the origin of the clothing worn by the dead young man and his companion. Is it not an easy matter to obtain some garments made in La Lune, then lure to Lincoln a simple peasant and his wife from some village well away from these parts, promising work or perhaps a small quantity of silver as an inducement? They are then abducted, poisoned and left to be found in a public place. And also stabbed after death. Poison is a woman's weapon, the sword a man's. The use of both points to both genders having a hand in the murders. De Kyme conveniently pretends grief, followed by rage, charging his wife and stepson with the slaying. He has accomplished his aim—to free himself of a barren wife and wed another on whom he may beget a son of his own loins."

Bascot had to admit there was an element of possibility in her conjectures. "The *secretarius*, Scothern, would have to be privy to the matter, if that is what was done."

"Not necessarily, Templar. You told me the letters were said to have been despatched with a retainer of de Kyme's, then by ship, entrusted to the captain. The usual way for any missive not of great import. But the letters may never have been sent at all, and the *secretarius* could simply have been told that an answer had been received without actually seeing it arrive. Scothern may have done no more than pen the letters and read the ones that came in answer. He need have known nothing."

"De Kyme is not literate. Someone else must have written the replies supposed to come from the boy's mother."

Lady Hilde shrugged. "Not very difficult to find a clerk in any town hereabouts to write a letter. He would not be interested in the contents, only his fee."

Bascot pondered for a moment. "It could be as you say. I must find out if the boy that was killed was actually Hugo. If, indeed, such a person as Hugo ever existed."

"A difficult task, Templar. The lands in Maine are in turmoil at the moment, what with our new king's continental subjects rebelling at every turn. And did you not say that the last letter claimed that the boy's mother was intending to embark on a pilgrimage? If the missives were falsified, this is a convenient ploy to cover her absence in La Lune. On the other hand, if the story is true, it is possible she may not be there to confirm or deny the truth of the matter."

"Yes," he said slowly, pondering. "Perhaps I can persuade the Templars to help. They have stations in nearly every large town in Christendom. I will ask the local master to send an enquiry on my behalf. To Compostella, if necessary. The Templar resources are large and efficient. If a deception has been carried out as to the boy's identity, it may be that they will be able to discover it, or even prove that the dead boy was genuinely de Kyme's son."

"A slim hope, and one that will take some time to uncover, even with the Order's help," Hilde replied.

"You mentioned two suspects, Lady Hilde. Who is the other?"

Hilde took some time to answer. When she did, her response surprised Bascot. "The other is Hugh Bardolf," she said.

At her companion's look of disbelief, she added, "You are a newcomer here, Templar. I have known these people a long time. Bardolf is a greedy man, greedy for power. He has a daughter, Matilda, and is touting for a husband for her with all the voracity of a ribbon seller hawking a tray of shoddy goods. She is not an unattractive girl, but spiteful by nature and, rumour has it, not above giving her favours lightly. But her father is an ambitious man. Whether he is aware of his daughter's unchaste behaviour I do not know, but even if he is, it would not deter him. He already has much land and wants more. De Kyme wants an heir and Matilda needs a husband. Bardolf would see such a match as a gift from God. And I do not think he would be averse to enlisting the devil's aid in helping him to accomplish it."

"It seems an extreme length to go to on the hope of a li-aison that could only be a tenuous promise at best," Bascot remarked.

"Ah, but is it, Templar? Has the fair Matilda already warmed de Kyme in his bed? That she is rumoured to have done the same with others might suggest that she has. And she is young, and of a good family, if not as high-placed as his own. She would be an ideal wife for de Kyme in her father's eyes and I am sure Bardolf could be persuasive enough to make Philip see it that way. But he would need to be free of Sybil first."

Bascot leaned back and drained the final dregs of wine in his cup. "You have given me much to think of, lady. And there is much that must be done, if I am to ascertain the whereabouts of all these people on the day the murders were committed."

"If you are agreeable, Templar, I would like to aid you in this matter. I am not as mobile as you are, even with your injured leg, but I am privy to one place that you are not. The solar. Women love to prattle and so do their servants. Between myself and Freyda there"—she gestured to the maidservant—"we could glean much from any tongues that can be encouraged to wag."

Bascot laughed despite himself. He could not imagine Lady Hilde engaging in cosy idle conversation with anyone. She was too intimidating. The old woman laughed with him. "I know your thoughts, Templar, but I can be amiable—if I wish. Will you accept my offer?"

Bascot told her he would and, as he bid her goodnight, found himself in a more hopeful frame of mind than he had been since the whole devil's brew had begun.

Twenty

✛

THE TEMPLAR LINCOLN HEADQUARTERS, OR PRECEP-
tory, was situated in an enclave just north of Eastgate, near
the Priory of All Saints. Behind a high wall with a stout
gate lay a chapel, dormitory, stable, storehouse, armoury
and a square patch of ground used for exercise. Early the
next morning Bascot presented himself at the gate and, after being admitted with a friendly wave by the guard on
duty, went through to the outer yard. The familiar stench of
horse dung and human sweat gave him a wrench of nostal-
gia and took him back to the day he had taken his vows to
join the Order. How happy he had been then, looking forward to the joy of using his strength and skill to fight for
Christ while at the same time satisfying his own longing
for the inner peace of a monk's life. Disillusionment had
been slow to come, but come it had, already setting in before he had been captured by the Saracens. Now he wished
he could return to that time of his youth and feel again the
sweet savour of promise.

On the practice ground two Templar men-at-arms, in long

tunics of brown, were putting a pair of new recruits through a drill with short sword and shield under the watchful eye of a black-robed serjeant. Two Templar knights, clad in the white surcoats that denoted their higher rank, stood watching. Of the third rank of the Order, that of chaplain, identified by tunics of green, only one was to be seen, hurrying towards the round stone building that was the chapel, glancing as he went at the top layer of a sheaf of parchment held between his gloved hands. Even though the day was hot, the gloves could never be removed, except to don a clean replacement, for the hands of the priests must always be kept in a pristine condition to serve Holy Communion.

From the stables came the shrill sound of a horse neighing in anger, followed by the thud of shod hooves hitting solid timber. Bascot went towards the sound. He was looking for the officer in charge, the preceptor, and if he was to find him anywhere it would be in the stable.

At the end of a row of horse stalls, illuminated dimly in the gloom, stood a group of men. Two were grooms, holding with difficulty the reins of a wild-eyed grey stallion. A Templar serjeant was trying to get a saddle on the animal's back, dodging to and fro in an effort to escape flying hooves and bared teeth. Watching the spectacle and, from the grin on his face, enjoying it mightily, was the preceptor, Everard d'Arderon.

"Come on, Hamo, get that saddle on his back," he yelled to the red-faced serjeant. "Not going to let a horse win a battle, are you? Get on with it, man."

The serjeant, as angry as the horse now, wrenched the reins from the frantic clutch of the groom and pulled the animal's head down cruelly, forcing it onto its forelegs. As the stallion let out his breath in a whuff of defeat, the serjeant threw the saddle on its back, gave his captive a savage kick in the testicles and pulled the straps into position, securing them before the horse could recover. Handing the reins to one of the grooms, he stepped back and watched with a satisfied smile as the stallion regained its feet and stood on wobbly legs, breathing hard.

"Well done, Hamo," d'Arderon said. "That will be a good piece of horseflesh once it's trained to use its temper against the infidel and not honest Christians."

Noticing Bascot's arrival, he gave a nod of greeting and walked over to where he stood. "Come to get a supply of *candi*, have you?" he asked with a grin. "I've just received a new batch, covered in marchpane. Come into the storehouse and I'll let you sample a piece."

Without waiting for Bascot's reply, the preceptor walked out of the stable and into the bright sunshine of the yard, not stopping until he reached the long low building that housed supplies of all sorts of commodities, from sacks of grain to piles of well-seasoned timber. The odours here were sweet, a pungent mixture of resin, spices and beeswax. As the preceptor rummaged about amongst a pile of hide-bound bundles, Bascot rested his aching leg by sitting on a tun of wine and watched, with something like affection, the man who had, under orders from the Templar Master in London, placed him in the household of Nicolaa de la Haye nearly a year before.

D'Arderon had been Lincoln's preceptor for almost three years, ever since a bout of tertian fever in the Holy Land had laid him so low it was thought he would not recover. To save him from the danger of a further infection, he had been sent back to England and given the preceptorship of Lincoln. Under his care was the recruiting of new postulants and the supervision of their instruction in the rules of the Order; maintaining and collecting the revenues from properties given as gifts to the Templars in the Lincoln area; and filling the many requisitions for supplies such as weapons, armour and timber to be sent to the Holy Land for the Order's use in the war against the infidel. The preceptor also, on occasion, acted as safe-keeper of monies that Lincoln's citizens wished to be sent abroad, perhaps in payment of a debt or as a gift to a member of their family. D'Arderon could, too, if he deemed it advisable, advance monies to individuals outside the Order for their own purposes. To avoid the stigma of usury, these loans were given without interest, but the amount stipulated under the terms of the loan was always a little more than the actual amount borrowed, in order to cover the cost of the Templar's handling of the arrangement.

Although the burden of all these matters was weighty, d'Arderon was a man of cheerful humour, with his threescore years sitting lightly on shoulders still unbowed and muscular, and he had a sincere liking for the young Templar knight who had arrived in Lincoln wounded in body and sore in heart.

"Here they are, de Marins," he said, straightening up and waving aloft a small leather sack. "These new ones with the marchpane are extra sweet—should be even more to your liking than the plain kind."

D'Arderon accompanied his offer with a wink of conspiracy. Although monks, Templars, unlike their nonmilitary counterparts, were fed well in order to keep up their strength for battle. But *candi* was not a part of their regular diet and was imported to England primarily for sale to the public, the proceeds of which went into the Templar coffers. Even so, it was not uncommon for one of the knights, or even a serjeant, to have a small leather sack filled with the sweets put aside for his own use. Although Bascot was not strictly within the Order at the moment, d'Arderon still kept a supply for him.

Bascot thanked him and popped one of the sweets into his mouth, relishing the taste. D'Arderon gave him an assessing glance as he did so and said, "You look in better fettle than when you first arrived. Life in the castle agrees with you, does it?"

Bascot shrugged. "I am treated well. There are meaner posts."

"And the boy—your waif?"

"He thrives. Like many poor urchins, he needed only food and shelter."

"And care," added d'Arderon shrewdly, "which you have given him."

"He has become a good servant," Bascot protested weakly.

"Aye. And who would not, with as gentle a master as you?" D'Arderon held up his hand to forestall more objections. "I will not repeat my assurances that if you return to our ranks we will ensure that the boy is well cared for. You have heard them often enough from others beside me."

He changed the subject deftly. "I hear you are investigating a case of murder on Lady Nicolaa's behalf. How goes it?"

Bascot gave the preceptor a straight answer. "Not well. That is why I have come here today, to ask the help of the Order."

"And I thought you came just for the *candi*," d'Arderon jested, taking one himself and crunching it between teeth still strong and white. "Tell me your problem, and how we may be of assistance. If it does not detract from Christ's cause, I will do my best to aid you."

Bascot repeated the gist of his conversation with Hilde the night before, and her suspicions that the identification of the murdered young couple may have been false. "If de Kyme did have a son by his former paramour, then it is vital that we discover whether the boy lived in La Lune and whether he did, in fact, journey to England with his wife. If there was no son, or if he is still alive and well, then . . ."

"De Kyme is behind the plotting and the murders," d'Arderon finished.

"Or he was gulled into thinking he had an heir who was then killed by his wife and stepson." Bascot stopped short. There were so many possibilities to the situation that he resisted enumerating them. He was sure only that finding out if the dead pair were who they were said to be was the logical place to begin and try to fit the pieces of the riddle together.

D'Arderon paced back and forth a bit, deliberating aloud as he did so. "I think I can help you. As you know, we have riders with despatches leaving every day for London, and often farther afield. As it happens, I have a missive to send to Maine this very day, to Le Mans, and I thought to send a couple of new recruits who need the edges taken off them. A trip through the turmoil over there will steady them up nicely. I'll add a message to the preceptor in Le Mans. Tell him to make enquiries about the boy with all speed and send his findings back to me immediately. Shouldn't take too long, twelve days at most, ten if I tell 'em that's how quick I want it done. Do the new lads good to feel a whip at their backs."

At Bascot's questioning look he added, "These recruits are for the men-at-arms rank. Got a feeling they were outlaws and joined up before Sheriff Camville could catch up with them. They're freeborn, of course, couldn't take them otherwise, but if they've been spending the last few months in the greenwood, the prospect of a comfortable straw pallet and free food would look good to them, never mind that they'll be clothed and armed into the bargain. They have yet to take their final vows and I want to test their mettle and their commitment before they do. One thing to enjoy the benefits of the Order, quite another to put up with the discomfort of hours in the saddle with the possibility of an ambush and an arrow in your neck all the while—and you know well that's what they'll face in the Holy Land. Saracens behind every sand dune. And just to ensure they don't run off once they're free of Lincoln I'll send Hamo with them. He'd slit a Christian throat just as soon as a Saracen's if he thought they were betraying the Order. I'll send your enquiry along with him."

"I appreciate your assistance," Bascot said, rising.

D'Arderon threw an arm affectionately about his shoulders. "We are all brothers in Christ, de Marins. And brother should help brother. Remember that when you finally make your decision whether to stay in the Order or leave it. You will find no such steadfastness in the world outside."

"I am aware of it, preceptor. And will not forget your kindness."

Bascot felt a tiny sliver of regret as he crossed the yard and departed through the gate. A part of him wanted to stay within the confines of the walls, to join d'Arderon and the Templar brothers at their communal meal in the refectory and engage in the camaraderie that would prevail afterwards. Then he thought of Gianni. Despite the preceptor's assurance that the boy would be looked after if Bascot should return to the Templar ranks, he knew that the young Sicilian, however well treated, would feel lost and betrayed if he left him. No, it was not a decision he could yet make. First he would complete his enquiry into the alehouse murders. Time enough afterwards to put his mind to the future.

After he left the preceptory, Bascot walked the long distance through the town and down to the shop of the cobbler to find out if his boots were ready. By the time he had reached the shop, and had been admitted by the shoemaker's wife, he was more than ready to take a seat on the same chair he had sat on before and which was, again, quickly proffered for him.

The shoemaker bobbed in deference, then brought from his workbench a pair of fine leather boots, highly polished, and knelt in front of Bascot to remove his old ones and slip the new pair on. They were soft and supple, encasing his feet snugly, but without strain. Bascot could feel, just slightly, the soft pads that had been inserted into the left boot and which forced a gentle pressure on his injured ankle.

"If it will please you to stand, Sir Templar, you will find a new comfort in your limb," the cobbler said.

Bascot did so and, as he came to his feet, felt surprise. Aside from a slight strangeness that the feel of the pads gave, there was no other sensation in his ankle. The pain had gone.

"You have the touch of an angel in your hands," he told the shoemaker. "Never since I sustained the injury have I been without a constant ache in that ankle."

The cobbler looked gratified but gave him a warning. "You will still find it there if you give your leg too much strain, sir," he said. "With normal walking or riding, the boot will help. Alas, it will not make your bones whole again."

"The boots are well worth your price," Bascot told him warmly. "Had I known of your skill, I would have become a patron when first I came to Lincoln. I would have been saved many hours of anguish."

The shoemaker's son, who had ambled in behind his mother to see the fitting of the new boots, enjoyed the compliment to his father. "Da's helped many a man that's had an injury, haven't you, Da?" he said. "Got a rare touch, he has, so everyone says."

"Hush, boy," the cobbler said with a slight impatience. "It is a sin to boast."

"I'm sayin' nowt but truth, and well you knows it," the boy replied. "And truth's not a sin, is it, sir?" He asked the question of Bascot, showing his long equine teeth in a grimace that passed for a smile.

"No, it is not," Bascot assured him. "And it is certainly true that your father has a talent for helping the maimed."

"He makes covers for them that has lost a hand, too," the cobbler's son went on, "to keep the arm from injury. And once he fitted a brace on a man that had broken his shoulder, so he could stand straight." The boy giggled. "He even makes hair shirts for priests sometimes, so that their misery fits them comfortably."

"That's enough, boy," the cobbler said sternly. "My aids

are between me and my customers, not to be spoken of lightly by the likes of you. Be careful that God, for your impertinence, does not strike you with some affliction my skill cannot help."

The threat subdued the boy and he stopped speaking, hanging his head in a sullen manner. Bascot, however, was interested in what he had said before he had been chastened into silence.

"Is it true that you have fitted priests with hair shirts, shoemaker?" he asked.

"Aye, one or two. Men's chests and shoulders come in all sizes, just like feet. It would not be proper for the hair shirt to be seen, since its exposure would defeat the spirit of humility in which it is worn. So I make them to fit snug under a priest's vestments."

Bascot acknowledged the sentiment, then said, "There was a priest in town that was attacked with a dagger and almost killed only a few short days ago. Father Anselm. Do you know him?"

"Aye, I do," was the reply.

"He was wearing a hair shirt when he was attacked. It is thought the shirt saved him from death. Was it one of yours?"

"Since you already know of its existence, it cannot be wrong of me to tell you about it. Yes, I made it for Father Anselm. Just a week before the fair began. And I thank God that I did so, for if it helped to deflect the dagger that struck him, then it was God's hand that guided mine in the making."

Bascot took a deep breath. Here was the possibility of more information, connected perhaps not only with the attack on the priest, but also with the murders. But he had to be careful how he asked for it. The shoemaker was a simple man, honest and truthful—and frightened of committing a sin. "Father Anselm is near death. The monks at the priory fear that he will leave this world without regaining

consciousness and never be able to tell who it was that assaulted him. A person that would strike a priest must be
caught. The crime is repugnant and calls out for punishment. If you know of anyone that might have wanted to
harm the priest . . ."

"He spoke no word to me of enemies," the cobbler
replied. "Indeed, he spoke little at all when he was here."

"You have no knowledge, then, of the reason he wanted
the shirt?" Bascot had tried to avoid the direct question, but
could find no way around it.

The cobbler looked at him with a shocked expression.
"No, sir, I do not. It would not have been fitting for him to
tell of it to any except his confessor."

The shoemaker's son burst out in a new fit of giggles.
"'Twas for lechery, Da. Everyone knows that, even if you
don't . . ."

"Silence!" The shoemaker rose to his full height, which
was still a good half-head shorter than his son. His rage,
however, made him seem taller. "Hold your tongue unless
you can find a better use for it than to slander a priest. Go!
Go out of my sight, and beg God for forgiveness."

The boy slunk out and the cobbler turned to Bascot with
an apologetic air. "I am sorry, sir. The boy forgets himself,
and also that you, too, are a man who has sworn himself to
God's service. I beg your pardon for his behaviour."

Bascot made light of the boy's remark. "I am not so old
that I forget on what a young lad's mind constantly dwells.
Were we not all once enthralled with the tumbling of a lass
and could think of nothing else?"

The shoemaker shook his head. "What you say is true,
but in my youth I would not have dared to speak so in front
of my elders. The young today have no thought for any but
themselves. It is a sad statement, but a true one."

Bascot changed the subject, paying the cobbler for the
boots and complimenting him once again on their making.

As he left the shop he saw the shoemaker's son standing over to one side, still punching holes in a piece of leather, but with anger this time. Bascot walked over to him.

"Did another speak of Father Anselm being lustful, or is it only your own imagination at work?" he said to the boy harshly.

Now fear replaced resentment in the boy's eyes. His answer came out in a rush. "'Tis the truth, I swear it. Da will not listen to what he says is evil gossip, but a friend of mine told me his sister complained to him of the priest, said that Father Anselm was always touching her when he got the chance. And not only her, but some of her friends. Accidentally brush their titties, or stand so close behind they could feel his member pushing into their bottoms, that sort of thing. We reckon that's why he got the hair shirt, and that it was some angry father or husband that stabbed him, after finding out he had been lecherous with one of their womenfolk."

The boy looked down at the piece of leather in his hands, now almost in shreds. "I wouldn't of said it if I hadn't been sure it was true. Da's always telling me I'm insolent, but even so I wouldn't make up a story about a priest, as well he should know."

"Perhaps you'll find it easier to get on with your father when you have gained a few more years," Bascot said, not unkindly. "It may surprise you to find that the older one gets the more we appreciate the wisdom of those we did not think possessed it."

As Bascot walked back up to the castle, marvelling at how easily his ankle bore his weight, he turned over in his mind what the boy had said. Had the stabbing of Father Anselm been nothing more than an outraged parishioner's revenge for liberties that no priest should take, or was it somehow involved with the deaths of the people in the alehouse? It seemed the more he delved into these murders, the more lust played a part—that of de Kyme and the paramour of his youth, Hilde's suggestion that Hugh Bardolf's daughter was unchaste, and now Father Anselm and his hair shirt. Was there a link between one deadly sin and another?

The midday meal was already in progress when Bascot arrived back at the castle. The fair was almost half-over and its momentum had slowed somewhat, as though taking a breath, readying itself to pick up the pace again as the final days approached. Nicolaa had obtained permission from the king to hold a tournament on the last day and now most of the conversation around the crowded tables was of the merits of one knight or another.

As Gianni came up silently beside him, Bascot pushed his way through to a seat next to the elderly knight he had been in conversation with on the evening that William Scothern had come to tell him of his suspicion of the identities of the slain young couple. As Gianni ran to fetch wine for his master's cup, the old man glanced at Bascot, wiped his straggly moustache free of gravy, then said, "Found out if it was young Conal who did 'em in yet?"

Bascot shook his head, taking a long draught of wine from his freshly filled cup as the old knight went on. "Look for a woman, that's what I say. Always a woman mixed up in secret murders. Bound to be. Especially where there's poison." He shot a quick look at Bascot from under his bushy eyebrows. "Was poison that killed 'em, wasn't it?"

"It is believed so. They were stabbed as well, but that was after they were dead."

"Aye, just as I said. Look for a woman. Though any female would need a man's help to kill four. Unless she were a witch, of course. Then she'd have demons to help her. I mind me of one time, back in '76 it was, when the old king was still alive, found six bodies, all laid out in a circle around an oak tree by the king's hunting lodge. Not a mark on 'em. That was a witch. Found her in a hut nearby. Had her familiar with her. A black dog it was . . ."

Bascot let the old knight's voice drift out of his consciousness and surveyed the company in the hall. On the dais Lady Nicolaa presided with her husband beside her. Tonight the sheriff was attired more resplendently than Bascot had ever seen him before, in a pale grey tunic with embroidered silver sleeves and a matching cap. In his hand was the familiar cup of wine. On his right sat Conal's uncles Ailwin and Magnus, while Nicolaa had her sisters Petronille and Ermingard to her left. Farther down the board sat Richard Camville, between Conal and Lady Sybil, and near the end sat Hilde, strategically placed between Hugh Bardolf and his daughter. Bascot could see her smiling and chatting with good humour and saw that her amiability had not passed unnoticed by Ailwin and Magnus, for occasionally one or the other of the brothers would glance down at her with a look of perplexity on their faces.

Gianni piled Bascot's trencher with the remnants of the stew that was left in the large bowl in the middle of the table. It was mostly root vegetables and gravy, for all of the choice pieces of meat had already been consumed, but it was tasty and Bascot ate it with relish, finding that he was unusually hungry. As he started on the next course—spiced eels simmered in their own juice—he felt a movement beside him and looked up to find Ermingard's husband, William de Rollos, beside him.

"I have been looking for you, Templar," de Rollos said, wearing an embarrassed look on his heavy-jowled face. "I thought to tell you that Bardolf did not have my support in his baiting of you yesterday at de Kyme's manor. Nor do I endorse his sentiments towards Lady Sybil and her son. If they are guilty—then well enough, they should be punished, but that remains yet to be proven. I want no part of that intrigue."

De Rollos was sitting on Bascot's sighted side and he could not see if the elderly knight on his right was taking an interest in their conversation or not. However, he felt Gianni at his shoulder, taking an interminably long time to prepare his plate and straighten his wine cup and napkin. He guessed the boy was acting as a shield against his neighbour hearing his conversation with de Rollos and dropped his voice accordingly.

"How did you come to be at de Kyme's manor?" Bascot asked de Rollos.

"Bardolf asked me to accompany him to one of his properties to see a new destrier he has acquired. As you know, there will be a tournament at the end of the fair. Although I do not intend to ride myself, Ivo has a fancy to try his sword in the melee. Bardolf thought perhaps I might be interested in buying the animal for my son to ride. We stopped at de Kyme's manor on the way. I would not have gone if I had suspected Bardolf would get embroiled in a drunken argument with de Kyme and his relatives. I thought only to get away from the castle for awhile, and to see if the horseflesh he touted was of worth. Ivo needs a distraction. He is much distressed at his mother's illness."

And so are you, thought Bascot, but did not say it. Instead, he asked, "Your wife—she is no better?"

De Rollos shrugged. "She has not been this bad since Ivo was born. Then I thought I would lose her—it was the sight of so much blood at the birth, you see. But these last years she has seemed much calmer. And was still so, until a few nights after we arrived."

"Did anything happen that might have precipitated her illness?" Bascot felt sorry for the man. Even though it was probable that theirs had been an arranged marriage, the Norman knight seemed genuinely fond of his wife, and cared about her welfare.

"Nothing that we know of," de Rollos replied. "When we first arrived she seemed glad to be in the company of her sisters again, and behaved as normal. Then, one night—I think it was the night of the day the bodies were discovered—she was found wandering near dawn along one of the passages in the upper keep, crying and tearing at her garments."

"Is it known how she came to be there?" Bascot asked.

"No. She was sleeping in a chamber with her sister Petronille and their maids. I had bunked down on the floor of the hall, for the keep was crowded and all the available chambers had been kept for the women or those who were elderly. Her maid came to me just as the sun was rising, telling me of her condition. Apparently Ermingard had got up in the night without waking anyone—presumably she wanted to use the privy. Neither Petronille nor the two maids knew how long she had been from her bed, but when one of them woke and found her gone they went searching for her. She was some distance from their chamber, and in the state that I have told you."

Bascot remembered how distressed de Rollos' wife had been on the morning she had entered the solar. "And she did not tell you where she had been?"

"No." De Rollos' misery was written plain in the downcast set of his jaw. "She just keeps saying over and over about something being the wrong colour, but what that something is, we do not know." He sighed. "I have no doubt she saw some blood somewhere and it has turned her mind. I will be glad when we are away from here and back in Normandy. Perhaps familiar surroundings will restore her to health."

Bascot was trying to find an answer that would lift the Norman's spirits when he felt a hand touch his shoulder and looked up to see Ernulf standing behind him.

"Brunner's been found," the serjeant said. "He's dead."

"Where?" asked Bascot.

"In an old shack near the leper settlement, just outside town off the road from Pottergate. He's been stabbed, but not after death like the ones in the alehouse. Blade took him straight in the heart while he was still breathing, damn his evil hide. He deserved to die slowly."

"And the girl—Gillie?"

"She was with him when he was found. Tied up and bruised, but alive. Frightened near out of her wits, though."

"Where is she now?"

"I've put her in the holding cell at the back of the garrison. Left two of my men with her and a chaplain. Thought you might want to question her."

"I'll come straight away," Bascot replied.

Twenty-one
✠

THE CELL INTO WHICH ERNULF HAD PUT GILLIE FOR
safekeeping was one that was usually used to keep the occasional drunkard or brawler locked up for the night. It had
a dirt floor and little furniture except for a hard pallet and a
stool, and a bucket for slops. The one window was fitted
with strong bars and the door with a heavy lock. Gillie lay
on her side on the pallet, the chaplain kneeling beside her
and speaking to her in reassuring tones. The priest looked
ill at ease. He was the chaplain that attended the small
church of St. Clement just outside the castle's northwest
wall and was more accustomed to giving comfort to the
men of the garrison than a young female.

When Bascot entered with Ernulf and Gianni, Gillie sat
up and began to entreat the Templar. "I won't catch the wast-
ing disease, will I, sir? Please tell me I won't. I didn't touch
any of the lepers, but we were very near to them. Brunner
made me go there with him. And he tied me up so I couldn't
get free. Will God punish me for being a harlot and make me
a leper? Am I damned, sir? Please, please help me."

Bascot hunkered down beside her. Her face was scratched and dirty, her hair tangled and laced with wisps of straw and her clothing torn and stained. Her fresh country expression was gone, replaced with the haunting look of fear. He was unused to wailing females but could understand the girl's terror. Leprosy was a terrible disease and no one knew how to cure it. Once the disease was contracted, the unfortunate victim was given the last rites just as though they were already dead and then they were consigned to live in a community with others that had been stricken in the same way, to stay there until they died. The leper community's only sustenance came from alms given by the church, and their care was entrusted to a few monks or priests brave enough to enter their dwelling place. They were not allowed to travel away from their hovels without ringing loudly on a bell to warn healthy citizens of their approach and they were forbidden to try and contact any members of their families. For all intents and purposes they were already dead and buried, their only joy of life what little comfort they could find in each other's company. He could see pity for Gillie etched on the faces of those around him, even young Gianni.

"Now be quiet, Gillie, and listen to me," Bascot said, searching for words of comfort. "If you didn't touch any of the lepers' sores then it is most unlikely you will get their disease. As for God's punishing you for being a harlot, you know as well as I that if you confess your sins and do penance, Our Lord will forgive you. Especially if you do not return to the life of a bawd."

Beside him the priest murmured agreement and, after a few minutes, between them they managed to calm the distraught young doxy.

Once she was sitting quietly, albeit still shaken and trembling, Bascot asked how she had come to be where she was found.

"Brunner made me go with him. He said that there was someone who would kill him, and me, too, if we did not hide. We left the stewe-house and went out Pottergate to where the lazar houses are. I was frightened, but he wouldn't let me go, and we went to this shack. It was a mean place, not as good as my da keeps his pigs in. There was no food, and not even a pallet to lie on. I told him I wasn't going to stay there, not only 'cause it were so terrible, but because the lepers were right there, just a short distance away. He beat me and then he tied me up."

"Did he leave the hovel himself?"

"Aye, he did. He had to because we had no food, you see, and he was as hungry as I. And he wanted wine, as well." She added this last with contempt. "He went out all wrapped up in his cloak. It was just on dusk. He told me he'd be back before long."

Gillie's eyes grew dark with fear as she remembered. "But he didn't come back. It got dark and there weren't no candles, nor could I have lit them if there had of been, tied up as I was. I tried to cry out, but my throat was parched from not having anything to drink, and I was half-scared anyway that if anyone heard me it would be a leper." She shuddered. "I ended up just crouching where I was, all bound with rope. Finally I fell asleep and didn't waken until I heard a noise outside."

"Was it Brunner returning?" Bascot asked.

"It was, but I didn't know that then. I heard voices, boots scuffing on the ground. Then there was a cry, and I heard a thud against the wall of the shack. Then silence. I was so frightened, I just lay there and didn't make a sound. It was morning before anyone came. A monk, from All Saints. He was going to the lazar houses and saw Brunner's body outside, I suppose. Anyway, he came in and found me and loosened my bonds." She looked at Ernulf. "Then the serjeant's men came and brought me here."

Bascot looked to Ernulf, who nodded. "The monk saw Brunner lying on the ground and went to see what ailed him. Found him dead and then the girl."

"I might have been killed, too," Gillie wailed.

"You're right, you might have been," Bascot said sternly to stop her breaking into fresh sobbing. "So you had better tell us anything you know about this matter or else Brunner's murderer may come looking for you."

"But I don't know anything, sir. Honest I don't. Brunner told me to tell you that pack of lies the day you came to the stewe-house. Only he didn't know that dead girl was pregnant, I swear, because he was as surprised as me when you said she was with child. All he kept saying was that there was someone who would do for him if he wasn't careful, someone high-placed, and that person would do for me too because I knew about the lies."

"He said someone high-placed, did he?" Bascot asked and Gillie nodded. "And he didn't know who it was?"

"I don't think he did," Gillie answered slowly, taking a moment to consider. "He just kept saying he had been given a warning and he didn't want to end up like the alekeeper."

"We found this parchment tucked into his hose," Ernulf said to Bascot, proffering a dirty piece of much-used vellum with black inky figures drawn on it. Bascot took the paper and looked at it. The meaning was plain, dead Wat with his skull broken and Brunner with a knife through his heart. When the stewe-keeper had received it he must have been alive and it had been sent as a warning. Now, it was the truth.

"The sad thing is that we nearly caught hold of Brunner while he was still breathing," Ernulf said. "Just this morning, at dawn, that little serving maid from the brothel come to the castle gates asking for me. Said she'd seen Brunner yestere'en and had followed him as far as Pottergate. He must have been coming back with the food. A loaf and some cheese was found beside his body. The little maid couldn't get away to tell me last night—trade was too brisk at the bawdy house—but came as soon as the doxies had finished their night's work and were all asleep. If only she'd come before, we might have got to him before the killer."

"Did you ask the maid if she saw anyone following Brunner?"

"I did. She says she didn't notice. She was too intent on following Brunner, but she couldn't go through Pottergate after him because the bawds would be expecting her back. Also, it was nigh on dark and she was nervous of going outside the city walls on her own. Her mother had sent her out for some wine, you see, and would be angry if she was gone too long. She's a good little lass, but scared of her mother, I reckon. Anyway, she did just as I told her to do, as soon as she could. Just a shame it wasn't earlier."

Bascot returned his attention to Gillie. "You're sure you haven't forgotten to tell me anything? A name Brunner might have mentioned, or something about his connection with the alekeeper?"

"I don't think so," Gillie replied, her sobs forgotten as she tried to remember. "He just kept saying over and over again that we had to hide, and stay hidden."

Bascot rose and, as he did so, she looked up at him, fear once again on her face. "What is to happen to me, sir? Am I to be punished for telling you those lies? I didn't want to, Brunner made me. He really did."

"I believe you, Gillie. And you will not be punished. You are free to go."

"But where, sir? If I go back to the stewe-house, whoever murdered Brunner may come after me there. What am I to do?"

There was rising panic in her voice and he saw Gianni tense. Memories of his own plight at the time Bascot had found the boy must not be far below the surface of Gianni's mind.

Bascot looked down at her and said severely, "Do you want to continue being a bawd, Gillie?"

The girl hung her head and gave it a little shake, then mumbled, "No, sir, I don't."

"Then do you want to go back to your family?" Bascot asked more gently.

Gillie looked up at him, tears streaking her face. "No, sir. Me da'll beat me and that old hag he married will crow in my face forever. 'Twould be near as bad a life as a harlot's." She began to plead. "Isn't there some honest work I can do, sir? I don't mind what it is. I'm strong and willing. And I can clean and cook. Please, sir, don't you know of someone who will give me a place?"

Bascot looked at Ernulf. He knew the serjeant had a strong protective streak in him, especially for women and children. "Is there any need for another scullery wench in the castle kitchen, Ernulf? Or perhaps a girl to take out slops and help with the poultry?"

As Bascot had known, Ernulf, after a sympathetic look at the distraught girl, nodded his head. "I'll find somewhere to fit her in. Just as well keep her under our eye for the moment, in case the murderer thinks she's a threat. She'll be safer within the castle walls."

The serjeant gave Gillie a grim look. "But you listen to me, girl. You'll be doing only the job of work you're given and nothing else. If I hear of you lying on your back for any of my men, you'll be out the castle gates before you can pull your skirts down, do you hear?"

Ernulf's expression softened as Gillie promised contritely that she would do just as she was told. He then gave her over to the care of one of the grinning men-at-arms who had been standing on guard at the door, admonishing the soldier to take her straight to the cook. The chaplain, seeming relieved that his services were no longer required, made a hasty exit leaving Bascot, Ernulf and Gianni alone in the dingy cell.

"Well, we've found Brunner, but we're no further forward than we were before he was dead," Ernulf said.

"Perhaps we are," Bascot replied, "even if it does not seem so."

"How's that?"

"When I went through the hall last night, after I had seen Lady Hilde, I am sure I saw Conal and his mother both still there."

"They were. I saw them myself. Conal was playing chess with Richard Camville and his mother was keeping company with Lady Nicolaa and her sisters."

"Then it should not be too difficult to find out if they stayed the night."

"Richard and Conal were still playing when I made my last rounds. The ladies had gone to bed."

"Then I am sure there will be witnesses aplenty to where they all slept, with the castle being as crowded as it is. Neither Conal nor his mother could have left through one of the gates without one of your guards seeing them, could they?"

Ernulf gave the question consideration. "Not if they left through one of the main gates. There is the postern, of course, but I keep it locked against intruders. It would be unlikely either of them would have access to the key, or could unlock it without making a disturbance. For all that it's small, it's not much used and makes a racket when opened."

"Then whoever killed Brunner, it could not have been either de Kyme's wife or his stepson," Bascot said. He looked again at the parchment he held in his hand. "The person that killed the stewe-keeper and sent this are one and the same. By implication of the drawing of the alekeeper, Brunner's death is connected to the murders in the alehouse. If it could not have been either Conal or Lady Sybil, then it is one piece of proof for their innocence."

Ernulf looked doubtful. "De Kyme will say they used a minion."

"So he will, but it will be a feeble charge unless he can come up with the person who did the deed and then connect that person with his wife or Conal. I think, Ernulf, that our murderer has made his first mistake. Find out for me, if you can, whether Philip de Kyme stayed at his manor house last night. And where his nephew and cousin were. Also Hugh Bardolf."

"Bardolf? Surely you don't suspect him of having a hand in this?" Ernulf said with astonishment.

Bascot explained to him Hilde's opinion about the baron. "Even if he is not the one who did the deed, he may know more than he is telling. Especially if he has hopes of marrying his daughter to de Kyme once Sybil and Conal are disposed of."

Ernulf nodded. Throughout the exchange Gianni had been staring at them, listening to every word. His young face was strained, his dark eyes full of consternation. He tugged on Bascot's sleeve, and made a quick flurry of movements with his hands, rubbing the skin of his forearms and face and pointing at Bascot.

"What's troubling the lad?" Ernulf asked.

"He is frightened of the leprosy," Bascot replied.

"But why? He has not been in contact with the lepers and neither have you."

Bascot gave a short laugh. "No, but he knows I soon will be."

The serjeant looked at the Templar enquiringly. "Sometimes I think the boy knows me better than I know myself, Ernulf. I must go to the leper house. It is possible that one of the inmates or the monks that tend them saw something that may help us in our enquiries. I do not imagine your men stayed in the area long enough to ask many questions."

"No, and nor do I blame them," Ernulf replied. "They came at the monk's request, got the girl and left Brunner's body to be disposed of by the Priory. No one in his right mind would go into a leper house if he didn't have to. And neither should you. Lady Nicolaa would not ask it of any man, nor will she of you."

"I am a monk, Ernulf, just as those who go to care for

the lepers. Few of them take the disease, for God gives them his protection. I must trust that He will do the same for me."

"Sometimes it doesn't pay to stretch the Good Lord's patience too far," Ernulf muttered.

Bascot laughed. "I will be careful not to take unnecessary risks, I assure you."

The Templar looked down at Gianni, saw the boy's eyes were filled with tears. He knelt down beside the lad, clumsy on his ankle. "Do not fear, Gianni. God has led me into this mystery, I must believe that he will protect me while I try to unravel it. Stay with Ernulf until I return. I will not be long."

Twenty-two
✦✦✦

Unfortunately, Bascot did not learn any more about Brunner's assailant at the leper house. At the lazar community he was directed in his visit by the monk who had found Brunner, a Brother Thomas. The monk was a rubicund man with a rolling gait, who looked as though he would have been more at home on the deck of a ship than tending the sick. His face was broad and fat, and his tonsure left the remainder of his hair sticking up like stubble in a shorn field. He had a ready gap-toothed smile and pudgy, capable hands. Only the gentle expression in his dark grey eyes belied the roughness of his exterior, along with the caring manner in which he treated his patients.

The lazar houses were within a low-walled enclosure and were of simple construction, but clean and dry. On the south side, at the far end of the main buildings, the enclosure opened out into a field in which there was a vegetable and herb garden and a byre which housed a few cows. Chickens clucked in a small coop and some sheep grazed in a walled pasture beyond the garden. Other monks were in evidence, tending to the chores of caring for the garden and animals helped by one or two inmates who were still well enough to do so, their diseased limbs wrapped in clean linen and large hats of straw shading their faces from the heat of the sun.

"The shack where the murdered man was found is beyond the pasture," Brother Thomas told Bascot. "There are a few tumbledown buildings there, which were once all that the lepers had to shelter them. When Hugh of Avalon became bishop of Lincoln some few years ago he was much distressed at the terrible state in which these poor unfortunates were living, so he chivvied the people of the town into giving enough material and alms to build the new hospice which you have just seen. He is a saintly man, the bishop. Would that all men were as good as he."

Brother Thomas led Bascot to the place where Brunner had been discovered. Gillie had been right, the buildings were hovels, most with caved-in roofs and insect-infested walls.

"It was I who found the dead man," Brother Thomas explained. "One of the sheep had strayed during the night and I was looking for it when I saw what I took to be a bundle of clothes in the grass. I thought perhaps some kind soul had left them as a gift for the community and went to examine them. It was then that I discovered the terrible deed that had been done."

"And the girl?" Bascot enquired. "How did you know she was in the shack?"

"I did not. I merely went in to see if the dead man had perhaps left some clue to his identity in there. Inside I found the girl, lying on the floor, bound hand and foot and too frightened to cry out for help. She was much distressed, poor creature."

Brother Thomas' face became solemn as he showed Bascot the interior of the shack. There was nothing inside, just a dirt floor on which was a pile of mouldy straw and the length of rope with which Gillie had been tied. There was no sign, either inside or out, of the blade that had ended Brunner's life.

"Do you have much trouble with beggars or other unfortunates using these shacks?" Bascot asked Thomas.

The monk's wide face creased into a smile. "No, we do not. There are few desperate enough to intrude so near the inmates of the hospice and risk infection. Besides, as you can see, there is little to make use of." He looked down sadly at the spot where he had found Brunner. "The slain man must have certainly been in dire circumstances to have sought refuge here."

"He was, Brother," Bascot replied. "And whoever killed him must have been just as desperate."

Bascot did not enter the hospice where those lepers too sick to leave their beds were tended by the monks. However, he still took the precaution of washing his hands in a laver of wine which was kept near the entrance. "We do not know how the disease is spread," Brother Thomas had told him, "but the ancient Greeks thought much of the cleansing properties of wine and so, under Bishop Hugh's instruction, we always wash our hands in it before we leave."

Bascot had thanked him and ridden slowly back to the castle, oblivious to the crowds in the town and conscious only on the periphery of his thoughts that his new boots made the effort of sitting in the saddle much easier. By the time he got back to the hall, tables were being set up for the evening meal and Gianni was waiting for him anxiously at the east gate instead of in his usual place among the dogs. Ernulf was nearby, talking to one of his men.

"The lad would not leave the gate, even when I tried to tempt him with something to eat," he told Bascot with a smile. "I reckon he thought you would be struck with the lepers' disease the moment you entered the hospice and be instantly confined there, never to return."

Bascot told the serjeant that he had discovered nothing

helpful and asked if it had been confirmed that Lady Sybil
and Conal had spent all of the evening and the night before
within the castle walls.

"It has," Ernulf said with some satisfaction. "Conal kept
company with Richard Camville until late, and then they
both retired to the same chamber together, along with another male guest who is staying here. Conal's mother went
to the room she shares with Lady Petronille and, unless she
be a wraith that can vanish through walls, never left it 'til the
morning. Because the chamber is cramped, Lady Petronille's maid had a pallet across the door. If anyone had left
the chamber in the night, she would have been woken."

"Then we know that they, personally, are innocent of
Brunner's death."

"It would seem so," Ernulf replied.

Alan de Kyme sprawled in a chair by an unlit hearth in
his small manor house, drinking a cup of weak ale, his foxy
face set in concentration. His wife sat nearby, repairing a
rent in one of her husband's old tunics while keeping a
watchful eye on their three children, who were playing
with a ball on the other side of the room.

"You've heard that the Templar has evidence that neither Sybil nor Conal were involved in this latest crime,"
Alan said to his wife.

"Doesn't mean they weren't involved in the other one,"
his wife responded shortly. She was like her husband in
features, with a similar pointed nose and sharp eyes, but instead of the flaming red hair that he possessed, hers was
dark, and her skin was sallow. She also had a less humor-
ous temperament than her husband.

"The Templar believes it does. He thinks the murders are
all connected—de Kyme's son, the priest and the stewe-
holder."

"If he knows so much, why doesn't he know who did
it?" his wife retorted sourly.

Alan de Kyme laid his finger alongside his nose in an artful manner. "Knowing is one thing, proving is another."

His wife's head came up sharply. "Do you think he does know, then?"

Alan shook his head gently. "I don't think so. But he's determined, I'll say that for him. If he doesn't find out it won't be for want of trying."

Alan's wife gave him a searching look from under her dark brows. "Do you know who it was, husband?"

"I could make a guess, if I had to," he replied in an off-hand manner.

"And who would it be, if you were to guess?" she enquired, her needle still, poised in midair as she waited for his answer.

"No, wife, not even to you will I name anyone. Could be dangerous. Look what happened to the priest and the stewe-holder. They knew who it was, like as not, and they were murdered because of that knowledge."

His wife looked thoughtful, then bent her head to her sewing once again, and kept her head lowered as she asked softly, "Alan, it wasn't you, was it?"

"Don't ask daft questions," her husband replied, the words sharp but his tone gentle. "I've enough problems without adding to them by skulking about murdering my cousin's bastard."

If his wife noticed that he had not given a direct answer to her question, she did not remark on it. Instead she turned the conversation to the problems he had mentioned. Holding up the tunic she was mending, she said, "This repair is all but done, Alan, but the fabric is overworn. I will need some cloth if I am to make you a new one, and also some material to sew clothes for the children. They will soon run naked without."

"I know, woman, I know," Alan said, a little testily. "If only that damned Jew had come here first before he got himself murdered we could have had the money he was bringing and denied receiving it to Isaac. It wasn't much, but with the loan the Jew will give us anew it would have got us not only some timber for the mill but a new ram as well as your lengths of cloth."

His wife sighed. "Are you sure you shouldn't ask Philip for the money instead, Alan?"

"Not the right time to ask," her husband said decidedly. "My cousin is awash with grief for a bastard son he never even laid eyes on. He's spent more on the trappings for laying that Hugo and his wife out in his chapel than he'd lend me in a score of years, the parsimonious wine-sop. Beeswax candles at the end of each bier, and not just one, mind you, but three. And the best of silk for the palls. No, I'll repair the mill with the money Isaac lends us, as we'd planned, and we'll have to hope for a good harvest this year for the rest."

"Perhaps Philip will make you his heir once his bastard's been buried," his wife opined hopefully.

"Not if Roger has his way, he won't," Alan said with a sudden grin. "Every time he goes to visit his uncle he brings that damned Arthur with him to dangle under Philip's nose. He doesn't realise Philip is usually too wine mazed to even notice the boy. Or Roger's fawning."

Alan held out his cup for his wife to refill. "And if you think we're badly off, you should see the condition of Roger's estate. The grain-stores are falling down, half his sheep have died from lack of care and I swear his stables haven't been mucked out for a month."

"Is he in debt to the Jews as well?" his wife asked.

"He is, and for more than the piddling amount I'm borrowing. If he doesn't come up with a payment on the interest soon, I think they'll be applying to the bailiff for redress."

"But he has that fine house in town," his wife protested. "How can he pay the upkeep on that if he is so far in debt?"

"I doubt he'll have it much longer if he doesn't find some way out of his troubles," Alan retorted.

His wife's face glimmered with resentment. "One solution would be for him to be named Philip's heir, wouldn't it?"

"So it would, wife, so it would. And it would be a way out of our problems if I was named instead."

Hilde was sitting in Nicolaa's solar, in company with Sybil and her attendant, Isobel. They were in a far corner of the room, well away from the huge fireplace, their only light a dim glow from the closest casement. At the other end of the chamber were a group of ladies, among them Nicolaa's sisters, Petronille and Ermingard. Most of the women were engaged in some pastime, embroidering or reading, a few others were gossiping and enjoying tidbits from trays of honeyed fruit. Two of the younger women were playing catch with a soft ball. Petronille was one of those sitting idly, watching her sister sort out the colours of a small box of embroidery thread. Ermingard had seemed better these last two days, and was bent intently to her task. Hilde noticed with a passing thought that she didn't seem disturbed in handling a skein of red wool, placing it on her lap with as much unconcern as she did those of blue or green.

"It is fortunate that the Templar has proved that neither I nor Conal could have been involved in the killing of that stewe-keeper," Sybil was saying. "It will take some weight out of the charge Philip has brought against us."

"Your husband can still claim you were responsible, and used a hired assailant to achieve your aim," Hilde replied.

Sybil leaned forward towards Hilde. "Yes, but at least we can prove that in this one death, neither of us was directly involved. And, as Nicolaa pointed out, all these deaths must be connected. To be cleared of one helps to clear us of the others."

Hilde made no response. She had little affection for Sybil, the only redeeming factor in her favour being that she had been Leif's wife and was Conal's mother. Hilde considered her a cold woman, although her fair beauty had been attractive when she was young, and was still, to a certain degree. Mentally Hilde dismissed the thought. Sybil was a Dane after all, and she was sister to Magnus and Ailwin. What else could one expect with such a bloodline?

She glanced at Sybil's attendant, Isobel, who was sitting with an open Psalter in her hands, her eyes downcast as she read. Now there, Hilde thought, was a completely different type of beauty to Sybil's. Warm colouring, rounded flesh, eyes the glowing colour of amber beads, all suggesting a passion that she either chose not to display or did not have. But if there was one thing that Hilde had learned in her long life it was that the appearance of a thing or person was often at variance with its nature. Her eyes flicked back to Sybil. Not for the first time she wondered if Conal's mother had been, after all, involved in the deaths of de Kyme's bastard and his wife. Conal had sworn to her that he was not and Hilde believed him, but Sybil had only denied the charge dismissively in her cool fashion. Was she involved with a man other than her husband, perhaps, and had persuaded her lover to remove the threat to her son's inheritance? Had she even helped him? After all, she had no one to account for her presence on the day the murders had been carried out.

On impulse, Hilde asked her great-niece-by-marriage a question. "Why have you stayed with Philip all these years, Sybil? No one would have blamed you if you had gone into a nunnery to escape a marriage that has gone more than sour."

Sybil gave her a glacial stare from her pale eyes. "If I had done as you suggest I would have given up any claim to the dower I brought with me. I could not do that. It is for Conal."

And Conal doesn't want it, Hilde thought. It was not your son you stayed for, madam, but yourself. Avarice is a strong trait in your family. You are just as grasping as your brothers, if more pleasant to look at.

Aloud, she said, "I have never been married, thanks be to God. But if I had been I do not think I could have found the fortitude to bed a man that held as much dislike for me as Philip seems to feel for you."

Sybil turned her gaze towards the women at the other end of the chamber. They were too far away to hear any of the conversation, but she lowered her voice a little as she said, "For all he rants that I have never given him a son, there have been few opportunities these last years to conceive one. In fact, there have been none at all since Conal was a young boy."

The statement didn't surprise Hilde. If the rumours about Philip de Kyme's excessive drinking were true, he must seldom be capable at the end of the day of bedding a woman. Especially a woman he appeared to have disliked from the very beginning of their marriage. Forcing her voice to sound jocular, Hilde remarked, "Then you might as well be in a nunnery. Many women in your situation would have taken a lover. There must be handsome young squires and sturdy grooms aplenty in a retinue the size of de Kyme's."

As Hilde spoke Isobel's eyes darted up from her book and looked with speculation at her mistress. Hilde wondered if her words had struck on a truth. But Sybil answered in a detached manner and the girl's eyes returned to her Psalter.

"I have been content alone," Sybil responded. "Were it not for the lack of a child, it would suit me very well."

"And Philip—is he chaste?"

"If he has a leman, I have not heard of her. But, truth to tell, I have never taken much trouble to find out. If he has one, he obviously hasn't sired a son on her, for I have no doubt if it had been so he would have boasted of the feat to all of Lincoln. And there would have been no need to send for Hugo."

Again Isobel's eyes gave a covert flicker in the direction of her mistress before returning to the written pages of her

Psalter. Some emotion had again been quickly masked. Was it speculative, as Hilde had first thought, or was there something else—contempt, perhaps, with maybe a trace of fear? Hilde nodded absently in agreement with what Sybil had said and turned her attention to the girl. "You are assiduous in your reading, Isobel. Do you not wish to indulge in a game, perhaps, like those two girls over there?" She nodded to the pair tossing a ball to and fro. "I am sure your mistress will excuse you if you wish to."

As Sybil started to give her assent, Isobel shook her head. "Thank you, lady, but no. I will gladly absent myself if you want to have private speech, but I have not a nature for playing games."

Sybil laughed. "I have exhorted her many times to entertain herself with something frivolous, Hilde. But she always declines, attending Mass twice as often as I or making herself busy with some other duty. It was with the greatest difficulty that I persuaded her to enjoy the fair that day I was so ill in Roger's house. As it turned out, I wish now that she had stayed by me. Her witness to my sickness would have proved my innocence in this whole affair of murder."

"Yes, that was unfortunate," Hilde responded absently, keeping her attention on Isobel. "Your diligence commends you, girl."

With a glance from her amber eyes Isobel thanked her for the compliment. Hilde studied her, remembering the looks the girl had flashed earlier at her mistress. It had been akin to panic, Hilde was sure. Did the maid know something about Sybil's habits that might prove incriminating, Hilde wondered? She resolved to get the girl alone as soon as she could and make an attempt to find out if a lover had been warming Sybil's empty bed.

Philip de Kyme stood in the small chapel that abutted his manor house and stared down at the spot where he had buried Hugo and his wife. A slab of expensive marble marked the place near the head of the nave, and it would be suitably inscribed by a skilled mason in a day or two. At the baron's side stood William Scothern, head bowed and hands clasped as he waited for his master to finish the prayer he was murmuring.

"Well, William," de Kyme said finally, "my only son is buried. I would wish it were my wife instead."

"She will be suitably punished by the justices, my lord," Scothern answered quietly.

"Aye, I am only sorry that her rank will probably prevent them from demanding her life," de Kyme replied. "Still, there is the comfort of knowing that my marriage will be dissolved. Not even our sanctimonious Bishop Hugh would demand I stay married to a wife who is guilty of murder."

"It will give you great pleasure to be free of her, my lord," Scothern replied smoothly.

De Kyme's wine-ravaged face lit up. "Aye, Will, great pleasure. The moment of our parting will be sweeter than a cup of nectar from the finest grapes of Auxerre. I will not carp at the cost of achieving it." He threw his arm around the shoulders of his *secretarius*. "And do not think I shall forget your loyalty throughout this matter. You have served me well, and shall be just as well rewarded."

Wine was also being mentioned in the Lincoln town house of Philip de Kyme's nephew, Roger. But it was about the lack of it.

"God's Blood, is there nothing but this soured ale to drink?" he demanded of his steward, an aging retainer with the shabby clothes and pained expression of a long-suffering servant.

"There was only a small store of wine put by, my lord," the steward replied. "And it was almost all used during the occasion of your uncle's last visit. The last was served at the evening meal yesterday."

At mention of his uncle, Roger's temper lightened. He

turned to his son, Arthur, who was keeping him company through the long hours of the afternoon, and said, "Philip's grief will ease now that he has buried his bastard. Soon, I think, he will realise that I am the only one of our family worthy to be named his heir. I should have been named so before this if my uncle had not decided to send for that wretched boy. Still, the bastard is well gone now, and not before time."

Arthur mirrored his father's expression. "Yes, father. It is your good fortune that he and the child his wife was carrying were murdered together. Once Lady Sybil and Conal are denounced there will be no one to stand in your way." The lad looked up at his father and said carefully, "Unless Sir Philip should marry again. He may yet father a legitimate child of his own."

Roger's heavy brows came down and met over the hook of his large nose. "He'll not marry again. Not while I am here to persuade him against it. I shall be his heir, and no one else, I tell you."

Arthur took a discreet course in his answer, recognising the blackness of his father's expression. "There is only you deserve to be such, Father," he said.

In the fine stone house of Isaac the Jew, Nathan was laying a soiled and malodorous purse in front of his brother.

"This is Samuel's?" Isaac asked, wrinkling his nose and touching the stained scrip with the tip of his forefinger.

"It is," Nathan said. "It is one I gave him myself."

"Where was it found?" Isaac asked.

"It was buried in the midden at the back of the alehouse."

"By the beard of Abraham, it must have been a brave man who searched for it," Isaac declared, moving back from the table to escape the stench that wafted up from the purse.

"It was necessary. The servant who found it waited until

the alewife was away from her yard, engaged with the attentions of her new admirer, Goscelin the baker."

"You were wise in your decision to search the premises, even though the Templar said he had done so and not found anything other than a scrap of cloth."

Nathan gave a grim smile. "There are places that a knight would not think of looking."

"So it seems," Isaac replied. "It was empty?" Nathan nodded. "And there was nothing else hidden with this?"

"My servant said not, although he claims he did not have much time to search the midden having, understandably, left it until last. But it may be that his stomach rebelled and he lacked the fortitude to be more diligent."

"I would not blame him, if that were the case." Isaac rose and walked a few paces, his robe billowing as he moved. Then he turned and came back to face his brother. "The Templar will have to be told of this," he said.

"I know," Nathan replied.

Twenty-three

✦

Bascot was thoughtful on his ride back to Lincoln from Alan de Kyme's messuage. The fief he had just seen was a small one, set some ways off the main road to Torksey, and gained by a narrow track that wound towards the central house and yard near the Trent River. As the Templar rode, he went over in his mind what Alan had told him. It had not been much. The baron's cousin had cheerfully said that he had been at home with his wife on the evening and night that Brunner had been murdered and, on the day that Hugo and his wife must have met their end, had been at work on his holding, preparing a few of his lambs for sale at the fair. His wife and two of his servants would vouch for him. Bascot knew they would be unlikely to gainsay his words, since their own meagre livelihood depended on him.

"I can't prove I didn't kill them, Templar," Alan had said with a crafty smile, "but neither can you prove that I did."

One piece of information was new, however. Alan had told Bascot that his manor house had been the destination that day of the Jew, Samuel. "He was to bring me a small loan of silver I needed for repairs to my mill," Alan had said. "He never reached here, although I don't suppose you'll believe that. I only wish he had. One dead Jew and no proof on him that I had received the money would have fitted me fine. But I never saw him. And that you can believe."

As he neared the junction of the narrow dirt road from Alan de Kyme's property and the Torksey road, Bascot noticed a small track leading back through the trees and thick underbrush in the direction of the river. He had seen a few such, all leading off the main road in the same general direction, and this was no different except it looked less used. Bringing his mount to a halt, he dismounted and walked a short way up the track. It seemed no more than a faint trail, with a few barely discernible marks of passage by either man or animal. He stopped and looked to the west, enjoying the silence and the fresh breeze while he thought. The river was close at this point, no more than a mile distant. Easy access for fishing. Or to snare the birds that inhabited the marshy ground close to the river. Or for someone who had need of a boat.

Bascot walked back to his horse and remounted. He believed he had just found the way that the dead Jew, at least, had been brought back to Lincoln.

Ernulf was waiting for him when Bascot returned to Lincoln Castle. "There is a Jew come for you. Says that Isaac sent him with a message. He won't give it to anyone but you."

The young Jewish boy waiting near the barracks was relieved to see Bascot. He had been there some time and being the only Jew in the midst of so many Christians was unnerving him. Hastily he handed Bascot the roll of parchment with which Isaac had entrusted him, then bolted off on a dead run out of the bail.

After reading the words written on the scroll, Bascot turned to Ernulf. "Send two men to arrest the alewife, Agnes. Bring her here and incarcerate her in your holding cell. Leave her alone, with no comfort of either food or drink. Then go yourself and fetch her sister, Jennet. Tell the sister that we have Agnes locked up and I wish to speak with her before I hand Agnes over to Roget. I'll be waiting in the armoury."

Bascot used the time while he waited for Ernulf to return to think. When Ernulf finally ushered Jennet in before him, Bascot was ready for her.

"You have been told your sister is being kept confined?" he asked.

Jennet nodded. "What is it that she has done, sir? I thought you were satisfied she had no involvement in those . . . those deaths."

"I was. Now I am not." Bascot walked to where shirts of mail hung on their crucifix-shaped holders. Beside them dangled the complicated trappings of a score of arbalests, the metal quarrels used to load them resting neatly on shelves nearby, well greased as preservation against rust. Lances were stacked in a corner, lengths of chain were coiled on the floor and a mound of leather wrist guards spilled from an open sack. Bascot picked up a sharpening stone from a pile that lay there and, taking his dagger from his belt, began to hone the blade, glancing at Jennet as he did so.

"Your sister has consistently lied to me. First about where she was on the night the bodies were left in the alehouse and then about the fact that she had nothing to do with the slayings."

"I know she lied in the first instance, my lord," Jennet said nervously, eyeing the dagger. "She was frightened, that is all. But she told the truth in the end, I am sure. Just as I am sure that she could not have had a hand in the murders. It is not in her nature, my lord . . ."

"Her nature, woman, is to lie." Bascot tested the edge of his blade with the ball of his thumb and replaced it in its scabbard, throwing the sharpening stone back onto the pile of others as he did so. "The dead Jew's scrip was found on the alehouse premises. It was in a place that she claimed to have overlooked the whole night long, so no one—neither her dead husband, nor the man she claimed killed him—could have put it there without her seeing it done. Does not that, along with all her other lies, suggest to you that she was involved in these murders?"

Jennet looked at him grimly. "If I were you, my lord, I would believe that it did. May I ask what you are going to do with her?" Her voice quavered slightly as she asked the question.

"For the moment, mistress, that depends on you," Bascot said. "I have no more use for your sister's caterwauling and pretense of grief. You will go to her directly and get the truth out of her. If what she tells you does not satisfy me I shall turn her over to Roget, who will, in turn, hold her for trial at the assizes. Until that time she will be held in the sheriff's gaol in the town, along with any other prisoners he may have there. I will give Roget leave to try any method he desires to persuade her to tell what really happened to her husband and the others. Do you understand me, mistress?"

Jennet's pale complexion turned ashen. "I do, my lord."

"Ernulf will take you to your sister and leave you alone with her for the time it takes him to drink a sup of ale. You will get this one opportunity, and this one only, to speak to her. If you value your sister's comfort, I suggest you use it wisely."

"I will, my lord." She turned to go but Bascot stopped her. "What was the alekeeper's trade before your sister married him?"

Jennet looked at him in surprise. "Wat? He were a wherry man, sir. Had an old boat he used to hire himself out on to haul goods for a short distance. That's how Agnes met him. She had some kegs of ale to be taken up the Foss-dyke to a customer who lived on the other side. Wat didn't make much of a living out of it. Reckon when he met Ag-nes he saw a good chance to improve himself, and have all the ale he wanted into the bargain. She always was foolish about men," she added bitterly.

"This boat—where is it now?"

Jennet shook her head. "I wouldn't know, sir. He had a place for it somewhere on the river, t'other side of the stone bridge. Agnes did tell me that they still used it sometimes, to carry her ale, but not so much lately since she had made herself such good customers in the town. Is it important, sir? Should I ask Agnes about it as well as . . . as well as about the other, sir?"

"Not yet," Bascot said. "If I fail to be satisfied with what she tells you, there will be time enough to ask her about the boat when she is in Roget's care."

Jennet suppressed a shudder, then went to where Ernulf was waiting by the door, squaring her shoulders as she came up to him. "Take me to my sister, if you please, ser-jeant. And you don't have to take overlong with your ale while you wait. I will make it clear to Agnes that there is no more time left to waste."

"Apparently, when the alewife found the three dead strangers on her taproom floor, she took the scrips of each one, removed what was valuable and burned or buried the rest," Bascot told Hilde later that morning. "There was some silver in the Jew's purse, a few coins in Hugo's and a comb made from bone along with a pot of unguent and the little brooch in the girl's. There was also a piece of parch-ment in the purse of de Kyme's son, with some writing on it, but Agnes cannot read, so she burnt it."

"Are you sure she is now telling the truth?" Hilde asked.

"I think so." Bascot smiled. "Ernulf waited outside while Jennet went in to Agnes. He said there was no crying or wailing from the alewife this time, just the sound of two or three hefty slaps being administered, and then she told her tale to her sister as meekly as a babe."

"So we now know it was intended that the bodies be identified as soon as they were found. The parchment was most likely one of de Kyme's letters inviting the boy to Lincoln."

As Bascot nodded in agreement, Hilde called to her maid, Freyda. They were sitting in the privacy of Hilde's chamber, with only the maid and Gianni in attendance. On the floor was a basket of plums which the boy was rapidly popping, one after another, into his mouth.

"Some wine, Freyda," Hilde ordered. "And some of those cakes you brought up from the kitchens this morning.

When the refreshments had been served, Hilde leaned back in her chair. "You have done well, Templar. Now, I would like to hear about the boat."

Bascot told her that the boat that had belonged to Wat had been found at a mooring near the Lincoln end of the Fossdyke. "It had empty ale barrels fore and aft, and a canopy under which it would have been possible to secrete three people, unseen by any passerby or the occupant of another boat."

"And you think that was how Hugo and his wife were brought to Lincoln? By boat?"

Bascot nodded. "I think they were brought upriver alive—probably willingly and thinking themselves making the last stage of their journey—then given a potion that either rendered them unconscious or killed them. They were then put into barrels on the boat, which the alekeeper offloaded onto his wagon before driving into town."

"Then the bodies were never at Roger de Kyme's town house?"

Bascot shrugged. "Perhaps, or not, it makes no matter.

Wat may have left them there while he made his other deliveries to prevent them being discovered on his premises. Or he may simply have left them on the wagon until night fell."

"But what about the Jew? It is certain he was never on a boat."

"No, but he was on the Torksey road, and close to the river. Whoever hired Wat needed to meet the alekeeper at some point, either to carry out the killing, or to help convince the victims that they were being taken to de Kyme's residence. If Samuel saw that person, or persons, making their way down to the river by one of the paths from the Torksey road, he would have been a witness as to their whereabouts at the crucial time. He could not be left alive to recall their presence later, and tell of it."

"Yes, it all fits," Hilde remarked. "What about the harlot's gown, and the stabbings? I can see no reason for either. Why not simply leave the bodies in the alehouse and the girl in her own clothing?"

Bascot allowed Freyda to refill his wine cup before answering. "I think it was done as part of the story that was told to Wat. He was a willing accomplice and expected to be alive the next morning when the bodies were found. He may have been told that the purpose of the slayings were for a different reason altogether—that the girl was a harlot, perhaps, and she and Hugo were, say, trying to extort money by threatening a person of importance with revelations of the baby's true father. It might have been that Wat was going to explain their presence in the alehouse by saying that Hugo had hired the taproom for a private meeting, and Wat had come down in the morning to find them dead. Slain by a person whose identity he did not know and had never seen. That would explain the gown, to convince Wat of the girl's calling. As for the stab wounds, just another piece of frippery to give weight to his story, and confuse him as to the real issue."

Hilde thought over what he had said, absently holding out her own cup to Gianni for refilling. The boy responded quickly, staring at the silver raven's head on her cane as he handed her the replenished cup. She noticed his look and laughed.

"Would you like to touch it, boy?" she asked.

Gianni nodded solemnly and went nearer, reaching out one forefinger to touch the gleaming metal reverently. Hilde placed her old hand, gnarled and bent with age, over his young one and gently curled his fingers around the beak. "You may hold it, boy. Keep it ready for me when I have need to use it."

Bascot thought that even the new shoes with the red beads had not brought such a look of delight to Gianni's face. Carefully he took up the cane and sat down on the floor beside Hilde's chair, holding the raven's head delicately between his hands, the staff of the cane lying across his knees. Hilde looked down at him indulgently, rewarded with a smile of such sweetness from Gianni that it took Bascot by surprise.

"You are the first person, lady," he said, "that I have ever seen him so at ease with."

"It is my age, and my sex, Templar. I am not a threat to him and so he is comfortable."

She returned to the matter they had been discussing. "Then you know the manner of the deaths, and how they were accomplished. But that does not bring you closer to the knowledge of who is responsible."

Bascot made his next observation carefully. "It is probable they came upriver from some town farther south—Grantham, perhaps, or Stamford, or . . . Newark."

Hilde's eyes flashed at him. "And Conal was in Newark on that day." She made the statement sound like an accusation.

"He was, lady," Bascot said gently. "And has yet to give an explanation as to what he was doing there."

"No, he has not," Hilde replied. "But I know where he was all the same." Bascot looked at her attentively. "Richard Camville told me, in confidence." She sighed. "And, if I am to share information with you, as you have done with me, I must reveal what I was told."

Bascot waited for her to continue. "Conal was insistent that he was innocent, and I believed him, but I knew that he was keeping something back, something that may have implicated someone else—his mother, perhaps. I tackled young Richard and he told me where Conal was, where he goes rather often, it seems. It is to visit a young woman."

As Bascot started to interrupt, she held up her hand. "No, Templar, it is innocent enough, and has no connection with the murders. It seems young Conal believes himself in love and, with the silly notions of chivalry that our king's mother has made popular with her songs and courts of love, he believes he is protecting the girl by keeping her identity a secret."

"Is she married?" Bascot asked.

"No, but she is a cripple," Hilde replied. "Her foot, at birth, was thickened and twisted, so that one leg is shorter than the other and she can walk only with great difficulty. Her mother died giving her life, and her father, who is a prominent goldsmith in Newark, has kept her virtually imprisoned in his house since she was born for shame at her appearance. Richard tells me that Conal met her on a day when she was sitting in her garden and, from the other side of the wall, he heard her singing. Intrigued, he climbed up to find the owner of the voice and saw her. Since then he has been meeting her secretly. Her father does not know of his attentions, only one elderly servant who is the girl's sole companion is privy to the liaison.

"Conal believes that if he tells of the girl, she may be forced to come and give witness before the justices. If that were necessary, she would be subjected not only to her father's wrath but to the gawking and ridiculing eyes of the

world. Conal has said he would rather be found guilty of
the crime than force that upon her. Richard believes it is
Conal's intention to make the girl his wife, and that he
would have done so before now but that he feared the scorn
that would be heaped on his mother's head by Philip de
Kyme."

Hilde leaned back in her chair. "What follies we commit
when we are young. I have told Richard to let Conal know
that if he wishes to marry the girl, he has my blessing. I do
not doubt that Magnus and Ailwin will be swift to give
theirs also, since the girl's father is prosperous and would
likely provide a rich dower for connection with a knight's
family. Once he has got over his anger at being deceived,
that is."

Bascot digested her words, then said slowly, "As wealthy
as her father may be, it cannot compare with that of Philip
de Kyme. Conal has, after all, only a young girl who loves
him and her old servant to prove the truth of his claim. It
will be said they are lying."

Wearily Hilde nodded her head. "I know, Templar. I
know. But for your purposes, at least, I implore you to believe him."

Bascot smiled at her. He could see that the fear of her
great-nephew's involvement in this crime had taken its toll
of the old lady's meagre strength. "I think I must do, lady.
If for no other reason than, as Conal himself said, that if it
had been he that had done the deed he would have merely
left the bodies to rot in the greenwood."

Hilde's spirits revived at her companion's acceptance of
Conal's innocence. "That is the thing that puzzles me,
Templar. If the young man was truly de Kyme's bastard
son, why the haste to kill him, and for his body to be
quickly found? Such elaborate trappings to despatch him
must have a reason. Even if he had arrived and been received with due honour by Philip, surely it would have
been easier to let fly an arrow during a hunt, or slip some

potion in his wine cup one evening. Why all the involvement of Wat and the alehouse? Why the need for such
speed?"

As Hilde finished speaking, Gianni, from his position
on the floor, tugged timidly at her skirts. She looked down
and Gianni folded his arms and rocked them back and
forth, as though he held a babe and were soothing it.

Hilde laughed. "Of course, lad. You are right. Hugo's
wife was pregnant. The child could not be allowed to be
born. That would have provided another heir that needed to
be disposed of." Her cornflower blue eyes flashed at Bascot. "Or Philip de Kyme knew the dead pair for impostors
and did not wish to be forced to have the child of a stranger
declared his grandson."

Bascot leaned back and rubbed the leather patch over
his missing eye. The more he discovered about the murders, the more complicated the matter became. It made the
empty socket where his eye had been ache with frustration.

Twenty-four
✛

Bascot sat with Hilde for a short while longer. She told him of her suspicions of Sybil and that she could find no gossip of Philip de Kyme's having a leman.

"Incidentally," she added. "Philip is back in Lincoln. He is staying with his nephew, Roger, who is riding in the tourney. Philip intends to come and watch him. He will not, however, go to the castle, since Sybil and Conal are there, but I understand he allows Will Scothern to visit his sister."

Since it would still be some days before they would have an answer from the Templar preceptor, d'Arderon, about Bascot's enquiries in La Lune, they then pondered on the question of whether Hugo and his female companion were impostors or not and, if they were genuine, who could have been aware of Hugo's intent to come to England. Even though William Scothern had insisted that he had told no one of the correspondence between the baron and his former lover it was possible, probable even, that Philip had spoken of the matter while deep in his cups.

"Apparently, he was always baiting Conal and Sybil,

saying he had the ways and means to free himself from them," Hilde remarked. "It would not have been surprising if he had revealed the existence of his illegitimate son while drinking with his cronies."

"I did not find out much else of pertinence," she went on, her face a mask of disappointment. "I did get the impression that Sybil's maid, Isobel, is hiding something, but what it is, or its importance, I could not determine. The girl wears her piety like a mask, shielding her thoughts behind her Psalter. She should have been a nun, for all she has the face and body of a temptress. Matilda Bardolf is rumoured to have had lovers, but there is no one named. She is enamoured of Richard Camville, so the gossip mongers opine, but he does not return her fancy. It is also said that she and Isobel do not like each other, but that perhaps is because I have seen the glances of appreciation that Richard gives to Sybil's maid. Since Nicolaa's son is appreciative of any woman with a soft cheek and pretty eyes, it seems rather pointless of Matilda to harbour enmity towards just one, but perhaps that is because he is often near Isobel, when he and Conal are in company together."

She sighed. "It seems I have not been as much use to you as I had thought to be, Templar."

Bascot assured her of his appreciation of her efforts, reminding her that although he had discovered how the murders were carried out, he, like herself, had come no nearer to uncovering who had caused the deaths. He left the chamber, the socket of his eye still aching, intending to return to the solitude of his own chamber, but coming down the steps of the forebuilding outside the keep, he met Ernulf coming in search of him.

"Anselm is dead," the serjeant said. "A young brother from the priory came to inform Lady Nicolaa. Breathed his last just before Tierce. The monk said that he never regained consciousness. Just slipped away, easy as you please. God assoil him," Ernulf added as he crossed himself.

"Amen," Bascot said, bowing his head for a moment in silent prayer.

"That now makes six murders we've had," Ernulf declared roughly. "The devil's loose in Lincoln for this fair."

"Where is Lady Nicolaa?" Bascot asked.

"She's in the herb garden with her sisters. Said to tell you to attend her there. She's much concerned at the priest's death, I can tell you. All this mayhem will not be well received by the king, or Bishop Hugh, come to that, when he returns." As usual, the serjeant's thoughts were for the discomforts his mistress would endure; pity for the dead came second to his loyalty to Nicolaa.

Bascot crossed the bail and made for the walled enclosure at the far end. A small gate led inside, where the sweet smell of herbs was strong and pleasant. He found Nicolaa and Petronille sitting on a stone seat in the light of the morning sun. Ermingard was on her knees beside a patch of mint, plucking the leaves and placing them in a small basket standing on the ground nearby. Bascot walked to where Nicolaa sat, the heady aroma of thyme pungent as his feet bruised the profusion of bushy plants that carpeted the enclosure.

Nicolaa returned his words of greeting absently. "This is a bad business, de Marins. We must discover who murdered these people, and the priest. Have you anything new to report?"

"Beyond what I told you of the boat and how I believe that Samuel came to be with Hugo and his wife, no," Bascot replied. "I am sorry for Anselm. Not only for the loss of his life, but that I had hoped he might be able to tell us who it was that attacked him. I have always felt that his stabbing was somehow connected to the deaths in the alehouse. He was close by. He may have seen something or someone, perhaps without knowing the importance of it, which made him dangerous to the murderer."

"Well, it is too late for him to tell us of it now," Petronille said sadly. Her kind face was drawn in sympathetic lines, unlike her sister Nicolaa's, whose capable countenance was tight with anger.

"The shame of it is that when Anselm was attacked, we took no note of the whereabouts of those we now believe may have been involved," Bascot said, his voice mirroring the futility evident in Nicolaa's face. "It was too soon. We did not know that the dead boy would be claimed as Philip de Kyme's son, or how the boy and the others had come to be in the alehouse. If we had, more attention might have been paid to those who may have had the opportunity to go to the church and attack Father Anselm."

"There was much activity that night, de Marins," Nicolaa said. "The town was in a turmoil preparing for the fair, and the alarm of the murders made for more confusion. There were many people in the hall—Philip and Sybil, Conal, Hugh Bardolf and his daughter, even Roger de Kyme, among them. Alan de Kyme was not there, but will most likely claim that, like the night before, he was preparing his stock for sale at the fair. But even of those who were present, it would be almost impossible now to remember if all were in sight all of the time. The church where Anselm was priest is not far away. Any of them could have slipped out for a space and not been missed."

"It was just before Vespers, was it not, that the priest was stabbed?" Petronille asked. "If we put our minds to it, Nicolaa, perhaps we can remember who was with us then. It will not give us any harm to try."

Nicolaa leaned back on the warm stone of the seat, closing her eyes for a moment in thought. "Gerard was talking to Richard, I think, and Conal was with them. Roger de Kyme I seem to recall seeing, but at what particular moment, it is hard to place. And shortly afterwards the representatives of the townspeople came with their complaints. And there was the storm, too."

She and Petronille went through as many of the people

they could recall as having been present, but could vouch for the constant presence of none of them. "Besides," Nicolaa added, "it will be easy enough for any of them to lie if they have something to hide . . ."

Ermingard's voice suddenly interrupted them. "*She* lied. I know she did because it was the wrong colour."

The two women and Bascot started at the words. They had all but forgotten the presence of the youngest Haye sister. She had been in a more composed frame of mind for the last two days, and had moved about the keep in company with Petronille in a withdrawn, but unmazed, manner. She looked at them now out of eyes clear of confusion, her words deliberate and coherent.

"What do you mean, Mina?" Petronille asked her. "You were not in the hall that afternoon, you were resting, don't you remember?"

Petronille spoke to Bascot. "My sister was very upset at the news of the murders. I persuaded her to lie down for awhile to calm her mind."

Petronille did not add that later that evening Ermingard had been found wandering the corridors in the middle of the night, but it was in all of their minds.

"The cloak," Ermingard insisted, "she said it was Sybil's, but it was not. It was the wrong colour. Sybil is all fair and light, like ice. She would never have worn it. A dirty brown colour, the shade of old dried blood." She shuddered. "And it was wet, I picked it up after she left. The blood stained my hands. Ah, I scrubbed at it, but still it stayed there, on my fingers."

Ermingard's voice faltered. Her expression became clouded. Petronille rose quickly and went to her, putting her arm about her. "Don't talk about it, lovey," she said soothingly. "It only distresses you."

"But I must. She lied, I keep telling you," Ermingard wailed.

"Perhaps if you tell us who it is you are speaking of we

could help you," Petronille suggested, trying to calm her sister's rising terror. But the only answer Ermingard gave was to shake her head and begin to weep.

"She will not tell you, Petra. She never does, no matter how many times we ask," Nicolaa said. "It is these murders," she murmured to Bascot. "That is what has unsettled her mind.

"Take her inside, Petra," Nicolaa said to her sister. "We should not have discussed the matter in front of her. I had forgotten she was there, how it might affect her."

Petronille persuaded the confused Ermingard to her feet, began to lead her towards the gate, but her sister balked a little. "It is not my imagination. She *did* lie. It was *her* cloak. *And* she is pregnant." With this last statement Ermingard's voice became sly, like a child trying to divert punishment by revealing a playmate's wrongdoing. "I saw her, winding strips of linen about her waist under her gown to hide the thickening of her flesh. She thinks no one knows. But I know. And I know what it will be like when she has the baby. There will be blood. Just like there was when I had Ivo . . ."

Ermingard's voice had begun to rise, the note of hysteria increasing. Petronille became a little more forceful, pressing her sister towards the opening in the wall, but with little success. Nicolaa rose and went to the pair. When she spoke, her voice was low and sharp, the same tone that Bascot had heard her use to a servant that had been slipshod. "Mina! You will be quiet and go with Petra and do as she tells you. Do you understand?"

Ermingard recoiled, as though Nicolaa had slapped her, but she calmed and slowly nodded her head. "Yes, Nicolaa," she said obediently, but then added in a low voice with a touch of her former defiance. "But I still say it was the wrong colour."

Nicolaa relented and patted her youngest sister on the shoulder. "We believe you, Mina. But now you must forget about it all and put your mind to something else. Petra will get you some camomile posset and read to you. You will like that, won't you?"

Ermingard nodded and finally allowed herself to be led away. Nicolaa returned to her seat by Bascot. "I love my sister, but I pity poor de Rollos. She is so confused. First the murders, then we learned that the dead girl in the alehouse was pregnant. It has brought Ivo's birthing back to her, and the attendant shedding of her own blood." She shook her head sadly. "It may be she picked up a cloak of such a colour as she describes and it was wet, and now she has muddled that and the birthing in her mind, believing it to be blood. Poor Mina. It cannot be easy for a husband to have such a one for a wife."

Bascot made no comment. The incident had deepened the lines of strain on Nicolaa's face. She rose and walked a pace or two, then turned to him. "Go on with your enquiries, de Marins. And let us pray to God most fervently that there are no more murders."

Bascot left, his head and eye socket still aching, wanting only the privacy of his chamber. With Gianni in tow he went back to the old tower and they climbed the stairs to their room. There he lay down on the narrow mattress of his bed while Gianni plopped down on the floor, taking from under his own pallet a small store of scraps of old parchment on which he practised his letters, along with a quill and pot of ink kept in a small wooden box. The parchment was much used, its surface scraped bare of ink at least two or three times and very thin. Gianni contemplated his last efforts, a copy of three verses from one of the Psalms, slowly tracing the words with his forefinger, brows furrowed in concentration, before putting the parchment down beside him and picking up the pen and beginning slowly and carefully to copy the words once more. Bascot felt the ache in his eye socket easing and enjoyed the cool breeze that was coming through the high slit window above him. Slowly his good eye closed and he felt himself slipping into a light doze.

This state of sleep he found enjoyable. In it the dreams that appeared in his mind were seen with two good eyes, not just the half-view of one. For a time the scenes were a jumble, a nonsense of pictures—the mane of a horse, the long face of the cobbler's son superimposed over that of the elderly knight he had dined with in the hall, a notion of the smell of the sea and the heaving of waves—all accompanied by an awareness of the light scratching of Gianni's pen. In his mind he saw the boy's hand as he played his stone game, the pebbles going up in the air, Gianni's hand palm side up, then palm side down, the constant reversing and turning as the pebbles were caught and thrown, balanced and then thrown yet again, over and over, the fingers young and supple, flexing and straightening. The motion mesmerized him and he felt himself slipping deeper and deeper into sleep . . .

Bascot was not sure how long he dozed, but felt himself dragged up from a deep slumber by the sound of footsteps on the stone of the landing outside the door and then a voice speaking to Gianni. Bascot opened his eye. It was Ernulf.

"Sorry to disturb you," the serjeant said. "Sheriff Camville sent me. He wants to know if you will consent to be one of the judges at the tourney tomorrow. Since most of the barons will have a son or some other relative in the melee, he cannot ask any of them for fear of bias. The winner's purse is a good size, and he must have men of experience and impartial judgement to fill the posts. As a Templar, your decision would be respected. He also intends to ask d'Arderon."

Bascot got up from his bed, his head still half muzzy from sleep. "Tell Sir Gerard I will be honoured to assist him, Ernulf. And grateful. It will be a welcome diversion for my disordered mind."

Ernulf grinned in response and left the chamber. Suddenly the room felt hot and airless to Bascot. Motioning to Gianni to continue with the practice of forming his letters, Bascot went out and up onto the roof. On the top of the tower the air was clearer and the sun beat down strongly. Although the breeze was fresh, it was warm, almost humid. Bascot limped over to the edge of the parapet, and leaned into the gap of the crenel, breathing deeply to steady the familiar dizziness that assailed him. He thought of the men that would be fighting tomorrow, young men, whole in limb and sound of faculties. He did not begrudge them their vitality for once he had been such as they, but he suddenly felt old, and it unsettled him.

He should not have slept in the afternoon. It had made him discomfited. The thought of disrupted sleep returned his mind to Ermingard. Her fear of blood, the nightmares she must endure, fuelled by the murderer abroad in Lincoln. He could feel empathy for her. Many times he had been near the edge of madness himself during the long years of his imprisonment by the Saracens. Slivers of his dreams intruded on his train of thought, disjointed now that he was awake. Again the water, but this time accompanied by the sound of rain, swirling in muddy pools. The glisten of a knife blade.

Bascot stood at the parapet, forcing himself to focus his attention on the panorama of Lincoln stretched out below him on the southern sweep of the hill. A flock of starlings swooped and wheeled above the buildings. He could make out the broad arc of Danesgate as it went down the slope past the small bell tower of the church where Anselm had officiated. Unbidden, his mind returned to contemplation of how to find the malefactor who was responsible for the murders. Somehow, he was sure, the priest had been connected to the deaths in the alehouse. But how? Somewhere there was a connection, some fact he had missed, or not taken note of. But what?

Bascot closed his sighted eye against the dizziness that resurged with the focusing of his thoughts, absently rubbing the leather patch that covered his empty eye socket. A red glow from the bright sunlight beating against the lid of his good eye suffused his inner vision, merging with the constant blackness of the unsighted side as he struggled to bring some order to his speculations.

Anselm had been the first to be told of the bodies in the alehouse, by Agnes, the alewife. The day had passed, during which he and Gianni had discovered that the bodies of the four dead had been brought there in the casks that were used to transport the ale. The priest had been alone and unharmed before Vespers, when Bascot had gone to the church and asked where Agnes could be found. Then, but a short while later, he had been stabbed, and Bascot had gone back to the church where he had met Roget and the alewife had told a little more of the truth she had been withholding. He had felt extremely angry, Bascot remembered, at having to order the screeching woman dragged back to the church in the rain.

The rain. Ermingard had said the cloak she had seen was wet. Whoever had attacked Anselm would have been caught in the downpour as he left the church. And the elderly knight he had sat with at table had advised Bascot to look for a woman. Could the offhand remark be right?

Ermingard had said the woman of whom she spoke was with child. Perhaps he should be looking for a pregnant woman. If Anselm was a lecher, had he made one of his flock pregnant? Then been killed by an irate male relative of the girl? But, if that were so, what connection would there be with the other murders? It was only his own instincts that made him think there was such a connection. And between Anselm and Brunner? The dead girl in the alehouse had been pregnant. Perhaps if she hadn't been there would not have been such haste to kill her. But once she was dead, and the baby with her, then why the urgency for the bodies to be found?

The view of Lincoln faded from Bascot's awareness as a new thought formed. Perhaps the haste had been not to kill Hugo's pregnant wife before their baby was born, but to have them dead before it was time for *another* woman to be brought to her birthing. He had been looking for the murderer amongst those who would benefit by becoming de Kyme's heir, but what if that heir had yet to be born?

His thoughts chased up and down like Gianni's hand in the stone game. That day in the solar, when Ermingard had become distressed—where had she been looking when she had become so insistent about the wrong colour? It had been suggested that it was the tapestry about which she had been rambling, but perhaps it had not been the bright colour of red depicted in the embroidered picture. Perhaps the person she would not, or could not, name had been present. Who had been there? Bascot thrust his mind back to that morning—his own embarrassment, the air of tension. Following that line of reasoning, the motive for the murders took on a different slant, and he juggled the people that he and Hilde had suspected with others hitherto dismissed as of no importance. The shadow cast by the sun on the stone of the parapet had moved a good measure before he suddenly threw up his head and took a deep breath of air. He had found the connection he had been looking for.

Twenty-five
⤞⤝

HILDE LISTENED INTENTLY AS BASCOT EXPLAINED WHO he believed had committed the murders and his reasons for thinking so. When he had finished, she nodded. "Yes, Templar. It all fits. Like a rotten plum hidden deep in a basket, hard to find until one tastes it and knows it to be rank."

They were sitting in Hilde's chamber, alone. Gianni had been left in Bascot's room and admonished to keep practising his letters while Hilde's servant, Freyda, had been sent to keep watch outside the door while her mistress and Bascot talked together. The old lady had herself poured the wine they were drinking from a pair of small cups decorated with silver gilt.

"Will you go to the sheriff with your findings?" Hilde asked.

"I cannot, not yet," Bascot replied. "First I must have proof. Even if Camville agrees with me, he must have some evidence to lay a charge."

Hilde held out her cup for Bascot to refill. "Such proof will be hard to find," she said.

"Unless we devise some," Bascot answered quietly.

Hilde's bright blue eyes regarded him. "You have thought of a means of doing that?" she asked disbelievingly.

"If my instinct is true and the stabbing of Father Anselm is connected to the other murders—for something he may have unwittingly seen or heard that constituted a threat—then I think I have. But I shall need your help to make it convincing, if you are willing."

"You shall have every assistance I can give you, Templar," Hilde assured him. She leaned forward. "Now, tell me what it is that I must do."

The great hall was crowded that night, full almost beyond capacity, just as it had been on the eve of the fair. All those who had been deemed to have any connection with the murders were present, even Philip de Kyme, who had been persuaded to join the company by Gerard Camville with the promise that his wife and stepson would be seated well away from him and warned not to approach the baron under any circumstances. Outside there had been a light shower of rain, not sufficient to threaten the tourney that was to take place on the morrow, but heavy enough to lessen the heat that had gathered by the end of the day. Once the meal was over, the trestle tables were cleared from the middle of the huge room and minstrels were summoned to play while members of the company danced or just listened to the music. Nicolaa and her husband presided over the company, making a point of moving about amongst their guests and engaging most of them in conversation.

Hilde was there also, leaning heavily on the arm of her great-nephew, Conal, as she walked about the room. Finally she asked him to seat her with a group of guests still sitting at a small side table, lingering over their wine in a desultory fashion. Hilde was unusually affable, leaning across to ask a question of one or the other of her companions, or to pay a compliment.

She sat for some little time in this manner, before leaning back and, under cover of the flow of conversation and
the strains of the music, said in a low voice to the person
who sat beside her, "I have much cause to rejoice this night.
Conal and his mother have been proved innocent, and the
identity of the true murderer discovered."

Furrows appeared between the brows of her companion,
but Hilde made it appear that she had not noticed and blithely
continued speaking. "It seems that the Templar was with
Father Anselm just before he died, and the priest told him
who it was that had stabbed him. De Marins believes that it
was the same person that killed de Kyme's son and his wife,
and says he has proof to support it. He told me privately
that the innocence of my relatives is now not in question,
although he would add nothing further. Of course, the Templar is a monk and must consider whether he can reveal
what Anselm told him in such extreme conditions, but
since he is not a priest he is not bound by the oath of the
confessional. I am confident that by morning he will tell
what he knows to Sheriff Camville and the murderer will
be arrested."

Hilde paused to let her gaze roam over the company before adding, with a smile of satisfaction, "Yes, even now,
de Marins is preparing to spend the night in a solitary vigil
before the altar of St. Clement's. God will guide him
aright, I am sure of it. By this time tomorrow, Conal and
Sybil will be free of the charge against them."

Just before midnight, Bascot put on the Templar surcoat
he had not worn since he had come to Lincoln. The red
cross emblazoned on the pristine white cloth of the coat
settled comfortably over his heart. He had not donned a
shirt of mail underneath, fearing it might warn the murderer he was expecting to be attacked and had, instead,
chosen to wear a well-padded gambeson under his dark-
sleeved tunic. With any luck it would provide as much, or

more, protection as the hair shirt Father Anselm had worn. Finally he smoothed his fingers through his hair and beard, adjusted his eye patch and left the room. The only weapon he carried was the short-bladed knife at his belt.

The sounds of revelry from the hall could be heard as he crossed the bail. The outbuildings were all but deserted, the servants of the castle either in attendance on the guests in the keep or asleep in their beds. Shortly before midnight Bascot let himself through the postern gate in the north wall and walked along the cobbled path that led to the small church of St. Clement. Near the entrance he could see two shadowy figures waiting for him. D'Arderon and a Templar priest.

As Bascot approached, the preceptor came forward and spoke quietly. "We are here, de Marins, as you asked. Where shall we keep watch?"

"The sacristy," Bascot replied. "The door is in the shadows. You can see out, but none can see in."

They went inside the church and d'Arderon and the priest crossed the nave, going to a small door near the altar. Just before he slipped inside d'Arderon turned and whispered a benediction. "God be with you, de Marins. And with this venture."

Once they were out of sight, Bascot knelt at the low rail in front of the altar, crossing himself and murmuring a prayer as he did so. The darkness inside the building was relieved only by the small glimmer of the sanctuary lamp and the larger brightness of one fat beeswax candle. Above the altar hung a wooden crucifix carved with the tortured body of Christ, the candle's light accentuating the hollows of the face and glistening upon the nails thrust cruelly through the hands. With one last plea for heavenly aid, Bascot stretched himself out full-length on the stones of the floor, face down and arms extended so that his body formed an imitation of the cross that hung above him.

As Bascot's cheek touched the coldness of the stone, he

was reminded of the night before he had taken his vow to become a Templar, when he had lain in just such a fashion. But then there had been gladness and joy in his heart, not stealth. This time, instead of meditating upon God and contemplating a future in His service, Bascot was laying his back open to an assassin's knife, hoping that the murderer of Hugo and the others would be tempted to try to silence him before he had a chance to reveal the name that Anselm had supposedly whispered on his deathbed. It was a wild scheme, as d'Arderon had said, but Bascot hoped it would work.

There was no sound from the sacristy, but Bascot could feel d'Arderon's presence as surely as if the preceptor were kneeling beside him. Since the laws of old King Henry stated that, other than a close relative, only a witness to the act of murder or attempted murder could lay a charge against the assailant, Bascot had asked the Temple for help in providing one. D'Arderon, on learning of the danger Bascot proposed to put himself in, had insisted on coming himself. He had brought a priest with him in case his services should be needed. Bascot fervently hoped they would not.

The stones beneath him smelled faintly of incense, along with a trace of the gritty aroma of leather and oil, a reminder that this chapel was used mainly by the castle garrison. Many a knee encased in mail must have bent in genuflection where Bascot now lay. It was a comforting thought. As the moments went by, the silence in the chapel became complete. Not the rustle of a mouse or the squeak of a bat could be heard. Only the faint exhalation of his own breath sounded in Bascot's ears, and the beating of his heart.

The stillness dragged on. If the murderer came at all, it would be in the darkest part of the night, after all the guests and residents of the castle were asleep, but it had been necessary to come well before that time to make the vigil seem genuine. Bascot felt tension gather in his injured leg and tried to relax his muscles to ease it, thankful for the leather eye patch that shielded his cheek from the stone beneath. He would have an hour or two yet to wait.

Slowly his mind drifted, returning to thoughts of his long imprisonment. Was the capture of this murderer the reason he had been spared for all those years? He thought of the cell he had first been incarcerated in, the dust, the heat, the constant drone of flies, the evil smirking face of his gaoler when he threw him, twice a day, a mouldy lump of some hard bread-like substance. He remembered the day he had been herded out of his cell, lined up with other prisoners, not a Christian amongst them, and been inspected by a Saracen noble on a prancing white horse. Then the whip that had lashed across his shoulders as he was driven forward with a few others to become a slave in an infidel household. The Muslim overseer into whose care he and the other slaves had been entrusted had taken delight in finding the most menial and degrading tasks for the Christian captive to perform. Bascot had been unable to contain the humiliation and rage that had engulfed him.

It had been for insolence that his eye had been put out and the same reason, later, had prompted his sale, and that of Benjamin's, to the captain of a pirate ship. He could still recall the monotonous rhythm of the ship's drum as he and forty others pushed and pulled the huge oars to its beat, their feet chained into place, terror in their hearts when the ship of a trader was attacked and they were locked in place, defenceless while the battle between the pirates and their prey raged around them.

It had been during a storm that he had escaped, one of the sudden forceful tempests that were common in the sea south of the island of Cyprus. For the better part of a morning, rain and wind had lashed them, the waves of the ocean boiling and foaming as though they were afloat in a huge cauldron. Finally the flimsy planks of the boat, long past need of caulking, had given way, letting the sea rush in to batter captors and slaves alike. Bascot remembered how the mast had come crashing down to where he and Benjamin, along with two others, were chained, knocking free the hasp that held their leg irons in place. As it slid loose, the mast had suddenly tilted, trapping Bascot's leg beneath it. Benjamin, already on his feet and preparing to dive overboard to freedom, had hesitated when he saw that Bascot could not move. Then the Jewish boy had turned and, putting all his weight to the mast, had freed Bascot's trapped limb. It had been at that moment that one of the Saracen pirates had stumbled across them and, raising his sword, had cleaved Benjamin's neck where it joined his shoulder. Amongst the struggling, howling mass of slaves and pirates, his leg useless, Bascot had found the strength to drag the guard down beside him and wrench the scimitar from the man's grasp. With one swift stroke he had disembowelled him. But when he turned to Benjamin, the Jewish boy was almost dead, the bright blood pumping out of his throat like a geyser, mixing with the slicing drops of rain and covering his body in a mantle of red.

Bascot had tried, with difficulty, to raise Benjamin up, but the boy had looked at him with his soft brown eyes, moved his lips once in an attempt to speak and died. A moment later the pirate vessel was pitching and tossing in its own death throes and Bascot was thrown into the raging torrent of the sea. He remembered no more until the next day, when he found himself on an empty strand of shore, his body lying half-in and half-out of the receding waves. Like flotsam he had been thrown up on the beach with other bits of wreckage from the pirate ship. It had been there, his ankle smashed and his lungs full of seawater, that some fishermen had found him and taken him to their village. They cared for him until he could be removed to the

Templar hospital on the island of Cyprus. The following months were misty in his memory, a blur of pain and fevered images, but he had not forgotten Benjamin, or the look on his face as he had died.

Bascot saw that look now, in his mind's eye, and murmured a prayer for the soul of the dead Jew. It might be blasphemy to do so, but if Benjamin had not freed his leg, at the cost of his own life, Bascot would not be alive now. He pushed his face into the stone. If he had been spared it must have been for a purpose. Was it for this night's vigil, this catching of a killer? Would the murderer even come? Had he been wrong in his assumptions, was the person he believed responsible for all those deaths innocent of it all? Was it another, even now sleeping the untroubled sleep of those without a conscience?

And, if he was correct, and the murderer appeared and succeeded in his attempt on Bascot's life, what would happen to Gianni? Hilde had assured him she would care for the boy and Bascot knew she would keep strictly to her promise, but how would the boy react? Would he go on as he had been, growing up strong and straight, happy in his studies? Or would he run away and revert to the urchin he had been when Bascot had found him, trusting no one, scrabbling with the rats for food?

Silently he repeated a paternoster and prayed to God for guidance and help.

In the keep, all of the revellers and servants were asleep. Except for one. A shadowy form rose from the dark confines of a chamber and stepped lightly and quietly through the snores and slumber-deep breathing of the other occupants of the chamber. The door creaked slightly when it was opened but, thanks be to God, no one was sleeping across the threshold.

Outside, in the hallway, by the light of a guttering torch,

a knife was pulled from its sheath, checked for sharpness and replaced. Then its owner crept down the stairs and out of the building.

Overhead moon and stars twinkled in a heaven devoid of cloud. It should be a fine day tomorrow and would have been an even better one had it not been for Hilde's carelessly imparted tidbit of information. Damn the Templar! Tonight's excursion would not be necessary were it not for his incessant poking and prying into matters that were none of his concern. Ah, well, he would not be a threat much longer. Soon he would join the others, join them in paradise—or hell.

The candle was burning low in its holder when Bascot heard the first sound. A tiny scrape as the door to the chapel was eased open, quickly stilled as the intruder must have paused to see if the sound had been detected. Bascot tensed his muscles, straining his ears and forcing himself to lie still as he heard the soft brush of one footstep, then another, then a pause. The intruder seemed to be still some feet away from him. Was it the person they sought, or merely one of the castle guests, sleepless and come to seek the solace of prayer in the hours before dawn?

Seconds passed like hours, then the footsteps again began their slow approach. If it had been a guest, they would have retreated at the sight of Bascot on the chapel floor in apparent communion with God. This was the one they had been waiting for, the person who had wantonly killed six people and would, without compunction, kill again. Bascot felt the muscles in his back twitch in protest at their vulnerability. He knew he must wait, wait until an attack was made, else the murderer would deny any intent of violence, claiming only an accidental intrusion into the chapel precincts. Wait, Bascot said to himself, wait. Ah, God, it was hard to do. He held his breath, heard the footsteps move again, bolder now, and quicker as they came nearer.

He heard the swish of a blade being drawn from a scabbard, felt, as though it were his own, the sudden intake of breath as his attacker steeled himself to strike . . .

Bascot judged the last second of safety, hoped it was enough, and rolled, pushing out with his good leg to give himself purchase on the stone of the floor, presenting his blind side to the blade that swept down in an arc above his head. He threw up an arm to protect himself, drawing the blade from his belt at the same time. From the direction of the sacristy, he could hear d'Arderon and the priest burst through the door, their shouts of warning, the ring of their mail-shod feet on stone. Steeling himself for the slice of the blade, he turned his sighted side towards his attacker and readied his own knife to thrust, just as the preceptor's fist crashed into the jaw of the person above him.

"By God," he heard d'Arderon shout in disbelief. "It is not a man. It is a woman."

Bascot pulled himself to his feet and bent over the figure that lay unconscious on the floor, the hand the knife had held thrown out to one side, the sharp wicked blade glittering in the candlelight a few feet away. Silently he pulled back the hood that covered the face of his assailant to reveal a mass of dark russet-coloured hair.

"I thought you said it was the *secretarius*, William Scothern, that you suspected?" d'Arderon demanded.

"It was," Bascot replied.

"Then who is this?" the preceptor asked.

"It is his sister," Bascot answered. "Isobel."

Twenty-six

✦

"So that little lass murdered them all," Ernulf said, disbelief on his weathered countenance. "Seems hard to credit."

He and Bascot were standing outside the door of the holding cell, where Isobel had been taken after she had been revived. Dawn was near to breaking and the castle servants were beginning to stir. From the direction of the poultry sheds a rooster let out a call warning of the imminence of daylight.

"That little lass, as you call her, serjeant, killed six people. After stealing the key to the chest where her brother kept de Kyme's private correspondence, and discovering that Sir Philip was sending for his illegitimate son, she calmly wrote and instructed Hugo and his wife to come to Newark, where she told them they would be met. She then hired Wat, and his boat, and had him ferry the couple up the river just past Torksey. It was her that went to meet the ale-keeper there, and gave the boy and his wife a draught of ale with a potion in it that would render them unconscious. She then smothered them with a piece of sacking."

"That was where she met the Jew? On the Torksey road?" Ernulf asked.

"Yes. It was Samuel's misfortune that he had stopped there, perhaps to take a break in his journey before going on to Alan de Kyme's. He must have seen her making her way to the river. Since she could not let her presence be noted, she persuaded him she needed assistance and took him to the river and onto the barge with Hugo and his wife. Samuel was given the same adulterated ale as the others and suffered the same fate."

"You said she claims her brother had nothing to do with the business. How did she explain her absence that day to him? If I remember aright, it was originally claimed that she and him had kept company together at the fair. That was why she wasn't there to give Lady Sybil a witness to being sick in bed all day."

"She told Scothern she was going to Parchmingate, to see a new Psalter at one of the parchment makers, and would meet him later. Scothern was not averse to leaving her to her own company. It seems he has been visiting the pretty young widow of a cloth merchant, and used the time to spend with her."

"And Brunner?"

"Isobel tracked him down much as we did. Remember, she was in the castle. She not only had the advantage of knowing what we were going to do, and when, by observing our movements, she also could glean information from her brother. She was clever, and careful. It is only by God's grace she did not get away with it."

"It is hard to believe she killed the priest. That takes an evil heart." Ernulf said the words with distaste. "It's like that verse in the Bible, about what is an abomination to our Lord."

"'A proud look, a lying tongue and hands that will shed innocent blood.'"

"Aye, that's the one. Well, she had all of those, I reckon."

Bascot thought of the serene look of hatred that Isobel had given him when she had come to her senses on the floor of St. Clement's nave. There had been no sign of remorse in her eyes, nor a trace of guilt. She had calmly risen, rubbed the bruise that was swelling on her chin and said, "Well, Templar, you have found me out. I hope you burn in hell."

In the holding cell he and d'Arderon had questioned her. She had told them all she had done, hiding nothing. She had found herself pregnant, she had said, and not wanting her child to be born a bastard had decided that she would gull Philip de Kyme into thinking the child was his and then would persuade him to marry her.

"First I had to get rid of the boy that my spineless brother had helped de Kyme to find. Then I needed a way to make the baron set Lady Sybil aside." She had shrugged, the heavy fall of her dark auburn hair spilling around her shoulders, her graceful hands folded and still in her lap. D'Arderon and the Templar priest had stared at her. She was beautiful, with alabaster skin and eyes the colour of burnt honey. It seemed impossible to believe she was so evil.

"It seemed to me that the easiest way to accomplish both aims was to use one end to achieve the other. And it would have worked, but for the alewife. Had she left their scrips in place, they would have been identified immediately and Sybil and Conal charged straight away."

For the first time she showed tension. Her fingers tightened one around the other until her knuckles turned white. "Damn the alewife. Wat said she was upstairs, in bed, but she wasn't. If she had been I would have killed her, like the others." Her eyes met Bascot's, glittering with intensity. "Just as I would have killed you."

Bascot had pointed out that even had Hugo and his wife been identified at once, it would have made no difference. Nicolaa de la Haye would still have ordered an investigation to either substantiate Sybil and Conal's guilt, or clear them of culpability.

Isobel had looked at him scornfully. "Yes, but such an enquiry would have been only cursory. There would have been no need for you or any other to pry and dig. She had no witness to attest to her presence elsewhere when the murders were done. I saw to that by putting a little of the juice of the same plant I used on Hugo and the others into her food. And her precious son was off to visit his crippled paramour, as usual. He thinks it is a great secret, but it was not difficult to discover why he goes to Newark, as that simpering bitch Matilda could have done if she had thought to lift her jealous eyes from my face for a moment. Conal and his mother would have been able to bring no defence to the charge against them."

"And you would have seen your mistress and her son accused and found guilty, knowing that they were innocent?" Bascot had asked incredulously.

"Of course," Isobel had responded. "Why not? We are all at the mercy of fate. My grandfather might have given preference to a male bastard, but my mother suffered the ill chance of being born female, and so was relegated to a life of low station. As, in turn, have I. I should be the daughter of a baron, not merely a companion to the unwanted wife of one."

Her composure slipped slightly and there was a tremor of passion in her voice as she added, "My mother should have been born male, and so should I. My brother is weak, satisfied to pander to the whims of a wine-sop. Were I a man, I would have used my sword to carve a fortune, not wasted my life scratching messages on pieces of parchment."

She had told them the rest of the tale quite willingly. She had murdered Wat—smashing his head in with one of the alehouse stools when he had turned to pour them both a cup of ale after bringing the bodies inside—to prevent laying herself open to extortion at some later time. She had murdered Brunner for the same reason, tracking him down in much the same manner that Ernulf had done, by talking to the serving girl from the bawdy house the evening before the youngster had come to tell Ernulf she had seen the stewe-keeper. There had been a smile on her face as she told them how she had intended to dupe Philip de Kyme into thinking the child she had carried was his.

"I crept into his bed one morning before he awoke. As usual, he had drunk more than his fill of wine the night before and was sleeping alone in a small chamber adjacent to the hall. Will had told me how he often had to help his master to bed because his wits were so befuddled. When Sir Philip woke up, I pretended we had slept together all the night through, and that he had enjoyed my body during that time. It was plain he couldn't remember if he had done so or not, and it was also clear he wasn't going to admit to his loss of memory. When the time was right he would have accepted the child as his, and married me to have his precious heir, even if it was a female."

"And who is the father of your child?" Bascot had asked.

Isobel had looked at him in surprise. "Why, Anselm, of course. That was why I had to kill him."

At that point, the Templar priest had begged d'Arderon's permission to leave. Even though used to hearing the confessions of dying men, he protested, never could he recall being privy to such depravity as was spilling from the mouth of this woman. He felt a great need of the solace of prayer. The preceptor gave him his leave and, shortly afterwards, he and Bascot left Isobel to the solitude of her cell, putting a pair of Ernulf's men-at-arms on guard at the door.

Now it was clear what Anselm's repeated muttering of the word "unclean" had meant. He must have been a lecher, just as the shoemaker's son had said, and that could have been the reason why he been removed to such a distance from his parish in Canterbury. After coming to Lincoln he had met Isobel and succumbed to the temptation of enjoying her body. Hence his wearing of the hair shirt; an act of atonement for his renewed lapse from grace. It was probable he had seen her when she attacked him, perhaps realised the depth of her depravity. The enormity of the sin he had committed had robbed him of the will to live. From Isobel's point of view, his knowledge of their relationship was a threat to her plans. She had to murder him, to keep him quiet.

"What made you think it was her brother that was guilty, Bascot?" D'Arderon had asked when they were once more outside.

"It was Lady Ermingard's mention of the cloak. And her insistence that the girl that had it was hiding the fact that she was pregnant. I had puzzled long over the implication that there was the need for a quick discovery of the bodies. When I learned from Agnes that she had removed the young couple's belongings, thus effectively obliterating any way of discovering who they were, it seemed that the requirement for haste had been very real. All had been done to ensure they were discovered and identified quickly. Why? Once the boy was dead, and the child his wife carried with him, any of the other people who might have had reason to benefit from their removal could have waited to convince Sir Philip of their worthiness at their leisure.

"There could only be one reason, and that was that another child was soon to be born that could fill dead Hugo's place. Since Philip did not seem to have a paramour, there was only one woman other than his wife who could be carrying his seed, and that was Isobel. She was in his household all the time, and of such a supposedly pious nature that she would not have been suspected of having a liaison with the husband of a mistress she appeared to be devoted to. Besides, Scothern was extremely nervous when I went to de Kyme's keep to see the letters that had been written to

Hugo's mother. His explanation was weak, but there was no doubt his fear involved his sister. I reasoned that it was Isobel who Lady Ermingard had meant when she had been talking about the cloak being the wrong colour. And it had been the sight of her, not the tapestry, that had prompted the same reaction that morning in the solar. Isobel was sitting right in front of it. Ermingard had also said that the cloak was wet. It started to rain just about the time that Anselm was killed. Anyone leaving the church just then would have been drenched. Therefore, whoever had done the stabbing must be connected with Isobel. And have knowledge of the whereabouts of Hugo and his wife, and the movements of Lady Sybil and Conal. I thought it must be Isobel's brother, William; that he had discovered the intimacy between his sister and his master, and also her condition as a result of it. To keep her from the shame of unwed motherhood he had devised a plan to get the baron to marry his sister by removing de Kyme's illegitimate son and also Sybil at the same time. The others—the alekeeper, the Jew, Brunner, Anselm— had been killed to prevent them making public any knowledge that would implicate him."

Bascot took a breath, tracking the thoughts that had led him to his conclusion that Scothern had been the murderer. "I also remembered that it was he who first came to me with the tale of Philip's illegitimate son, and the possibility that the murdered boy could be him. If he had not come forward, the identities of Hugo and his wife might never have been discovered. But Isobel was well aware of my investigations and it was at her urging that he asked Ernulf if the origin of the cloth had been ascertained, and it was she who prompted him to tell me of de Kyme's letters to his former paramour. She had to have their identities made known.

"When Lady Ermingard spoke of the cloak, I reasoned that if Scothern had stabbed the priest and his garments had become drenched in the downpour that fell just moments after he had done so, then Isobel had suspected her brother's involvement and had been trying to protect him by saying the cloak belonged to someone else. In fact, the cloak was her own."

He paused as a sobering thought struck him. "It is fortunate that Ermingard never spoke Isobel's name. She might have been murdered as well, if she had. Perhaps, in her confusion she sensed that her knowledge was dangerous and although she knew it was important to convey it, still had the good judgement to keep part of it back. It is thanks to her, however, that the purpose of the murders became clear, even if I ascribed that purpose to the wrong person."

"The trail you followed was a true one, you just scented the wrong quarry," d'Arderon said.

"Yes. I looked for a woman in the riddle, but never for one moment conjectured that it was a woman who had, on her own, carried out the murders. And it must have been by God's own intervention that William was directed to tell his sister of the prepared speech that Hilde related to him last night."

"Scothern could easily have been guilty," d'Arderon opined. "Isobel said that her brother used to visit the alehouse while she went into Anselm's church, supposedly to attend Mass. And Scothern knew Wat, was even the cause of Isobel making the alekeeper's acquaintance when he ordered some of Agnes' ale for the baron's table. But it is hard to believe that he knew nothing of what Isobel had done."

"No, it is not," Bascot objected. "You have seen for yourself that she is clever and has a consummate skill at hiding her emotions. Scothern is a simple soul, cautious of incurring his sister's anger, and respectful of what he believed was her pious devotion. It would have been an easy matter for her to gull him, just as she gulled Philip de Kyme, and, indeed, the rest of us."

D'Arderon had left Bascot to go in search of a cup of ale to slake his thirst when Ernulf had joined the Templar, Gianni trailing behind him.

"I've told Lady Nicolaa and the sheriff what happened in the chapel last night. And Lady Hilde, too. She had not yet been abed, but was sitting up waiting for news of how you fared. She said to tell you that your task was well done, and she would have speech with you later."

Bascot acknowledged the words, but was looking at Gianni. The boy was strangely subdued, staying near Ernulf and looking at his master with watchful eyes. Last night Bascot had only told the boy he had Templar business with d'Arderon, and that Gianni was to keep Hilde company for the night. The lad must have discovered where Bascot had really been from the speech of the adults around him, but instead of being relieved to see his master whole and sound, he seemed distrustful and suspicious of Bascot. The Templar sighed inwardly. Gianni was a child yet and, to his mind, his protector had lied to him. The boy saw it as a breach of trust between them.

Twenty-seven

·✠·

CHE TOURNEY WAS TO TAKE PLACE ON A BROAD STRETCH of level ground outside the castle walls to the northwest. It was the place where, nearly sixty years before, King Stephen had defended his right to the crown of England against King Henry I's daughter, the Empress Matilda. Bascot arrived just before Sext, in company with d'Arderon and two other knights of the Temple. There was a huge crowd gathered to watch the spectacle, many already seated under the trees that bordered the river on the far side, eating food they had brought with them and drinking from flasks of ale or wine.

There was a good host of knights entered in the tourney, which was comprised of only one event, the melee, a mock battle between two opposing teams of knights. Although the entrance fee was steep, the purse for the winning side was a large one, and contestants had arrived not only from the area surrounding Lincoln, but from as far afield as London and York. The merchants of Lincoln had donated a bolt of cloth and a new saddle to be awarded to the knight declared champion of the tourney. These prizes were well worth fighting for, as was the ransom that a knight would collect from any opponent he unhorsed. Many a contestant would go home the poorer, not only for the loss of his entrance fee, but also his destrier and arms, given in pledge until he should pay the silver he owed to the knight who had captured him.

Since the fighting of the melee was frowned upon by the church, King John, when granting the licence to hold it, had made certain stipulations. The tourney was to be kept within a confined area so that neighbouring farms and fields would not have their crops destroyed by the hooves of the war horses, and any knight deliberately wreaking harm on an opponent that was already unseated was to be fined and disqualified.

Bascot's task, and that of the other Templars, was simple. First they were to oversee the drawing of the lots that would determine on which side the contesting knights would fight. Then, when the two teams were drawn up on each side of the meadow, they were to give the signal for the tourney to begin. Once the battle was underway, they had only to decide which knight, in their opinion, fought with enough valour to be declared champion. Since the team that would be adjudged the winner was the side that had the most combatants remaining at the end of two hours, the champion could be chosen from either side, whether that of the victorious or the defeated.

Bascot went to join the crowd around the large canopied stand that had been erected on the eastern side of the field. In it would sit Nicolaa and her husband, along with some of their guests. The common people would spread themselves along the perimeters of the meadow, fending for themselves as best they could if the mock battle came too near. A festive atmosphere lay over the whole event as well as an air of eager anticipation. Tents had been erected on the surrounding hillside for the use of the combatants and among these strolled minstrels, vendors of food and wine, and hawkers of everything from ribbons to horseflesh. The buzz of conversation, the strains of music from the troubadours' instruments, the neighing of the horses and the clang of metal was a din that floated heavenward into the balmy summer air. On the surface of the meadow the daisy-starred grass rippled in a slight breeze, its beauty soon to be trampled into oblivion.

As the sun neared its zenith and the time for the commencement of the tourney approached, the crowd became silent. Nearly one hundred combatants paraded before the stand and received a ribbon—either green or yellow—that would be tied to their arms to identify on which side they belonged. Bascot and the other Templars sat on their horses overseeing the affair, all clad in surcoats of white. Most of the contestants were young, with only one or two older knights, battle scarred and grim, among them. Richard Camville rode past, mounted on a magnificent roan, and received from his mother's hand a ribbon of green. On his shield the Camville silver lion quartered with the Haye twelve-pointed red star glittered as the sun struck it. Conal was close behind him, and given a strip of ribbon that was the same colour. In the stand, beside Nicolaa, sat Hilde, her face alight with joy as she watched her great-nephew, resplendent in chain mail and a surcoat of blue embroidered with a black raven, adjust his helm and take his place next to Richard at the south end of the field.

Beside Hilde was a golden-haired girl with a rosebud mouth, a light veil of gauze shielding her features. Bascot had seen Conal lift the young woman out of an enclosed litter a short time earlier, then carry her and seat her tenderly beside his great-aunt. Bascot supposed the girl must be the goldsmith's daughter, removed from the aura of secrecy in which her father had kept her and openly declared by Conal as the woman he loved. Hilde had welcomed her warmly, smiling and taking the girl's hand in her own before looking around defiantly to see if any of her neighbours should dare seem critical of her approval. Conal's mother, Sybil, and her two brothers, Magnus and Ailwin, were noticeable by their absence.

On the other side of Hilde was Gianni, the elderly lady's hand resting familiarly on the boy's shoulder as he clutched her silver-headed cane close in his arms. It pleased Bascot to see his servant thus, but he felt a strange sense of loss. It was as though the boy had deserted him.

Roger de Kyme came next in the parade of entrants. He was riding a black stallion with thick hindquarters. The animal was nervous and snorted at the close proximity of the crowd, ears twitching. Behind Roger rode his cousin, Alan, mounted on a wiry grey with a small head and alert eyes. Ivo de Rollos was there, too, watching with anxious eyes as his mother, Ermingard, handed him a ribbon with an air of puzzlement about what she was doing. All three received ribbons of yellow. It took nearly an hour for the rest to pass by and receive an identifying scrap of material.

During this time Bascot let his gaze roam over the crowd. It was a motley company, merchant alongside tinker, and prostitute standing cheek by jowl with clerk. He spotted Agnes, the alewife, in the crowd, her face white and subdued as she stood with her sister and family. Agnes had been released from gaol only that morning, Isobel's confessed guilt the alewife's warrant to freedom.

Nearby, and a small distance apart from the others, were Isaac and his brother Nathan. They were watching the line of combatants with hawk-eyed interest. There was no doubt that many of the entrants had borrowed the price of their fee from the moneylenders. The Jews would keep a sharp tally of who, among those pledged, emerged the victor or had the misfortune to be among the vanquished.

Across the field, Bascot saw the barber-surgeon who

had attended Anselm's wound after he had been attacked. The little man was wearing a gaudy gown of red and blue, his clean-shaven face gleaming and his grey locks carefully coiffed. On his arm was a woman that Bascot supposed must be his wife, a plump matron with a merry face and red cheeks. Near to them was the cobbler from whom Bascot had bought his boots, his horse-faced wife munching on a pasty while her son ogled the young girls in the throng. On the ground, under a tree, sat the mercenary captain, Roget, and the reluctant harlot, Gillie. They were sharing a flagon of wine and laughing. When Roget saw Bascot looking his way, he raised an arm and waved.

It was as the tourney marshal was lining up the two teams of combatants that Bascot heard his name spoken. Looking down, he saw William Scothern standing beside his mount. The clerk's face was drawn and miserable. Slung on his shoulder was a bundle and he was crumpling a soft-crowned cap between ink-stained fingers.

"Sir Bascot, I come to beg your pardon for my sister." The young *secretarius'* demeanour was dejected, his voice a stammer so low that Bascot had to bend down from the saddle to hear him.

"It is not my pardon you must beg, nor yours to have the doing of it," Bascot replied.

"I know that, sir," Scothern replied, "but I feel I must do it anyway. If I had been more vigilant, less preoccupied with my work . . . and other things . . . perhaps my sister would not have done what she did."

"That is between your own conscience and God," Bascot said, not unkindly. "None but He can help her, or you, now."

Scothern shook his head in misery. "Sir Philip has gone back to his manor. He did not ask me to accompany him and, even if he had, I would not have gone. There was a time that he told me he valued my loyalty. I thought he was speaking of my assistance in bringing his illegitimate son to Lincoln. But it seems he believed I knew that Isobel had warmed his bed, and appreciated my not letting it interfere with my devotion to his service." The clerk's face was a picture of misery. "How could he have thought me to be so base?"

The question embarrassed Bascot, and instead of attempting to answer it, he asked Scothern if he had been to see his sister.

Scothern nodded. "She is the same as ever, tight-lipped and contemptuous. I asked her what I was to tell our parents and she only replied that I could make up whatever lie my clerk's brain deemed suitable."

"Did you speak to her of what she had done?"

Again, Scothern nodded. "She took relish in telling me all the details. How she had told the alekeeper that Hugo was Lady Sybil's illegitimate son by a secret lover and that the boy was threatening to expose her, demanding money for his silence. She said that she was acting for Lady Sybil. Wat believed the pair were to be found dead, apparently poisoned, to remove the threat from Isobel's mistress. Poor fool, he believed her. Even when she made him get the harlot's gown, he swallowed her tale."

Scothern's eyes filled with tears. "She told the alekeeper that it was to disguise the identity of Hugo's wife, so that no one would know of the couple's connection to Sybil, but she said to me that she did it as a jest. 'All women are harlots,' she said to me. 'Only men are free to enjoy their lust where they may. If a woman does it, she is named a bawd.' She sickened me."

Bascot felt sorry for the clerk. He had honoured his sister, believed her to be chaste. How hard it was to find that one so near to him in kinship could have such a divergence of spirit. Isobel had been right when she had said that she should have been born a man. Bascot had known many men-at-arms, and knights, that fought not for the exhilaration of battle or the glory of winning, but simply because they had a lust to spill blood. Surprisingly, or perhaps not, they were the most valued warriors, for they fought without honour or conscience and often dealt the stroke that decided the outcome of a fray.

As if echoing his thought, Scothern continued talking about his sister's odious crimes, as though he could erase the memory by speaking of them aloud. "I asked her why she had stabbed the bodies after death. There had been no need to desecrate them so, I said. She laughed at me, said it had been a necessary practice, that she had needed to know how to deliver a knife-stroke for when she should kill Anselm. Her lover. A priest. Ah, how will God ever forgive her? She will end in hell, and there is none that can prevent it."

Bascot sought to divert the young man's anguish. "Where do you go now, William?" he asked.

"I will stay in Lincoln until the charge against my sister is heard," Scothern replied. "After that, to my parent's home, I suppose." He looked up at Bascot with eyes red from weeping. "Do you think they will hang her?"

"You know the law as well as I, William," Bascot replied, feeling a surge of pity. "She committed not one murder, but six, and all of those with prior intent. The best Isobel can hope for is the loss of a hand or foot and banishment."

Scothern nodded, his eyes looking in the direction of the helmed and mailed figures of the knights that were massing in lines and hefting their lances at each end of the sward. "If I had done as Isobel had wanted, and taken up the sword instead of the pen, perhaps she would not be where she is today."

There was no reply that Bascot could find to make. He could not say that the boy was suited to the task he had chosen and that his sister, God forgive her, had been suited to hers. As the marshal signalled for a warning trumpet to sound, the *secretarius* mumbled a farewell and turned away. The last Bascot saw of him was as he pushed his way through the crowd at the edge of the field, looking neither to one side nor the other, a forlorn and lonely figure.

Three short blasts of a trumpet forced Bascot's attention back to the tourney. A hush fell over the crowd as they waited for the melee to begin. Blunted lances bristled like the quills of hedgehogs above the heads of the knights, their destriers pulling at the restraint of their bridles as they pawed the earth with impatience. In the brightness of the summer sun, painted shields and polished helms sparkled and flashed. Overhead, and far above, a lone hawk soared and wheeled against the blue sky. Suddenly the long wail of a massed set of trumpets split the air and a second later, a huge shout rose up from the throats of the crowd as the two teams of knights lowered their lances and shot towards each other like quarrels loosed from opposing crossbows. The ground trembled beneath the thrum of the horses' hooves, then seemed to tilt as the two waves of armoured men met in a crash of shields and splintering lances. Fallen horses screamed and men cursed as slowly those riders who had retained their seats emerged from the tangled mass.

Bascot wheeled his mount up one side of the field, feeling the animal beneath him prancing in the excitement of the moment. On the other side d'Arderon was following the same course, the other pair of Templar knights making their pass in the opposite direction.

Riderless horses bucked and plunged through the confusion and those knights who had fallen yielded up their shields to a team of heralds busily noting names and escutcheons. Those still in the fray raced their horses back to their respective starting positions, then wheeled their mounts in preparation for the next charge. Bascot watched the second clash of muscle and steel with envy in his throat. How well he remembered the thrill of battle, the great surge of exhilaration that coursed through body and mind as one's lance found its target. Even with the memory of Isobel in his mind, he knew there was no joy that could replace it. Was he, like many another, guilty of lust, the lust to kill? Had God allowed him to justify it by leading him to join the Templars in the war against the infidel? Had he been wrong to turn away from such a life?

On the field, Richard Camville unhorsed his fourth knight. Conal was still in the saddle also, as were Roger de Kyme and Ivo de Rollos. Alan de Kyme had fallen in the first clash. Although swords and lances had been blunted, and the sharp flanges of maces wrapped in coarse linen, there were still many combatants who had suffered cuts and bruises, and one or two with a broken arm or leg. Leeches from the priory were tending the wounded in the shelter of the trees, salving mangled flesh with ointment before wrapping the injuries in strips of cloth. As the first hour wore on, those being cared for by the monks became more numerous, and by the time that the marshal called for a brief recess, out of the one hundred knights that had begun the contest, there were only some forty left. Of these, only fifteen still had ribbons of green fluttering from their arms. It looked as though the yellow side would be the victor.

Bascot and d'Arderon dismounted and drank a cup of wine at the edge of the trees. "Richard Camville looks to be champion," the preceptor said, "even though it appears he might be the only one remaining of the greens."

"He has a good arm," Bascot agreed, "and so does Conal. They are both young yet, and whole of body."

The preceptor looked sharply at Bascot. "You speak as though you are an old man, too feeble to hold a lance. Let me tell you that there are men here with a score more years than you who could take those youngsters in one pass. Gerard Camville for one, myself for another. Youth is no master to experience. Your fighting days are not over, Bascot, nor is there any need for them to be. And I do not think you want it so."

D'Arderon had been speaking roughly, almost with anger.

Now he paused to draw breath and continued in a gentler tone. "I saw your face when the melee started, Bascot. You would have been out there if you could. And would be as formidable as ever. There's many a paladin that has lost an eye and found no lessening of his skill. Why do you not come back to the Order, where you belong? Your brothers in Christ would welcome you with hearts full of gladness."

Bascot smiled at his mentor, aware of the truth in his words. "I know, my friend," he replied softly. He could not explain to the crusty old campaigner the maelstrom of emotions that beset him. D'Arderon would not, could not, understand. "But I must find my way as God wills it," he tried to explain, knowing his words were unconvincing. "I am not yet sure what it is that He has called me to do."

"There is no doubt of His purpose for you in my mind," d'Arderon answered promptly. "You were called to fight for Christ and kill Saracens. And you can't do that in Lincoln."

The trumpets sounded for the continuation of the melee and the two Templars resumed their roles as judges. As the next hour wore on and the sun grew hotter, it was plain that some of the knights were tiring. With the time allotted nearly at a finish, only Richard Camville and Conal were left of those who had worn a green ribbon, with some fifteen left on the yellow side, headed by Roger de Kyme. Ivo de Rollos was still in the saddle, but he carried his shield awkwardly and it was clear that he had injured his shoulder. Still, with grim determination, he kept his seat and rallied for what would be the last and final charge as Richard and Conal wheeled their horses at the far end of the field and, with a great shout, drove their steeds at the bunched mass of opposing knights.

Lances had been discarded some halfway through the battle. Now the knights fought with sword and mace only. Richard carved his way through with an easy sweep of his blade, finally unseating young de Rollos and delivering an-

other knight such a blow with the edge of his shield that the
man tumbled to the ground. Conal was not so fortunate,
however. He met with Roger de Kyme, shield to shield, and
although the younger man had the advantage of a longer
arm, de Kyme had more strength of muscle. Within two or
three seconds, the flat of Roger's sword had dented Conal's
helm and knocked his sword from his grasp. Hilde's great-
nephew had no choice but to yield.

As if by common consent, the remainder of the knights
fell away as Richard Camville turned to face the man who
had unhorsed his friend. They both set at each other with a
will, reach and strength equal. The crowd rose to its feet,
sensing that this was the match that would determine who
was champion. Blows were rained by each man on the
other with devastating effect until slowly, very slowly, it
could be seen that de Kyme was beginning to tire. Richard
seized his advantage, renewing his onslaught until Roger's
shield was battered and dented, with its owner struggling
vainly to protect himself behind it. Finally, Richard spurred
his tired mount forward and dealt his opponent such a blow
to the head that de Kyme dropped his sword and slumped
to the ground. A roar welled from the throats of the crowd
as Richard Camville turned alone to face the remnants of
the opposing team. Not one of them took up the challenge.
In one movement, they all dismounted, signalling their decision to yield by laying up their swords and removing
their helms. Richard Camville had won the day for his team
and also the prize for champion.

When the tourney was over, the prizes awarded and a
merry celebration well on its way, Bascot returned alone to
Lincoln Castle. He was weary, not only from a night without sleep and the rigours of his vigil in the chapel, but also
from the disquiet that d'Arderon's words had put into his
mind.

The bail was nearly deserted, with only a few guards at their posts on the wall, and a lone goatherd milking one of his herd. Bascot made his way to a small dank chamber set at one side of the old tower where, under cover of a stout stone arch, one of the castle wells was situated. With the aid of a bucket, he filled a large padded wooden tub with cold water, then stripped off his clothes and stepped into the soothing coolness. On a small table several tablets of soap made from wood ash and tallow were kept, and Bascot helped himself to one, scrubbing vigorously with a brush as he lathered away the sweat and dirt that had collected on his body. The water was quickly lined with scum, and once he had finished cleansing himself, he emptied the tub out onto the ground and rinsed himself off.

As he did so, he thought of d'Arderon's words again. Was the preceptor right—should he rejoin the Templars? Ruefully he looked down at the tub from which he had just stepped. He would have to go back to wearing the sheepskin drawers and lambskin girdle the Saracens had forced him to discard. There would no longer be the pleasure of washing his naked body all over as he had just done. A small price to pay for vowing service to the Lord? Perhaps. He did not know. As for Gianni—the boy was growing up, already there had been a rift, if a slight one, between them. Bascot had been too lenient, treating the lad as if he were an equal and not a servant. If the boy were to stay in his service, he—Bascot—would have to be more severe, show Gianni his place, not let the lad usurp his authority. Had he the heart to do that? Again, he did not know.

He picked up a piece of rough linen from a pile that lay beside the supply of soap and began to towel himself dry. Life was difficult to understand. He knew that if he left the Order, he would be rootless, like a puff of sea spray blown onto an arid shore, left to dry and disappear forever. All the time he had been in the Holy Land there had always been, at the back of his mind, the thought of home—his father and brother, a new generation come from his sister-by-marriage's swollen belly. Through imprisonment and torture there had always been that comforting thought, that he did not matter, he was only another soldier for Christ, his father's line would carry on without his help. When he had returned to England he had been bowed, but not completely broken, looking forward to the consolation of his family, the security of the walls of his father's keep. Within that sanctuary he would have been able to build up his strength, recover his faith and return to the Order.

But now it was all gone, and with it his life, his meaning. It was he who should have died, not them. The pity he had felt for Gianni had been from the comfortable perspective of a knight of Christ and the member of a solid living family. It had been his intention to leave the lad in his father's care, knowing the boy would be well looked after and would thrive. But instead he found that he and Gianni were two of a kind, both adrift, both lost and homeless. Perhaps that was why he had become so attached to the child, using him as an anchor against his own uncertainty. Sweet Jesu, where did his future lie? He did not know what it was that God wanted him to do, nor less did he know what he himself wanted.

He looked down at the wet ground, felt the pain surge in his ankle now that his boot had been removed. Outside the bathhouse door the bail was deserted. Flies droned, the weak bleating of lambs could be heard in the afternoon heat. A discarded rag rolled lazily across the doorway. Did he belong here, in Lincoln? Part of it, yet not a part? Apart—wasn't that what he had always been, as a child in the monastery, in the loneliness of his vows to the Order? Or was he wrong, was he a part of something after all? And if so, of what? He reminded himself of the vows he had taken—poverty, chastity, obedience. The first two were easy to follow, but the third. . . . How could one be obedient when it was not clear in what direction that obedience lay? God had guided him unerringly through the web of lies and deceit that had surrounded Isobel Scothern's crimes and, he had to admit, the fact that he had been the means whereby the souls of her victims had been granted retribution was very satisfying. But had he truly been an instrument of the Lord's will or was his gratification causing him to be guilty of the sin of pride? He wished God would give him a similar assistance in determining the path of his own destiny.

Bascot folded the towel and replaced it, then turned to pick up his clothes. As he did so, he caught the sense of a slight movement at the entrance to the bathhouse. It was Gianni. Slowly the boy came forward, holding Bascot's clean tunic and hose in his arms. Without a change of his solemn expression, the lad held up the clothes for his master to take, then turned to fold up the discarded and soiled ones. When he had finished and Bascot had dressed, he raised his face to his master and Bascot could see tears welling in the lad's eyes.

"Does Lady Hilde no longer require your presence?" Bascot asked and Gianni shook his head. "Did she tell you to come back here and attend me?" Again the boy moved his head from side to side, then suddenly knelt and put his head down to his knees in an attitude of subjection.

Bascot reached down and lifted him gently. "I think it is time we had something to eat. Go to the kitchens and get some food. Afterwards, you may practice your letters while I sleep. Then we shall return to the tourney field and join in the festivities."

Gianni raised his head, a smile beginning to form tremulously on his lips. With a quick movement, he had straightened and was running towards the castle kitchens, Bascot's dirty clothing bundled under his arm. The Templar reached into the pouch at his belt and took out a *candi*. He felt light-headed—a transient, fleeting sense of freedom. It was not permanent, he knew, but he enjoyed it all the same. Perhaps God was giving him a direction after all. For the present, at least, he would remain in Lincoln.

Epilogue

✦

ᕼAMO, THE TEMPLAR SERJEANT THAT D'ARDERON HAD
sent on Bascot's quest to discover the truth of dead Hugo's
identity, returned, as the preceptor had ordered, ten days
after he had left. As expected, the young couple that had
been slain were confirmed by the boy's mother as Philip de
Kyme's illegitimate son and his wife. The distraught woman
was herself prostrate with grief after receiving William
Scothern's letter telling of her son's death only the day before Hamo's arrival. She still planned to make a trip to the
shrine of St. James in Compostella, this time to pray for her
dead son's soul instead of to give thanks for his good
fortune.

Isobel Scothern was never brought to answer the charge
of murder before the king's justices. The morning after the
tourney she was found dead in her cell, a cup on the floor
beside her which the infirmarian from the Priory of All
Saints declared to contain the dregs of a strong distillation
of foxglove leaves, a deadly poison.

The elderly monk, called from his patients to examine

the murderess' body, had gently closed Isobel's lids over her sightless amber-coloured eyes, murmuring as he did so, "By committing a mortal sin she has escaped her earthly judgement, but I fear her heavenly trial will be far more terrible. May God have mercy on her soul."

A few days later, without ceremony, Isobel Scothern's body, with the child she had carried dead in her womb, was buried in a patch of unhallowed ground at the edge of a stony field outside the walls of Lincoln.

Author's Note

✢

The setting for *The Alehouse Murders* is an authentic one. Nicolaa de la Haye was hereditary castellan of Lincoln castle during this period and her husband, Gerard Camville, was sheriff. The personalities they have been given in the story have been formed by conclusions the author has drawn from events during the reigns of King Richard I and King John.

For details of the town of Lincoln, I am much indebted to J. W. F. Hill's *Medieval Lincoln* and, for information about the Order of the Knights Templar, to John J. Robinson's very definitive book, *Dungeon, Fire and Sword*.

MAUREEN ASH was born in London, England, and has had a lifelong interest in British medieval history. Visits to castle ruins and old churches have provided the inspiration for her novels. She enjoys Celtic music, browsing in bookstores and Belgian chocolate. Maureen now lives on Vancouver Island in British Columbia, Canada.